DOCTOR ARNOLDI

DOCTOR ARNOLDI

by

Tiffany Thayer

Introduced by
Chris Mikul

Foreword by
Richard A. Lupoff

RAMBLE HOUSE

TO

CHARLES BLACKBURN SIMS,
*the hairy ape, because it was he who told
me to read "Breaking Point", by Michael
Artzibaschev.*

ISBN 13: 978-1-60543-712-5

ISBN 10: 1-60543-712-3

Introduction ©2013 by Chris Mikul

Foreword ©2013 by Richard A. Lupoff

Published: 2013 by Ramble House

Cover Art: Gavin L. O'Keefe

Preparation: Fender Tucker

INTRODUCTION

by Chris Mikul

Look, you don't have to read this book if you don't want to. You could put it on the table over there and forget all about it. You could 'accidentally' let it fall behind a chest of drawers and not find it again until you move house years from now. You could even throw it out the window, and it need never trouble your dreams. I won't mind. It's entirely up to you.

What's that? You're still here? Well, okay, if you're sure . . .

As you have probably gathered by now, *Doctor Arnoldi* is a very strange book, and its author, Tiffany Thayer, was a very strange man. He was born in Illinois in 1902, the son of actors, and became an actor as well, having some success as a juvenile lead in a Civil War play called *The Coward*. While his acting career eventually petered out, with his last role a comic turn in an obscure 1936 film, *The Devil on Horseback*, there remained something of the actor, something flamboyant and larger-than-life, in everything he did.

In the 1920s Thayer worked as a reporter on the *Chicago Tribune*, where he met Ben Hecht, who would become a friend and literary mentor. He landed in New York in 1926, and started writing fiction. He wrote crime stories for the pulps, and in 1930 brought forth a novel called *Thirteen Men*. It told the stories of twelve men whose lives converge when they become jurors at the trial of a thirteenth, a mass murderer. It was bold, vividly imagined, strikingly original and sexually frank (a hallmark of all Thayer's works), and it became a book that 'everyone' read. Thayer's literary career was off to a good start.

A man of prodigious energy, Thayer spent the rest of the 30s turning out big, splashy, often risqué novels which saw him dubbed 'the bad boy of American letters'. *Call Her Savage* (1930), about a half-white, half-native American girl with a fiery temper and a problem with men, was probably his biggest hit after *Thirteen Men*. (It was filmed with Clara Bow in the lead role.) *Thirteen Women* (1932) is a tense crime story about a group of women terrorised by a fellow pupil at their former school. *One Woman* (1933) chronicles the adventures of a reporter trying to reconstruct a dead woman's life from the names and numbers in her pocket book. *An American Girl* (1933), a farce involving a fictional European kingdom and a Hollywood film crew, was one of him most notorious works thanks to its orgy scene (with monkeys!). And *One-Man Show* is an intriguing fantasy about a man who acquires great artistic talent after nearly being killed in a car accident. Some critics praised Thayer for the vigour of his writing and ability to delineate character (he received particular praise for his female characters). But most pilloried him for the sexual content of his books, calling him crude and coarse. F. Scott Fitzgerald wrote of how "curious children nosed at the slime of Mr. Tiffany Thayer in the drug-store libraries". Thayer, who saw himself as working in the cheerfully uninhibited tradition of Rabelais, ignored such criticism. "I can't help myself," he said. "I am incorrigible."

Thayer moved to California in the 30s to try and break into screenwriting, but had little success. By the end of the decade, tired of Hollywood and, it seemed, of novel writing as well, he had returned to New York. He made good money working for an advertising agency, and directed most of his energies to the Fortean Society, which he had founded in 1931. This promoted the writings and ideas of Charles Fort (1874-1932), a pioneering compiler of anomalous phenomena—strange lights on the sky, mysterious appearances and disappearances, rains of frogs and other creatures—anything for which science did not have a ready explanation. From 1937 onwards, Thayer published a Fortean Society journal, called *Doubt* from the third issue, in which he printed Fort's unpublished notes on strange happenings. But the magazine's real purpose was to give Thayer an outlet for his own crankish views. A born contrarian, he railed against numerous aspects of society, denouncing vaccination, nuclear power, airplanes, you name it.

And he was secretly writing a novel, too, but not just any novel. Thayer intended *Mona Lisa*, which was set in sixteenth century Italy, to be the longest novel ever written. The final manuscript – all handwritten – clocked at 46,000 pages. The first three volumes appeared as *Mona Lisa 1: The Prince of Taranto* in 1956, but alas, Thayer's readers had slipped away by then, and the book was a flop. He was trying to cut the remainder down to more manageable size when he died of a heart attack in 1959.

Thayer never wrote the same book twice, and as well as the novels from the 30s described above there were others, even more unconventional, that were never going to trouble the bestseller lists. *The Greek* (1932), for example, is a staggeringly egotistical production in which Tiffany Thayer—he's the book's narrator—helps a Greek aristocrat become the emperor of the USA, then, as his attorney general, reshapes the country to his own liking (legalising polygamy and pornography, but banning books on the grounds that people want things more if they're banned). *Kings and Numbers* (1934) is even odder, a collection of anecdotes about the ancient Athenian statesman Pericles and his descendants which is simply puzzling.

Then there's *Doctor Arnoldi*, which is unlike anything else Thayer ever wrote. But then, it's unlike anything else anyone ever wrote.

Thayer got the idea for *Doctor Arnoldi* after reading the Russian writer Mikhail Artsybashev's 1913 novel *Breaking-Point*, and indeed lifted his title character straight from it. In Artsybashev's book, Arnoldi is an ageing, overweight, world-weary doctor who lives in a small town in Siberia. At

night, its young men gather at a club to drink vodka, squab-
ble over women and complain about how little there is to do
in the town. They look up to Arnoldi as a wise father figure,
but when they ask him questions about weighty philosophi-
cal issues, his usual reply is "I don't know."

Breaking-Point is a book steeped in death. Two of Arnoldi's patients, an elderly professor and a faded actress, die
protracted, agonising deaths. Meanwhile, an engineer named
Naumoff argues to anyone who will listen that life is futile,
happiness an illusion, and the only reasonable response to it
all is to kill oneself. The philosophy of 'Naumoffism' is
hotly debated by the others, and even more so when six men
and women of the town commit suicide in rapid succession.

Near the end of the book, a student named Tchish is discussing these events with Dr. Arnoldi. Tchish has always
been one of the fiercest critics of Naumoffism. He is an ar-
dent socialist who dreams of the revolution, when the working class will rise up and there will be happiness for all. Arnoldi is predictably dismissive of such ideas.

>   Dr. Arnoldi sighed. "Oh, you'll get tired of that, too,
> one day."
>   "You're an awful pessimist, Doctor! Really, you're
> worse than Naumoff," he cried.
>   "Perhaps."
>   "Then why don't you shoot yourself, Doctor?"
> sneered the little student.
>   Again the doctor fixed his small, expressionless eyes
> on him. After a time, he answered:
>   "Why should I shoot myself? I've been dead for a
> long time as it is!"
>   Tchish started. A strange chill floated through his soul.
> At the moment he really experienced a dream-like sensa-
> tion of sitting and conversing with a dead man.

Later, Tchish is in his room, pondering their conversation.

>   Dr. Arnoldi was right: he had been dead a long time al-

though he went about and spoke. At least he recognised he was dead. Whereas thousands and thousands move about the globe, like worms on a carcase, and never know that they are walking corpses whom someone has let loose in the world in malicious irony till at last they are really shovelled into the grave.

I am sure that when Thayer read that paragraph, a little spark flashed in his brain. It set off other sparks, and they spread and flashed into a vast and awful vision which he knew he would have to get onto paper. And so he set about the task with his usual gusto, transporting the lugubrious doctor from the Steppes of Russia to the tenements of New York, and fleshing out the nightmarish vision in grim, relentless detail.

Doctor Arnoldi generally horrified reviewers. It was never reprinted and virtually disappeared without trace, so that the original edition is today extremely scarce. But, like a mutilated corpse that won't lie down, here it is again. It's not for the faint-hearted, but if you're up for it, you're in for quite a ride.

FOREWORD

by Richard A. Lupoff

Some fifty or sixty years ago I came into possession of a copy of *Doctor Arnoldi,* by Tiffany Thayer. I'd already read several of Thayer's other—and earlier—books. Of course I'd read *Thirteen Men.* That was *de rigueur.* But also *Thirteen Women, One Woman, Three Sheet, The Greek,* and Thayer's admirable anthology, *33 Sardonics.* At that point in my life I was an enthusiastic science fiction fan and learning that a mainstream writer (well, more or less) had once written a science fiction novel (well, more or less) set my young heart to fluttering.

The book looked intriguing in its bright yellow and black dust jacket with three magenta-toned character portraits. I opened it and started to read, and I was swept into the story. I don't want to give away too much, and I'm sure that you already know this book examines the "Death takes a holiday" theme.

I'll do nothing more to give away the plot than to alert you to watch out for the hamburger scene. Oh, and I'll add that I wish Thayer had developed the subplot of interplanetary travel that he barely mentions and then abandons with a passing tip of the hat.

Some time after I'd read *Doctor Arnoldi,* it and the rest of my modest Thayer collection somehow slipped out of my grasp, an event which I soon came to regret. Like the late Vincent Starrett, who repeatedly sold his book collection to meet pressing obligations only to start scouting up the very books he'd just parted with, I went on the prowl for Thayer titles, especially for *Doctor Arnoldi.* For decades I searched, and found a few, but none were copies of *Doctor Arnoldi.* It seemed that the book was headed for literary extinction.

Then—somehow—Chris Mikul, that admirable book scout and critic, not only found a copy, but found one in a pristine dust jacket. The yellow and black background and those three magenta heads had been rescued from Limbo. I do hope that the original jacket is reproduced for the spiritual and aesthetic elevation of readers new to this book and its spectacular design.

I was astonished to discover that Thayer did not actually create the character of Dr. Arnoldi, but lifted him bodily from an earlier book by Russian novelist Mikhail Artsybashev. Did Chris Mikul unearth this scholarly gem after years of diligent search, or did he already know of the *Breaking Point / Doctor Arnoldi* connection? My lobe of curiosity is positively tingling to find out, but then, on the other hand, sometimes it's better not to know.

Tiffany Thayer in general and *Doctor Arnoldi* in particular have been controversial for decades during which time Thayer has drawn the ire of the famous and influential. It's no secret that Dorothy Parker, writing in *The New Yorker,* said of Thayer, "He is beyond question a writer of power; and his power lies in his ability to make sex so thoroughly, graphically, and aggressively unattractive that one is fairly shaken to ponder how little one has been missing."

William Tenn devoted an entire essay to *Doctor Arnoldi,* concluding, "If you ever find a copy, give it to some sf fan you dislike. Your reward will be the baffled misery in his eyes after he's read it."

As for me, I can only paraphrase Tiffany Thayer's own opening words of *Thirteen Men,* the first words of Tiffany Thayer that I ever read:

Doctor Arnoldi is the damnedest science fiction novel you ever read. Not the best or the worst, but the damnedest.

I implore you to read *Doctor Arnoldi.* Once you've done so you may decide that you adore this book, or that you despise it, but you will not be indifferent to it, and one way or the other I guarantee that you will never forget it.

DOCTOR ARNOLDI

As Sid Lyman pressed your pants he'd tell you what was wrong with the social system and the economic structure of the United States. Whether you listened or not you'd hear about it, for Sid's voice was strident as a police siren and he talked about nothing else. "Pass the salt," was enough to start him, and anything more involved than that just kept him spouting that much longer. Happy Suderman made his living by an erratic sort of performance as a reporter on the New York *Ledger*. These two roomed together in Greenwich Village and never left off asking themselves and each other why they did so.

They made a strange combination, so strange, in fact, that neither man could become accustomed to it, although the relationship had existed three years. Happy's plaint usually took the form of self-abasement. "What a sap I was when I picked you up! If you worked that pressing machine half as hard as you do your jaw, you'd *own* the place in two months."

"I don't want to own it. I don't want to own anything." When Sid made a statement of that kind he always tensed his body so that his head vibrated, giving his voice an annoying tremolo whine.

"You Bolsheviki bastards don't know what you want!" Happy had said a thousand times, but every May Day he went to the police station and paid his roommate's fine. Sid accepted this largess from the paid cat's-paw of the capitalist-subsidized press, accepted it as his due. Confronted now and again with the grand total of dollars he owed the reporter, Sid flew into a rage and stormed out of their rooms. That was the limit of human endurance. The mere fact of legal tender raised him rampant, his own defalcations set him braying. And that should have been Sid's crest, a rampant ass, abray.

The hours these two kept were so irregular that sometimes days—up to six or seven—passed without either seeing the other. It was after a peaceful holiday of this kind that they met one afternoon in their rooms.

"Hello! Aren't you home early?" asked Happy.

"Bankers and brokers leave their offices at this hour every day. Why shouldn't I?"

"Because you're a pants presser, I guess."

"Not any more. I quit."

"You quit?"

"As a protest."

"A protest! Who do you think you are, Gandhi?"

"My Cause is just as important. I have quit my job, I will deny myself *bread,* to impress a very great man, a very great Russian."

"The hell you say!"

"Dr. Arnoldi, a famous Russian surgeon; did you ever hear of him?"

"Seems to me I have."

"He is here!" Sid's voice rang like a clarion through the apartment.

"And you quit your job to impress him, huh?"

"He must speak to the workers. He must tell us about the glorious revolution. *He* saw it."

"Maybe he wants to forget it."

"No man who lived through it can forget it."

"Maybe he'd like to try."

"He must not! We must keep their example always before us. They pointed the way."

"I wish you'd impress me by going back to work. The rent's due next week."

"Never! I stood before him and said: 'Dr. Arnoldi, as a protest against your indifference, to show you that the Cause of my brother workers is more important to me than life itself, I will not return to my work, I will deny myself even the necessities of life, until you consent to address us.' "

"You'd be in a mess if he took you up on that and then talked on the wrong side. What makes you think he favors the Cause?"

"In Russia—in Russia, before the revolution, he gave up a position at court, a princely income, the highest honors! to return to his native village and minister to his own poor people."

"Originally a peasant?"

"Yes."

"Oooh, yes. I remember him now. Dr. Arnoldi. I should say I do! And you asked *him* to speak—to get up in Labor Temple or somewhere and harangue your misfits? Why, you damned fool, he's an intelligent man!"

"That is why we need him. That's why I am willing to starve—"

"Starve! On my money."

"I will not touch your money, or your food; I will leave this house—"

"What's his address?"

"The doctor's? What are you going to do?"

"I'm going to see him."

"What for?"

"I'd like to talk to him. I cut my wisdom teeth on a story about him."

"What do *you* know about Dr. Arnoldi?" Sid made a skinny little statue of Scorn.

"I know that if you got the whole pants pressers' union to go on a hunger strike, he wouldn't walk across the street to break it. I didn't know he was in this country, but if he is, it's because he couldn't stand your precious Soviet!"

"Have a care how you speak about the Movement!"

"Where does he live?"

"On Canal Street."

"What number?"

"I don't know the number; it's over a furniture store."

"Canal and what?"

"About three blocks from the Bowery."

"Well, why didn't you say so?" Happy slammed the door

behind him but Sid opened it at once.

"Tell him I have not gone back to my lathe! I have put aside my tools—as a protest."

"Y'don't press pants on a lathe, you half-wit!"

2

THE DOCTOR would not be the one to tell how he got here. One thing had led to another. He had lost everything, but he would not talk about it. Happy was fascinated.

"What really became of the Czar, doctor?"

"I don't know."

"But what do the Russians think—the people? What do they think became of him?"

"Some say this; some that."

"What is your opinion?"

"I have not formed an opinion." His thick, old fingers measured beer from a bottle carefully so the lees should not rise from the bottom. He had made the beer himself.

Happy finished his glass, and after an unprofitable half hour went to the corner drug store to call his city desk. Dr. Arnoldi had no telephone. "I've got a swell human interest yarn about a fat old Russian doctor who lives in a dump on Canal Street. Remember Dr. Arnoldi?"

"Never heard of him."

"Well, *I* have, and there's a peach of a story there, but he won't talk."

"If he won't talk where's your story?"

"I'll get it."

"Don't let me stop you . . . Does he really amount to anything? What does he say about the Soviet?"

"He says it's all one. The peasants will never be happy— nor very unhappy. He says—'They won't get very far either way.' "

"I guess he's right. Call back in an hour."

Happy's feet moved again toward the dingy entrance of the rooming house. Funny old poseur! What did he think that attitude was going to get him? "*I do not know.*" Playing sphinx so people would think he knew a lot. Like Coolidge. Saying nothing so he'd look profound. Some subscribed to the *Literary Digest* from the same motive; or carried the *American Mercury* on the subway.

Happy decided to try the neighbors. He could get the background of his story of this man's ways in America from the delicatessen—the druggist—the other roomers in the building. He could build Arnoldi's character to suit himself; help the old man spread that silent-mental-giant pose, if he wanted it spread, show him moving among mortals and workaday people like a dimly remembered dream. What good was publicity going to do an old codger like that, anyhow? Did he think that tongue-tied futility was going to get him a chair in some college? He no longer practiced medicine, so it couldn't be patients he was trying to attract.

Happy turned into the delicatessen. "Pack o' Camels." . . . He grinned in spurious friendliness at the Jew. "Great old guy, th' doctor upstairs; eh?"

"Psss—yeah?" Obviously the fellow in the white apron did not know who was meant, though he answered the grin with one of his own and nodded his head, almost chuckling. "Yeah"—vacantly.

"Been here long?"

"Hm?"

"Has he lived up there very long?"

"Hm? Who? Who you mean?" He lost no countenance upon being caught lying.

"That fat old doctor that lives upstairs. The Russian."

"Oooh . . . Ha! I t'ought you meant the other fellah."

What other fellah? But Happy ignored that.

"Is he a doctor?" the face over the white apron asked.

"Sure. Didn't you know that? A Russian doctor. Very famous over there."

"Tch-tch. So? They got doctors everywhere, I guess."

"Great old guy," Happy tried his original conversation-opener again.

"Yeah—fat!"

Haw haw haw—"Yeah," Happy made wide gestures with

his hands, "awful fat."

"Yeah."

"You know him pretty well?"

"Me?"

Happy was on the point of making him take the Camels back. "You're Russian, ain't you?"

"Me?"

"There must be some easier way to make a living than this!" the reporter muttered.

"Noo. I'm German. German-Jew."

"Uh-huh. I thought maybe you were Russian, you know, and Dr. Arnoldi had talked to you."

"Arnoldi?!! Oh, you mean *him!* . . . Oh, Arnoldi. Yeah, great guy."

We will now sing the Twenty-third Psalm! "Yeah. Him. Ever talk to you?"

"Sure, sure. He used to come in my place—every day."

"Doesn't come in any more?"

"Oh, no. He don't come downstairs at all no more. He can't walk."

"Can't walk?!"

"Noo. Can't walk . . . Too bad. Great guy."

"What's the matter with him—he can't walk?"

"I don't know. His legks."

"Is that so? Well, how does he eat?"

"Ve deliver. For a while I didn't, but it got so I had to. The drug store sends sandviches and soda . . . What are you gonna do?"

"Yeah, there's somethin' in that. How long's it been since he couldn't walk?"

"Oh, him . . . Six months I guess. Six months he ain't been downstairs. He walks around in the house, I guess."

Happy remembered the ancient carpet slippers on the puffy, swollen feet, as Arnoldi sat sipping homemade beer. "Where's the nearest malt and hops store around here?" he asked.

"Hops? I got a good grade Bavarian hop . . ."

"No, no. I don't want any. I want to know where Arnoldi

gets his."

"Um-hmmmh! So! He's bootleggin' maybe, huh? You gettin' the goods on him, eh?"

"Aw, f'Chris' sake, no!"

"Well, I don' know." The Jew waddled away with a wise smirk. He had nothing more to say.

Happy sighed heavily as he turned again into the street. Hello! Did *that* live up those dingy stairs? The reporter watched a girl pass through the door of Arnoldi's building. She opened a mail box in the hall, one of the few with doors which still locked. Neat, he classified, neat and trim. Who was it she looked like? Nazimova? Sort of. A little taller. And that one who worked with Gary Cooper in—in—oh, what the devil? What was her name?

Quick, energetic steps were taking her up the first flight of stairs that Arnoldi had not descended in six months. Well, interviewing the neighbors came under the head of business. She had been in that third box.

A calling card of the sort printed while you wait, 50c a hundred, revealed—in Old English type—that the mail of Mr. and Mrs. Willard Kent stood a slightly better chance of reaching them if put in that box than if put in any of the others.

"Mrs. Kent," Happy grimaced, "you are about to receive a gentleman of the press." When a key rasped, two floors overhead, he followed her up the steps.

The door was still ajar. Myra was putting her packages on the table. Happy tapped lightly and remembered to remove his hat. "Mrs. Kent?"

"Yes."

She *was* pretty; taking off her hat now. And that wave looked natural. The rich brown color surely was.

"May I trouble you a moment—for some information?"

Another salesman. "I have all the Fuller brushes I need."

This grin of Happy's was not forced. It had taken prizes. It was good to see.

"I'm not selling anything. I'm a reporter."

"Oh, yeah?" She could say that without seeming hard.

"Truly I am."

"Well, I haven't killed anyone."

"Oh, I'm not from the *Mirror!*"

"Excuse me."

"Do I look like a man that'd work on a tabloid?"

"You look like a boy I used to know, named Bill."

"Did you like him?" He shouldn't have said that, Happy Suderman decided as she stiffened a little and ceased to smile. He shouldn't have said it just yet anyway. "But I wondered if you could tell me anything about Dr. Arnoldi, the old Russian who lives upstairs."

"Oh, yes. He lives in front on the top floor."

"Yes, I know. I—I've been up there. But he won't talk about himself. I want to know something about him. How he lives; what he does all day. He was rather famous, you know; but now he doesn't practice any more—and they tell me downstairs that he can't walk. Did you know that?"

"Um—well—he doesn't climb the stairs much. Oh— won't you sit down?" She closed the door behind him and Happy crossed deliberately to a meager sofa. "But he can walk all right."

"Just—just can't go up and down."

"Yes. I was talking to him—oh—two or three days ago; he wanted to go to an exhibition of Rivera, you know, that Mexican's paintings? But by the time he'd made it down this far he was all tired out. Poor old man. He rested in here for a while and I helped him back upstairs to his room."

"Gosh."

"Oh, it was just too pitiful. He wanted to go *so* much. He's very old. I only hope I shall be able to keep my interest in things at his age, paintings, good things to eat and drink. I admire him."

Happy's brows were knitted closely. "You'll just have to forgive me, Mrs. Kent, I can't help it; do you mind telling me what you're doing in this place?"

She scowled with her brows but her mouth smiled. "Why, what do you mean?"

"What do I mean! Haven't you seen any of your

neighbors? Talked to them? The women, I mean."

"Of course." She understood, to be sure, but she was going to get it as nearly in writing as possible. She was going to make him explain it every word, lusciously.

"Well, they are the type one expects to find—eh—in these surroundings. A little smudgy, you know? Voices that catch on things; babies, what-not. You aren't like that."

"Thank you very much."

"Oh—it's—all right. I mean it. You—you don't belong here. Oh, I know, you've heard that before. Why don't I pull a Cadillac out of my hat? . . . Well, cheer up. I'm part seer, see? and I'm predicting Cadillacs for you. You have what is known as 'The Cadillac eye'—If I'm not too personal."

"I'm afraid you are; much too personal."

"Well, let's get back to Arnoldi." She hadn't thrown him out; in fact, she liked him. Count that day lost—

Myra sat in a straight chair at the table. "I don't know much about him. You say he's quit practicing; that's true. But I know of one or two cases here in the building, maybe three people, he has treated—no money, you know?"

"How long have you lived here?"

"This is the second year."

"Is that so?"

"Yes—two years in February."

"You—have to sign a lease?"

"Yes. One year."

Happy moistened his lips and smiled at her, much too personally, by intent.

"We sign from May to May," she said, embarrassed.

"May to May?"—*so* interested.

"Now stop it," said Myra, not at all harshly, "I don't want to be prudish or—or silly, but you are far too intelligent—and too nice—to start flirting with me so crudely three minutes after we've met."

"You're not going to tell me we haven't been introduced!"

"I was considering just that."

"And I wasn't aware that I was flirting *crudely.*"

"Oh, well, I didn't mean that you were winking or whistling at me, but your manner—"

"My manner told you, and I told you myself, too, that you were altogether too beautiful and intelligent and select for this atmosphere. You don't belong here and you know it."

"I don't mean to stay here."

"What does your husband do?"

"Mr. Kent is an engineer."

"On the Erie?"

"He is connected with one of the contractors putting in the Eighth Avenue subway."

"Fresh out of school . . . You aren't very old."

"Not nearly as old as Dr. Arnoldi."

"Bother Dr. Arnoldi. Let's talk about you."

"Mr. Reporter—see there? I don't even know your name."

"Name's Suderman."

"Suderman what?"

"Happy Suderman."

"Happy!"

He nodded. "But I didn't write *The Song of Love* or *Song of Life,* or whatever it's called. Ever read it?"

"*Songs of Songs.* Years ago."

"It is pretty old."

"But ever new," Myra murmured and rose abruptly. "I think you had better go. The superintendent's wife will be able to tell you a great deal more about Dr. Arnoldi than I can. You'll find her in the rear on the first floor."

"I'll bet a dollar she's ugly." He rose, but stayed at the end of the sofa.

"We-ell, Earl Carroll isn't clamoring for her."

"Tell me about your husband. Was I right? Isn't he young? Not long out of college? And aren't you helping him get his start?"

"You make it sound offensive; just the way you say it."

"Ten years on New York dailies."

"Ah! Bitter, bitter life!"

"That works two ways, doesn't it?"

"Why should I let you make me feel like a fool?"

"Oh, please—I—I'm sorry . . . I'll go." Happy picked up

his hat. "Please believe that I'm sincerely sorry for making fun of anything dear to you. It's a nasty habit of mine. I beg your pardon, humbly."

"You can't even apologize without burlesquing. You are the most insincere person I have ever met."

"I know *when* to be sincere."

She studied him appraisingly. Taller than Willard, and, yes, considerably better looking. Needed flesh, especially about his chin and neck. But his eyes were very expressive. Gray, she thought, but color was unimportant. She had always admired that type of man, even before she had married Willard.

"Do you have the time?" Myra asked. Dared he believe his senses? That, certainly, was an innocent and innocuous question. But the thoughts or half-thoughts it might reveal were flattering to Happy and delectable in other ways as well. This very pretty young married woman whose life was no bed of roses had admitted him to her apartment in her husband's absence, had permitted the conversation to take a distinctly personal turn, had looked him over appraisingly, permitted a slight glow of pleasure or satisfaction to be sensed if not actually seen as the result of her scrutiny—and then her mind had turned to a consideration of the time of day. All of which might mean nothing, but—on the other hand—might mean that she was estimating the period of time until her husband should homeward wend his more or less weary way.

Happy cocked one brow at her, then looked at his watch. "My old granddad used to say: 'Half-past kissing time; time to kiss again.' "

"Your watch is very fast."

He looked up quickly.

"Are all reporters like you?"

"I don't know," Happy said, crossing the room to her in three rapid steps. "What do you think?" His long arms held her, bending her back carefully so that if he had not been strong and sturdily poised, her loss of balance would have made her stumble. She could have fallen. Involuntarily, her arms clasped his shoulders and a kiss of no mean proportions was well in progress on her lips before she had catalogued the exact nature of the attack. The answer to her question reached Myra psychically. Indeed, all reporters were *not* like Happy Suderman. Scarcely another news-gatherer in town could have accomplished this recent maneuver with such accuracy, *éclat* and despatch. One futile wriggle showed her that a struggle would not only be useless, but would also, very likely, make her look ridiculous. Practically the only way out of the embrace was a sudden squat, which would inevitably sit her on the floor with a bump she preferred to avoid. His stance anticipated her movements in every other direction; anticipated them and through its unbelievably efficient organization took a disconcerting advantage of each one; making her a party to his designs, making it seem that she moved within his arms—like an old and somewhat inventive friend—while he laughed at her all the time. Her choice, then, lay between accepting the kiss in supine disinterest and squatting abruptly. Remaining absolutely still, Myra decided, was the better course for several reasons. The kiss of itself was highly entertaining; her first from anyone save Willard since the ceremony more than four years back. It would be over the sooner without a struggle. And sitting suddenly might destroy his equilibrium and bring him tumbling atop her on the floor. Perhaps he had allowed for that too. Even if he hadn't, once down, he damned soon would. Anyone so adept at accommodating the movement of a limb or the flexing of a muscle as was this Happy Suderman, would surely quicken his accommodations and increase the speed of his adjustments once he was horizontal.

Having resolved so much with entire accuracy, it is impossible to determine why Myra suddenly sat. Yet, she did—and quickly too—since the success of the effort depended entirely on the surprise element. The kiss, by consequence, came to a sliding finish along her nose and Happy pitched clumsily in an attempt to hold her up. Pitched, almost righted himself, sagged and slumped in a heap, half covering her, but not heavily enough to injure either of them. Then, somehow, they were laughing, and when Happy would have resumed the kiss, her fingers covered his mouth lightly. "Aren't you silly?"

"Have I hurt you?"

"No! But this is no place for us. Get up."

"Kiss me first."

"The idea!"—but she was laughing.

"Please?"

"No. The idea!"

"Then I shan't let you up."

"Very well . . . Oh, see here!" Myra frowned and jerked away. "This is too utterly absurd. Help me up instantly or I shall not only have you discharged but arrested as well." Myra had ceased to laugh.

Happy held her shoulders against the rug and watched her eyes narrowly. "You're not entirely convincing," he said. "I rather think you like it."

"Yes?" she snapped. "We'll see. Kissing is one thing. Wrestling like—a—a pair of—"

"Well, wrestlers," Happy helped her.

"Let me up!"

"You mean right now?"

Myra felt the need of a complete change of front. She was angry. Angry with herself for permitting this man that first liberty of an intimate remark. But he didn't scare well. And he was not the cave-man of legend nor the sex-starved criminal of the tabloids. The proper attitude would save this day, save it and eventually turn it to her advantage. For, if he was attracted to her person as much as his eyes said he was (and that kiss too must have had an idea back of it) she could become mistress of this situation and place herself in a position of power over him the moment she hit upon the correct pose.

She allowed her eyes to soften and her lips to tremble slightly. "This is no way to go about it," she chided him. "After all, I don't mean to be taken on my living-room floor."

Happy quirked his head to one side and waited. His expression was a perfect simulation of puzzled wonder. "What was that?"

"Let's go in there," she indicated the bedroom with her eyes. "I don't like it here."

"In there?"

She nodded—and relaxed her lids seductively.

"In the—bedroom?"

She nodded again—and sighed.

In one, continuous, almost catlike movement, Mr. Suderman was on his feet with Myra in his arms. She clung about his neck, and as he carried her through the door she prepared to take advantage of her first opportunity for freedom. He laid her gently on the bed and leaned over her, seeking her lips again. It seemed to Myra that this one additional kiss was probably necessary to further her aims. He must be convinced that he had won her—so his vigilance would relax. That's what Myra told herself. So she kissed him. She— *kissed* him; convincingly. She almost believed herself.

"Let me slip out of this dress," she whispered, and the quaver in her voice was not entirely spurious.

He grinned at her. "All right," he imitated her whisper. "While you undress I'll call my office. May I?"

She nodded quickly. "Go ahead."

That was, of course, the give-away. Happy was no novice. He kissed her ear in farewell, walked into the living-room and picked up his hat. He heard Myra slam the bathroom door and slide a bolt. He let himself into the outer hall, chuckling. "Dear Dr. Arnoldi," he said aloud, "you certainly have interesting neighbors."

On the floor above, a slattern waved a broom at the dirty carpet. "Good afternoon," said Happy. "Is there a doctor in the building?"

Good afternoon! No one talked like that! Rheumy eyes widened to take him in.

"Is there a doctor here?" he asked again.

"You want a doctor?"

"I want to know if one lives here."

"Mmm—no. Not here."

"Sure, eh?"

"Sure. There's a—a dentist on the corner."

"Yes, but no doctor here?"

"No-o-o."

"Who lives upstairs, in front?"

"Oh, Dr. Arnoldi."

"DOCTOR ARNOLDI!"

"Yes, but he's an—a—well. There's no doctor here. You have an accident?"

"No. I'm all right. But if he isn't a doctor, why do you call him 'Dr. Arnoldi'?"

"I don' know. Everybody does."

"How long has he lived here?"

The dirty maid gave Happy one piercing look and began again to threaten the carpet with her broom.

"How long has the doctor lived here?"

The reporter got not so much as a glance. Dust rose in a suffocating cloud around his head.

One flight below, Myra sent words through the very fiber of the wooden bathroom door. She told Mr. Suderman to be off. To take his noxious presence away and never to bring it back. That she was a respectable married woman, in love with her husband, to whom she was faithful in thought and in deed. That his kisses were being washed from her lips with water, toothpaste and Listerine, and that he might wait and rot a-waiting before *she* would unlock that door. This—and much more—she told Mr. Suderman as he scratched his head, well out of ear-shot, and wondered if it was worth while to go into the Doctor's apartment again and try to get him to talk.

He knocked at every door on the two top floors without receiving any response. Further pursuit of the neighbor angle was impossible. As he passed Myra's door on his way out of the building, he tried the knob. She stood on the far side of the room looking daggers at him. "Do you mind if I use your telephone?" he asked, smirking openly.

"Only my sense of humor saves you," she said. "I should

hate you."

"And you don't? I thought surely you would."

She shook her head slowly.

"May I come in?'

"What for?"

"The telephone."

"There's a booth downstairs."

"Thank you." He started to close the door.

"Come in, you fool!"

"Fool?"

"Yes!"

"But am I?" He closed the door behind him and leaned against it.

"Come over here and sit down." Myra, herself, sat on the sofa and indicated a place beside her. As he joined her she said: "You leave me no pride."

"Forget it."

Then their attention was absorbed by another kiss and it was only by the merest chance that *he* thought, some time later, to lock the outer door.

The city desk was incensed when Happy finally called in. "Where in hell have you been? You know damned well you're supposed to call in here every hour or so. You layin' up with some dame?"

"Why, Mr. Pratt!"

"Well, your voice sounds like it. Get down to Eighth Avenue and Fourth Street as quick as God'll let you. There's been an explosion or something in the subway."

"O.K., boss."

"Dja get that Arnoldi story?"

"I got a swell lead. I've got to see a party down here to-morrow."

"Well, get over to this cave-in now. Tell me about that later."

"Right."

Myra helped him dress. And Happy did not mention to her that his new assignment related to an explosion or something on the new subway, lest she worry about her husband. Happy was thoughtful that way.

3

IN THE NEWSPAPER OFFICE, Happy interrupted his own typing to tell an amazed group around him the one exciting feature of the subway story. "The five of them were buried there— and I mean *buried*—for over two hours. The firemen couldn't work on account of these beams; see? When they *do* get 'em so they'll hold, in they go and one at a time they bring out these birds that should, by all that's holy, be dead as flounders. They hadn't breathed—they *couldn't* 'a' breathed for two hours, and—so help me, Jesus—not one of 'em is dead. It's a God damn miracle, that's what it is.

"Three ambulances are waiting. They been there all the time. Four or five extra doctors and the first-aid boys from two stations. Do they go to work?! You never saw anything like it. When these doctors see there's life in those bodies yet—*how* they work! This young guy; what's his name? Tucker? Operated on Bamberger at noon? *He's* there. They cut belts and tear off buttons. Go over 'em. One guy's back is broken in two places. Get that! His back is busted in two places and he's been buried damn near three hours, dirt and stuff packed in his nose and mouth, and he's *alive!*

"They snake 'em all off to hospitals and, I just got it, two of 'em have already regained consciousness. Tucker is runnin' around like a chicken with his head cut off."

"They tell me Bamberger's gonna live too," one fellow said. "That's what gives Tucker the worms so bad he can't be still. He thinks he's a genius or somp'n."

"Suderman!"—his master's voice.

Happy ripped the unfinished story out of the machine and hurried to the city editor's side. "Comin' up!"

"What does Evans say about these guys bein' still alive?"

"*Evans!* Good Lord, he ain't a doctor."

"He's Health Commissioner. He's got to make a statement."

"I'll call him."

"Of course, call him. Don't be so damned intelligent. It ain't becomin' in a reporter. The public don't know their Health Commissioner couldn't remove a tonsil. Get him to tell you how five men could be buried so long and stay alive."

"Right."

"Get some other big opinions. We'll feature it. Get this Arnoldi to say something."

"I'll try."

"What'd the coroners say?"

"Aw, those birds are like a pack o' *prima donnas*. Tucker was there, see? an' all the others are just waitin' for a chance to slit his throat."

"Bamberger lived, didn't he?"

"That makes four breaks he's had in two weeks."

"You'll need help . . . Sol! . . . I'll put Sol on the Tucker angle. You stick to the hospitals and expert opinions. My knee has given me hell all day—an' you know what that means." For it was the city editor's cherished faith that when the joint of his left knee, once injured, ached and gave him no rest, a story of unusual proportions was on the cosmic hob.

Egmont Evans, County Health Commissioner, expressed appropriate amazement at the story of the Subway Miracle. He had a few kind words for Dr. Allardice Tucker (they were both Democrats), whose consummate skill at surgery had saved so many lives in the past few days, including that of the famous philanthropist, Nathan Bamberger, after his life had been despaired of by a group of the most eminent brain surgeons in the world. Dr. Evans' pronouncement almost indicated that it was his belief that Dr. Tucker's presence at the scene of the accident had been sufficient to stay the hand of Providence.

Happy started for the West End Receiving Hospital, mulling over his notes. Not until then, as he read over the names of the five injured men, did he realize that one of them was Myra's husband, Willard Kent, 408 Canal Street. Happy

stared through the cab window at the passing crowd, unsee-
ing. Even as they had dallied and embraced and caressed
each other, Willard had been bent over a conduit with several
tons of assorted gravel, earth and other debris stopping his
nostrils and holding him crushed and motionless, thirty feet
below the street.

She would be at the hospital. She would be at his bedside,
gripping the almost lifeless hand of her legal mate and hating
the man who had inspired her to an afternoon of madness;
hating herself for succumbing. A pretty pickle. Out of all the
available women in the five boroughs, he had had to choose
one whose husband was going to be killed that afternoon.
Well, if he did die, it might not be so bad. Myra would forgive herself, and him, in time. But—if he lived—there was
an end to that relationship immediately, and it had been a
more than ordinarily pleasant relationship. In fact, as Happy
reviewed the afternoon's events in sequence, he felt that seldom if ever before had a neater combination of male and female been effected. He paid the taxi off, mourning the un-
timely demise, the almost stillbirth, of a great physical love.

In the main corridor he passed the head doctor, Franklin
P. Jocelyn, on his way out of the place. "Hello, doctor; has
Willard Kent died yet?" Jocelyn's seamed face wrinkled in
tolerant amusement. "You fellows are *born* without hearts,"
he said oratorically. "One year at your jobs destroys your
kidneys . . . Your genitals rot off before any of you attain
thirty years, and your brains petrify at thirty-one . . . What's
left but stomach and bowels? Your lights are like hams,
smoke-cured. Your stomachs are perforated with gin-
ulcers . . . Just ambulating pus-sacks—and when you ask after a patient's health, you say: 'Is Willard Kent *dead* yet?'
. . . And my son had the nerve to tell his mother and me last
night at dinner that he was going to be a reporter. I'll kill him
first."

"Yes, doctor." Happy nodded his head patiently. "All true.
Too true. But what I wanted to know was whether Mr. Kent
had left this vale of tears or not. Do you know?"

"He was alive half an hour ago," the doctor chuckled.

"*Tucker's* up there with him now. That's almost a guarantee of a recovery, according to you boys . . . Say, how does it happen I didn't get a publicity break when I was his age? I was pretty good; but none of you demons of the press ever took me up. *Tucker performs 'miracle operation' on multi-millionaire!* If you don't stop inflating him he'll need a pair of those lead shoes deep-sea divers wear to keep him on the ground."

"It isn't all hooey; is it, Jocelyn? That Bamberger operation was on the level, wasn't it?"

"It's made history. Nobody ever saved one before."

"That's what I thought . . . And say, five men have never been buried like this—and lived—Jocelyn! I've got an idea. When was the last death in the hospital?"

"Last night."

"In the night . . . Have you got any cases that *should* have died since? I mean—have you got anybody you are pretty damn sure is gonna check out?"

"I've got an appointment. What are you driving at?"

Happy looked at the doctor a moment without speaking. Then, "Nothing," he said quickly. "So long,"—and he walked rapidly to the elevator.

Tucker, whose body was small, if his ego was swelling to keep up to his reputation, was giving the floor nurse instructions as the reporter alighted from the lift. They spoke. "Is he going to live, doctor?"

Tucker arched his black brows in affronted consternation and his short mustache bounced as he answered: "Kent! Live! Of course he'll live." And Happy was presented a back to stare at. He made a face of mockery at the surgeon and tapped gently on the private-room door.

The nurse admitted him cautiously and they spoke very low. "He hasn't regained consciousness."

"Has his wife been notified?"

"Yes. She's on her way."

"Tucker says he's going to be all right."

"All right!"

Happy nodded.

"His lungs are a jelly. He's breathing in about half an inch of each."

"Crushed?"

"Every rib. He's had one continuous hemorrhage since they brought him here. I think his heart is punctured."

"Then what the hell keeps him alive?"

The nurse poured herself a glass of water from a pitcher on the table. "Tucker," she said, and drank.

Happy's "idea" received this new support blandly. "Have you ever heard of such a case before? Lungs and heart smashed to a jelly—and the patient continuing to live?"

"Never."

"I'll be back." He went to the telephone in the visitors' room and called Bellevue. "Let me talk to Dr. Sterne . . . This is the New York *Ledger* . . . Miss Cohen, then . . . Hello . . . Hello, Miss Cohen? This is Happy Suderman, the *Ledger?* Listen; how long has it been since anybody died at Bellevue?"

"How long?"

"Yes. What time today was your last death?"

"Just a minute . . . That's a funny question."

"I know it is, but I've got a funny idea. I think the world's gone cockeyed, and I'm just checking on it."

"Hold on a second, I'm looking it up . . . Ten o'clock this morning. There were four this morning between nine and ten, but none since then."

"Is that unusual?"

"Um-m, no-o. No. It might happen like that. There's nothing unusual about it."

"It's nearly five o'clock."

"I know."

"Suppose you went through all of tonight without another death; would *that* be unusual?"

"Well, it *has* happened."

"And all day tomorrow?"

"What are you trying to find out?"

"I don't dare tell you. You'd call me mad. I'll be over to see you later . . . Good-bye."

He called the Homicide Bureau. "This is Suderman, the *Ledger*."

"Nothing for you."

"Look!"

"Yeah?"

"Have you fellows had any kind of a call at all since noon today?"

"There was a fracas in Harlem about one o'clock. Somebody got it."

"Shooting?"

"Yeah—but the *Ledger* got it."

"I know, but did the man die?"

"Naw, not yet."

"Where was he shot?"

"Why, we thought it was through the head, but I guess it was jus' a scalp wound."

"Where is he?"

"St. John's."

"Thanks."

"They must be no work at your plant."

"There's plenty."

Happy called St. John's Hospital. "Suderman, the *Ledger*. There's a man there, shot about one o'clock in Harlem?"

"Just a moment."

"Hello."

"Yes, Mr. Suderman. He's here. Colored. Johnson Maxwell."

"Where was he shot?"

"Cranium. Left side."

"Through the head!"

"Yes. Oh—the bullet is still in his brain."

"And he's alive?!"

"Hold the wire just a moment."

The "moment" seemed an hour to Happy.

"Yes—still alive. The doctors are quite excited about it. There's a special appointment; if he lives until seven tonight, Dr. Tucker is coming up to extract the bullet."

Tucker again! And he wasn't going to *try* to extract it.

There was to be no probing or vulgar fishing around. If the black proved his eligibility for attentions so august by living until that conceited little sawbones had finished his dinner, Dr. Tucker would come up and *extract the bullet.*

Happy returned to Kent's room. The nurse was reading *Western Stories Magazine;* the husband breathed in short, gurgling puffs, three or four hundred to the minute. A tiny stream of red ran from one corner of his half-open mouth into a pad of gauze. The reporter watched him a painful moment. So that was Willard. Blondish, pale; not much chin. In his present condition, Happy considered, not a very dangerous adversary. He had to get the hell out of there before Myra showed up. This was going to be tough enough for her without his presence to complicate matters. Happy gave the nurse a card. "Will you please call me at that number when you go off duty?"

At the precinct police station, Suderman pursued his mad hunch. Four or five officers gave advice and he called eight city medical examiners, three of whom were in. None knew of a death since noon. The Board of Health corroborated these statements. When he hung up after that conversation, he faced the uniformed men with a gleam in his eye. "You are going to read the God-damnedest story in tomorrow's bulldog that's ever been in a newspaper," he said. "The world's gone cockeyed."

4

DR. ARNOLDI was finishing a solitary dinner when Happy knocked again at his door.

"Come in," he said, and sipped more hot tea from an old glass. "You, my friend."

"Yes. May I come in?"

"Of course."

Happy sat in a straight chair from which a back-rung was missing and waited.

"There has been an accident," said Arnoldi. "The husband of a lady downstairs has been badly injured." He spoke deliberately, as if setting his words next to each other like bottles on a shelf. The expression of his face did not change. "Will you have some tea?"

"No, thank you."

"Beer?"

"Not now, thanks."

"If you did not come for my beer, it must have been for my company. Not many young people call on me any more."

"I came back because I wanted to tell you something."

The old doctor smiled and almost winked at his tea as he lifted the glass again to his mouth.

"Yes?" So many people had told him things from time to time, all through his life.

"When you were a practicing physician and surgeon, you witnessed many sad, painful—heartbreaking scenes. You saw much suffering."

The fat face moved up and down once or twice. A swallow of tea.

"Those near to the sick people often suffered more than your patients—and sometimes *you* suffered most of all."

"I?"

"Didn't you?"

"I was often uncomfortable in the face of anguish. Their eyes would look at me, asking 'why?'—asking *me* why!"

"And you couldn't explain."

"Who can explain?"

"Which would you say was the sadder spectacle, in your experience, doctor, life or death?"

Arnoldi slipped a long Russian cigarette between his lips, where it hung, oddly out of place, like a broom-straw in a cake. "But, life, of course."

"Then the story I have come to tell you is the saddest you have ever heard, for, Dr. Arnoldi, it has become impossible to die."

Still there was no change in that phlegmatic face, no alteration visible behind his clever eyes. He struck a match deliberately and applied it carefully to the end of his cigarette, another home-made product; the little machine for their manufacture sat on a shelf to the left of the window.

"I am not surprised. Their God would be deaf indeed to ignore their prayers always . . . How do you know?"

"There hasn't been a death in New York City since noon today, although the usual number of accidents, shootings, operations—all types of illness—all of man's maladies have continued at the usual rate."

"Only one afternoon? Perhaps Death is taking a short vacation."

"Perhaps—but it is unprecedented. There are seven or eight million people here, in Greater New York, and I have been checking since five o'clock. Not a single death has been recorded. I covered the accident to the lady's husband. This one downstairs. He is lying in a hospital now with his heart pumping blood out of his mouth, his lungs a pulp, yet he lives."

"And you have other evidence. I see that."

"Have you read about this fellow, Tucker? Have you seen him become the wizard? The miracle worker? We've been crazy. It isn't Tucker! His patients *can't* die!"

"I see what you mean."

"But do you see what it means to mankind? Do you see the effect on our morals, our laws, our institutions? Good Lord, Arnoldi, it changes everything! If man can't die what's to become of him? We can't preserve bodies that are beyond use or repair just because they—er—*pulse*."

"Can't we?"

"How can we? My God, doctor. It's indecent. It's ghastly. Can you imagine—"

"I think we can."

Happy paused and studied the Russian, thinking. The old rhetoricians' quibble came back to him from his college days: Which is the greater number; those living or those dead?—and he saw vast fields of naked bodies, piled like cord-wood, all—pulsing.

"Yes," Arnoldi repeated, "I think we can . . . I think we will. If your conclusion is correct, and through some omnipotent change of heart we are to have corporeal immortality here on earth, man will preserve the bodies; wait and see."

"He will; won't he?"

Arnoldi nodded, ruminating, then spoke with little interest. "Yes—he'll keep them."

"As a doctor, Dr. Arnoldi, can you offer any explanation of this phenomenon? Suppose, for the sake of argument, that I am right. How is it possible? How will physics, official physics, assimilate such data?"

"I don't know."

"Oh, please; of course you don't know, but won't you guess? They *will* assimilate it. They won't shut up shop. No recognized science is going to go bankrupt without a fight. What will they say?"

"Why don't you wait and see? You won't have to wait long—if you are right."

"How will the average man take it? Without the fear of death, how will he govern his life? What will the preachers say?"

"Man will like the idea at first, until he learns what it means."

"What *does* it mean?"

A tired old smile, one that had been in the doctor's family for many years, hovered across his face. "That depends upon how widely your calamity is spread. If the entire world is affected, it may mean that we shall have to go hungry."

"But we couldn't starve."

"No."

"It wouldn't matter whether we ate or not."

"That is a dreadful prospect," the doctor said sadly, moving the greasy plates lovingly toward the center of the table and munching a crumb of spice-cake he had overlooked. "I suppose the race would adjust itself to that in time . . . Won't you join me in a bottle of beer?"

"Thank you, I will."

Arnoldi pushed his chair back laboriously and stiffly.

"Oh, let me get it," said Happy, jumping up. "Where? . . ."

"Thank you," the old man said, relaxing. "In the ice-box.

The top . . . That large green bottle will do very well—
careful! if you shake it, the sediment rises. Try as I will, I
can't eliminate that entirely."

"That we had this afternoon was very clear; good, too."

"Thank you! I am rather proud of my skill as a *braumeis-
ter*."

"You have a right to be. Did you make your own beer in
Russia?" Despite the gargantuan implications of his new assignment, Happy had not forgotten that there was also a human interest story in this waning savant.

"No. Your prohibition made me take it up. That was your
amendment's one virtue; it made the individual responsible
for one of his major pleasures."

"And you think it's important that the individual develop
his skill, his various talents?"

"Important? No-o—not important."

"Desirable?"

"Since I can no longer hold a knife steadily enough to operate, I find brewing a pleasant pastime."

"You are human, then. You get a satisfaction from match-
ing your wits with Nature. You are proud of your skill at
chemistry. And when I praise your beer you are flattered."

"Perhaps . . . Something like that."

"Oh, come; admit it. That takes the place of the gratitude
your patients expressed after you had treated them successfully? Their praise was sweet—and now you miss it."

"I don't know . . . I don't remember."

"Don't remember?! As a young man?"

"Oh—then."

They sipped their beer in silence for a moment. Happy
studying the big man as if his head and shoulders looming
over the edge of the table would finally reveal the true nature
of his character if contemplated long enough, as the Buddha
resolved all the mysteries from creation to his day simply by
looking long and solemnly at his navel:

"So the man downstairs is to be one of the first of these
half-dead, these living corpses?" Arnoldi asked wearily.

Happy assented. "He's that now."

Dr. Arnoldi closed one eye to escape smoke from his cigarette. "She is a very pretty woman. Have you seen her?"

"Eh?—Yes. Yes, I've met her."

"She's with him?"

"I think so."

"She would be with him . . . I hope you are wrong, young man."

"Wouldn't you like to know that you would never die?"

Arnoldi's eyes held the reporter's as amusement curled his lip. "What difference could that make to me? I have been dead for many years."

"It will make a lot of difference to *me.*"

"What difference? What will you do?"

Happy felt for a moment as if the doctor were humoring him, as if he were a child. "Well," he said resentfully, "I'd quit caring about a lot of things. I'd have less consideration for others. I'd live recklessly."

"Would that make you happier . . . More beer?"

"Of course it would." Happy pushed his glass forward. "Why, look, the secret's not out yet. No one knows about it; Tucker, maybe. What's to stop me from doing some daredevil stunt—like Lindbergh? I know I can't get killed. Why shouldn't I—fly to the moon or—or something? I can be a hero, internationally famous."

"Hadn't you better wait until you see what becomes of these injured men who cannot die? You wouldn't want to live for eternity in constant pain."

"My God! Perhaps they'll have to keep some of these—these living corpses (we need a name for them, don't we?) under the influence of morphine for—for *years.*"

"And the supply of morphine may be insufficient, in time, as the food will be."

"I think I'm going mad, doctor."

"Try not. You will need your wits, all of them, if this comes to pass. We all shall."

"Tons of anesthetics will be needed. *There's* relief for unemployment. Thousands of men and women will be needed—there won't be enough nurses and doctors. The *race* will be serving its own—er—comatose, *comatants*. Does that express it? Comatants."

"Comatants . . . Suppose consciousness remains in some?"

"I don't want to suppose anything of the kind! The longer I think about this the worse it gets."

Arnoldi spread his thick fingers and gestured, broadly. "Do you see it? . . . It isn't a pretty picture."

"It is the most terrible situation man has ever faced. What will he do? What *can* he do?"

"Nothing."

"It would have to be made legal to bury the worst cases. It would be necessary."

"Bury them—alive—eh?"

"They wouldn't be *alive!*"

"They wouldn't be dead."

"We—we'd *have* to."

"I'm afraid you don't know your fellows very well, my son. I don't think they'd do that."

"But, in time they couldn't avoid it. There wouldn't be room for everyone. The world isn't big enough."

"Perhaps it is this which will push us on to interstellar exploration. If the world, Earth, gets too small to hold us all, perhaps we shall discover another place—Mars?—some other place."

Happy stood up suddenly, his blood pounding in his ears. "I—I must find out. I'll check further. This thing can't happen—it's too horrible."

"Man prayed so hard for life, long life. It is very sad to have one's prayers answered . . . More beer?"

"No! No, thank you. I must go. Good night." He started away without his hat, then returned for it. "May I come back later, doctor, when I have learned more? I'm going to telephone."

"Come any time, son. You are always welcome." The picture of the old fat man wiping beer from his lips with his swollen fingers followed Happy Suderman into the night.

5

AS A CAB took him uptown, Happy thought of Myra. He should have left a note, slipped it under her door.

Probably her family lived out of New York. Her speech had suggested the Middle West. She could have no intimate friends among her neighbors, certainly. Acquaintances about town somewhere, of course. He dared not face her. Not now. Not under these circumstances. Sight of him would enrage her; he knew that . . . Unless she was friendless—and that seemed impossible.

Somewhere ahead, in the street, out of sight, there was a tremendous crash! Glass splintered—and Happy screamed. Screamed like an hysterical woman. His driver turned curiously, grinning. "Never touched you," he said.

"Watch the road, you idiot!" Happy snapped. "You want a smash-up?"

"What's a coat o' paint?"

Three lanes of cars edged and sidled and moved slowly around the wreck. Happy's face was contorted with terror as his cab eased by the tangled, crumpled mass of wood and steel. "Jesus!" he said. "Get out of here, quick."

"Nervous?"

Happy did not answer.

"They got it, all right. That guy must've been drivin' blindfolded . . . Well, somebody gets it every day." Happy remembered an old song: *"Somebody's Dying Every Day."* There would be new songs now. What would Tin-Pan Alley do with *this* theme?

Happy walked by the information clerk at the door of the *Ledger* office without a word. His eyes were fixed, set, all but sightless. The old man on duty chuckled. Suderman was pretty drunk; pretty drunk even for Suderman.

At the city desk, the reporter plucked the night man's sleeve.

"Hello, Happy."

"Hello . . . Blake; listen."

"Yeah?"

"Blake—listen."

"You must of got an early start. I thought you were workin' on the Miracle story."

"Listen, Blake."

"Yeah, boy, I'm listenin'. You're settin' a lousy example for my reporters, Happy. Thank God none of 'em are in but Baxter."

"I'm not drunk. I've got the story."

"No-o! You ain't much drunk!"

"Blake, something terrible has happened. The more I think about it, the worse it gets."

"Baxter," Blake called. "What's happened that's so terrible, Happy? Don't look like you'd be upset, an old head like you."

"Wait'll I tell you."

"Shoot!"

"Blake, people can't die any more. We're all going on, living forever, sick and well, rich and poor. No matter what happens to us—we can't die."

Blake was reading copy, humoring him. "Well, don't let it go to your head," he said. "How many s's in 'possession'?"

"Four."

Blake looked around and up at Suderman, like a duck watching a soaring hawk. "Now I know you're drunk. There ain't a reporter in town uses more than three."

"All right, kid me." Happy's arms hung limply at his sides. "You think you want to live—tonight. In a year you'll be eating dynamite, trying to *blast* the life from your body."

Baxter came up to the desk.

"Take Happy home; he's pretty sick . . . Call me from his house. Try to get his story out of him."

"O.K . . . Where does it hurt the worst, Happy?"

Suderman only shook his head.

"Don't let him drink any more, Baxter. He's on the verge of pink elephants."

His genial comrade took Happy's arm as if to steady him. "Come on, boy, let's go . . . You ain't so drunk."

"I'm not drunk at all, but if this gorilla wants to throw a

swell story it's nothing to me. He'll read it in all the other papers tomorrow. Come on, I'll tell *you* about it."

"Don't forget to call back here, angel! Mother'll worry till she knows you're safe."

"O.K., boss."

"And don't sniff any of that stuff he's on! It ain't healthy."

The two reporters left the room—and the building. In the street Happy asked: "Did you see the Obits?"

"Nuts to *you*."

"No reflection. Did you see 'em?"

"No."

"Tomorrow there won't be any."

"Just as you say, boy. What do I know?"

"Look at me, Baxter! Do I look drunk? Do you smell anything on my breath? . . . You know I don't sniff anything."

"Well?"

"Baxter, it's on the level—and that's what's damn near killing me. Nobody's died—anywhere—since noon today. Babies bein' born all over the world at the same old rate— but nobody's dyin'. You get that, Baxter? You see what it means?"

The other reporter backed away a few steps, his cheeks turning pale. "You—you go on home by yourself, Happy. Get some sleep."

"Oh, go to a telephone, you sap! Ask any hospital in town! Ask for a nigger named Maxwell at St. John's. Tucker took a thirty-eight caliber cartridge out of his brain an hour ago—and he's gettin' well!

"I was on that subway story. I wrote it. Did you see it? Do you read the papers? We slugged it 'Miracle'! Why? I'll tell you why. Because those five men were as good as dead an hour before the bodies were found—and one of 'em ate dinner tonight. You think I'm crazy? Come on—we'll call the Cook County Morgue in Chicago. Come on." He dragged the unwilling Baxter back into the building and into a telephone booth. "You call 'em," Suderman directed. "Then we'll *both* be crazy."

Then they called Denver and Los Angeles and Dallas and Augusta. They went on from there, calling Mexico City, Tampico and Toronto and Montreal. Cables to Europe began to hum and Australia was asked for data.

"It's just North America," Baxter said finally, as he staggered, sweating and haggard, from his booth. "From the Canal north . . . What the hell do you suppose it is?"

"The Gulf Stream! How do I know what it is? But it's true, ain't it? Nobody's died on the whole damned continent since noon today."

"Do we dare to break a story like that? Suppose it's just coincidence? Will you write it or shall I?"

"Write your head off," the older reporter consented. "I got other things on my mind."

Happy went to the rooms he occupied with the radical pants presser.

"Did you find him?" the young man asked shrilly from his pillows. He was propped up in bed, reading. "What did he say? Will he come?"

"Who?"

"Dr. Arnoldi! Did you tell him I quit my job?"

Suddenly Sid Lyman and all his disgruntled kind were uproariously funny to Happy Suderman. He laid back his head and roared his bitter mirth. "*You* quit your job!" Ho!—how he laughed. Again and again.

Sid put his skinny feet out the side of the bed and began to vibrate with rage. "What is so funny about that? Stop! You sound like a crazy man."

Abruptly, Happy's merriment ceased. "You got me into this!"

"Got you into what?"

"Listen! It doesn't matter whether you work or not. It doesn't matter whether you *eat* or not. You can't die! *I* can't die. Nobody can die any more."

"Well, how did I get you into it?"

"It was you who sent me to Dr. Arnoldi. I met a woman there, in that building. Did you see her? A beautiful girl with brown curls? A woman much too good for those surroundings?"

"Too *good!* Too good for those surroundings! How is she any different from my mother? No woman is too good for any surroundings! These hovels are not fit for swine! But we'll leave them behind. You wait and see. We'll live in the palaces, the Park Avenue mansions! Capitalism is doomed!"

"Oh, shut up!"

"The great May Day is coming!"

"The great May Day is *here,* you little snipe. Didn't you hear me tell you? Death is no more."

"What are you talking about? Is this something Dr. Arnoldi has invented?"

"No! God's turning somersaults! Everything's upside down. Something has hit us! Hit North America, and it is impossible to die."

"You're fooling—but, if you are not, how does that alter our misery? Must we go on, now, indefinitely, suffering? Is this the crowning achievement of Privilege? That the slaves shall never die, never be delivered of their yoke by the merciful hand of death? That was all we ever had to look forward to."

"That will all be changed now. There will be no slaves, no classes."

"What will change it? Nothing but revolution will ever abolish class distinction."

"You think not? Consider this: If what I say is true, our present civilization is doomed. We will be reduced in less than a decade to the law of the jungle, the law of claw, club and fang. Brute strength alone will have value, physical might will make right as it has not since the mastodon passed. You, you insignificant little whiffet, will be shouldered aside and left to pulse in a gutter somewhere, wherever you fall."

"Who says this? Who says death is no more?"

Happy advanced part of his evidence.

"It is a great day for the worker—I think," said Sid. "A great day."

"It is the worst of all possible days for everyone. You are

still asleep."

"I think it is a great day because we outnumber them. We can take what is ours and they cannot stop us; all the factories and the mills, all the prisons and the stores and the banks! If what you say is true, they cannot kill us. We send our legions against them and the first ranks succumb, to imprisonment, to being maimed and beaten. New ranks of workers follow those—like the waves of the sea. Our numbers are endless! They cannot stop us now." A fevered madness lighted his eyes and he stripped himself quickly of his pajamas. "Who knows about this? Are the papers out yet?"

"No."

"I am going to Union Square. I am going to tell the comrades."

"The comrades are all in bed!"

"I'll get them up! They must learn about this first, before Privilege has time to mobilize against us."

"You wouldn't be so damned anxious to get crippled if you'd seen a few things I've seen today. You may go on for eternity, you know, every breath a piercing, burning agony."

"They will have to treat the wounded. Common humanity demands that."

"In two weeks there won't be any *place* to treat them. In a month there won't be any medicine to treat them with. There aren't enough doctors and nurses in the world to take care of the sick—if nobody dies."

"But what's to become of us? Eventually, I mean. We wear out. Our bodies and minds wear out."

"But life remains."

Sid stopped dressing with only one leg in his pants. "The streams will be polluted. Water supplies—city water supplies will fail! The streets will be choked with—bodies!"

"Now you're waking up."

"What are we going to do?"

"The same thing we've always done; *wait.*"

"Wait—forever?"

"Wait until this passes. I figure it's sun spots or something; they change all the time."

"Maybe we're passing through something, a—a strata of the air."

"You'd think that would affect the whole world. So far this has hit only North America."

Sid was moved beyond the power of expression. "Jesus!" he said, and continued his dressing.

"Congress will pass a law against intercourse. Marriage will have to be abolished."

"They can't stop that!"

"They'll have to!"

"But they *can't.*"

"Well, we can't go on having babies! You damned fool! Something has to be done."

"Castration! They—they'll have to castrate all the men."

"Well, you won't mind that."

"They can't; can they?"

"The doctors will all be too busy."

"Say! That's right too." Sid stared at the wall a moment, then admitted defeat. "It's too much for me."

"Life was never too much for you before, was it? This is the first time I ever saw you when you didn't know the answer."

"What does Dr. Arnoldi say about this?"

"He doesn't know."

"Doesn't know what?"

"Anything. He says it can't matter to him because he has been dead for years."

"It's all right to talk like that—but, say, he'll find out there's a difference, won't he?"

"I don't know."

With his hat in his hand, Sid stopped. "What are you going to do? Just sit here? With this going on? Aren't you going out and see what happens?"

"Nothing will happen for a while. You'll find the streets just as you left them. It's still against the law to park near a fire plug. Nothing will happen until the public begins to realize what this means."

"I'm going to Union Square."

"If you get arrested, I warn you, I will not bail you out. If you try to start a revolution tonight, you'll lie in a cell and rot before I'll come for you."

"I—I'm not going to start—a revolution. I'm just going to see if anybody else knows about this."

"Ask the nearest policeman."

Sid was gone. Happy looked out of their window over low roofs and rectangles of light which were the windows of other mortals, men and women proceeding about the routines of their lives. In the morning they would read the papers incredulously, stupefied by a thought too gigantic for assimilation. What *would* they do when they could no longer disbelieve? When, day after day, the papers continued to announce that immortality seemed at last to have become a physical and unavoidable fact, what would they do? Would it affect a single generation as much as he had at first supposed? Were such things as water famines possible—within a few years? Would engineers and scientists be equal to this new demand upon their powers? If housing and public utilities *could* keep pace with the increasing population, how long could Nature stand the strain? Coal and iron and oil were not limitless. Statisticians had predicted the exhaustion of these resources, setting the date so far ahead that no one had worried. But—now! The forests would be mowed down like hay! Where was the acreage sufficient for grazing all the beef and mutton which would now be needed? If babies were prohibited, would an age limit for feeding be imposed? No more baked beans after you are one hundred years old! Nothing!

Happy rubbed his aching head and walked around the room two or three times in blind circles. "I wonder if it's hit animals, too. My God! Suppose we have to eat *live* food!"

The night sounds of the city which had always passed with Happy for "quiet", even for *silence,* reached his consciousness and he listened intently. Wasn't there a difference? Had New York always sounded like that? The sky! Happy craned out of the window at the stars. "Well, I don't know much about where you should be, but you look all right to me. There's the Big Dipper."

Down the hall, a door slammed, and Happy whirled, crouching; his breath held; his fists clenched. A man walked along the hall. When those steps had died out, Happy relaxed. The walls and the familiar furniture of the room mocked him with their expressionless stolidity. "What in hell am I afraid of?"—but reason was powerless to quiet his nerves, his palpitating heart.

Glancing furtively behind him at every shadow, Happy gained the street and went again to Dr. Arnoldi's. He realized as he climbed the stairs that he must call his mother before the newspapers excited her too much. She was dependent upon him for the exegesis of all the day's events, for her political opinions and all her attitudes toward miscreants, convicted or at large. Mrs. Suderman always reserved judgment until she could speak to her son. What could he tell her about this?

The doctor had washed his dishes and disrobed, putting on a suit of unbleached pajamas of a sort of balloon cloth, part silk, before resuming his seat and a game of chess. He was his own opponent. The air of the room was thick with a singular odor, bitter and discomforting. "You are making yourself ill, my friend," he said to Happy who stood just inside the door, gaunt and staring.

"I?"

"It won't do any good, you know."

"My God, doctor, why don't you open a window in here?" Arnoldi raised his brows.

"Excuse me—please?" Happy had not meant to be rude.

"A window?"

"Don't you find it stuffy?"

"I hadn't noticed."

"May I?"

"Do."

Happy gulped the night air. Arnoldi moved a bishop very deliberately on his chessboard.

"Has anyone died yet?" The doctor was but making conversation. His speech was hardly a question.

"Not yet," Happy croaked. "No one."

"Vodka—or beer?"

"Nothing, thanks."

Mildly dismayed by the cleverness of his adversary's last move, the massive Russian hunched over the table and studied his game intently.

Myra knocked at the door. It was ten minutes before midnight. She spoke before entering, but Happy had no time to hide.

"Hello," she said. "You still in the building?"

Arnoldi rose, stiffly.

"Sit down, dear," she said.

"You know my young friend; do you?"

"Yes," Myra answered, her face as still as if carved from marble. "We met this afternoon." She did not look at either of the men, but sat suddenly in a chair and leaned her head back in exhaustion. "He's better now," she said, anticipating their question. "The flow of blood has almost stopped." She removed her hat with a quick, nervous gesture, as if it hurt her head.

"I'm glad to hear that," Happy said. "And I should like to tell you how sorry I am."

"Thank you . . . Dr. Tucker says he will live. Isn't he wonderful? Dr. Tucker, I mean."

Suderman and Arnoldi exchanged glances. When neither spoke, she raised her head and looked at them, looked from the drawn, taut muscles of Happy's face to the commiserating eyes of the old doctor. "What is it?" she asked. "What's the matter?" Unaccountably, *her* heart was racing. She dreaded to hear either man speak. The imminence of some disastrous revelation which her trouble caused her to imagine would be personal vibrated in the surcharged atmosphere. "Why don't you tell me?"

Happy took a step toward her and stroked her hair once, tenderly, frowning, scowling, to prevent any emotion from touching his features. "Myra," he said huskily, "something terrible has happened."

A low, soft moan escaped her. "He's dead! Ooooh, *God!*

They—they called? They called—while I was coming home."

The reporter shook his head. Arnoldi looked away from the face of his lovely neighbor; looked away and cleared his throat. "He isn't dead," Happy said. "He isn't going to die. He can't."

Her smile, piteous, grateful, loving, wrung the reporter's heart. He could scarcely go on. "Is—is death—the worst thing you can think of—happening to a man?"

Myra was puzzled. "It's—well—it's the *last* thing. The final thing. Even if he's always crippled, I'll love him." She realized that he might find that difficult to believe—and hurried on: "That's the truth! No matter what I have done; no matter how poorly I have shown my love; it's true. If he never walks again as long as he lives, I'll serve him, I'll work for him, I'll love him truly and faithfully, him and no one but him—as long as I draw the breath of life."

Happy turned to their host. "We shall have to learn to talk all over again. A thousand figures, a thousand words have lost their meaning."

"Love hasn't lost its meaning," Myra declared, vaguely defensive.

"You don't understand, my dear," said Arnoldi tenderly. "Mr. Suderman has something to tell you."

"Mr. Suderman has told me quite enough for one day!"

Arnoldi raised puzzled brows.

"Please," Happy begged. "This is different."

She glared at him.

"This concerns all of us . . . Death has stopped. It is no more. No matter how badly injured your husband may be, he cannot die. No matter how much I want to, I cannot die. No one can die . . . There is a new order."

His words were almost without meaning to Myra. She watched him narrowly, expecting some sudden maniacal display; a mad laugh, a leap, a contortion. Nothing happened and she laid her head wearily back against the chair, and closed her eyes. Not to die! What a stupid thing to say! Two things were sure; death and taxes.

She opened her eyes slowly. The young man had dropped into a chair and buried his face in his hands. The dim yellow light from a single bulb hanging from the ceiling of the ugly room wavered in her sight and her stomach growled noisily. She smiled at her old friend, the doctor. "I guess I've forgotten to eat," she apologized. "I didn't want to leave Willard . . . They made me go."

"You must sleep," Arnoldi said. "Food can wait. Perhaps you shouldn't eat—just yet."

"I'm not really hungry." Her voice was plaintive, tender. Happy jerked to his feet and strode to the window overlooking a dismal, unlighted back court.

Myra asked silently of her host what strange agitation so troubled his other guest. She touched her forehead lightly and made troubled eyes. But with her curiosity there was mingled another question: Could this male without morals to whom she had responded without shame—could he have told the doctor of their intimacy? Men did that. Some men. She thought he had seemed of another stripe, but now he was plainly insane. If he had told the doctor—Why should he tell the doctor?—Could his restlessness and wild talk be the result of their afternoon together? Was he, after all, an extremely decent young man? And was he wrestling now with conscience—even as she was?

Arnoldi did not answer her look. He smiled dully, meaninglessly. She studied Happy's back, which told her no more. His hands were clenched behind him; his head pressed the coolness of a pane of glass. She rose and tiptoed to the Russian's side. "What is the matter with him?" she whispered. "He seems to be out of his mind."

Arnoldi nodded. "Perhaps he is."

"Is he—upset about this—accident?"

Another nod. Myra tried to think. Was he in love with her? Really? A surge of compelling tenderness moved her a step toward that silent back. That must be it. The intimacy of that afternoon, the melting contact, the communion of their psyches, had welded him to her. Now he suffered for her, suffered in despairing futility, fearing to be misunderstood, helpless to comfort. As Myra thought these things, a sensation akin to one she had known that afternoon returned and carried her to his side. "You mustn't feel so badly," she said softly, laying her hand on his shoulder. "Please don't."

His eyes were hard and fathomless. "Oh, I'll be all right," he said between clenched teeth. "I'll be all right a little later, when this damned thing resolves itself—when I understand or *think* I understand what's going on . . . You don't get it yet. You can't. It will hit you tomorrow after you read it in the papers. It will be that way with everyone. It will come to them slowly. Some won't ever get it."

What was this? About death? What had he said? "I—I just didn't want you to—to feel badly—about us," she said so low she thought Dr. Arnoldi would not hear. They were behind the doctor, who did not move but sat silently staring into space through the chessboard.

"You're charming," Happy ejaculated. "Just charming . . . I wonder what this is going to do to you. No!" he stopped her from speaking, "don't say any more. You are overwrought. I couldn't take advantage of you—tonight. You mustn't be kind to me until later. Wait. Wait several days. Wait until you see some of the pictures I see already. *Then* if you feel kindly toward me—let me know."

"You go to bed," Arnoldi ordered suddenly without turning. "Both of you go to bed."

Myra blushed.

"That's grand advice," said Suderman. "I'm taking it." He moved into the center of the room and the girl stepped back against the wall, abashed. His gruffness bruised her. She had offered something; *what* was not entirely clear to her; and he had spurned it, whatever it was. She let her body relax against some shelves of old books and watched the reporter find his hat. He was a very sick man, she decided. His eyes burned instead of seeing. His lips were never in repose. His fingers wandered. This was not the same person who had so masterfully seized her, so certainly and surely and confidently managed and governed and manipulated every muscle, nerve and thought a few hours before. This man was little short of a nervous wreck. The doctor was right; he needed sleep. If he could sleep with his tousled head in the crook of her arm, his flaming eyes closed with her cool kisses, he would be healed. He needed that. So gentle and understanding, he had been, so sensitive. Why shouldn't she do that for him? Why should hoary convention prevent so pure a motive from ministering to so great a need? Would he misunderstand her proffer of that solace? Where else might troubled man find such relief? such comfort? such repose? *He* might find it in arms more familiar than hers. Myra knew nothing about him. Perhaps his wife would tender far more satisfactory service.

Perhaps he was hurrying off to go to another woman.

She gave him her hand as he came to bid her good night. "I shan't sleep a note," he said grimly, "but I damn sure mean to try."

"Do you live far?" Myra heard issue from her lips.

Happy blinked several times in an effort to focus his sight on her eyes which searched his for comprehension.

"I live in the Village with a radical pants presser. He's going to talk to me all night long."

A key slid into his palm.

Through the fog of weariness and misery that beclouded his brain, this was not clear. How could it be? Happy Suderman was a man. When a woman gave him the key to her rooms she said, in essence: "I want you." He fumbled with that thought a moment. Flattery emanated from the key, ran up his fingers, inflated him and almost cleared his head. It was good to know that the effect of those two hours had been not entirely one-sided. He was glad to have left the mark of his personality upon her. But what manner of woman was this who could invite him to her bed while a husband she claimed to love lay in battered unconsciousness, breathing blood instead of air? Happy had held her in different esteem. As he had looked at Willard's all but dead face on its hospital pillow, he had reasoned that only the man's death and the passage of time thereafter could possibly bring about a renewal of that pleasant relationship. Happy had thought thus highly of Myra. He had said to himself: "If this man recovers, my goose is cooked. She will never see me again." Yet, here and now, with Willard's fate still undecided, in her mind, and without any aggression from him, she offered herself. Happy could not see beyond that. Being a man, he could not identify womanly tenderness dissociated from sex. With internal mechanisms still readjusting themselves after physical interchange with this woman, he could not attribute her interest to any motive save lust.

Myra weighed these contingencies, yet she gave him her key. Perhaps woman is inured to misunderstanding. Perhaps she is blind to consequences when the pure desire to serve unselfishly urges a course of action. Perhaps some yet-to-be-discovered glands and filaments did seek their complement selfishly and without her knowledge. Perhaps there is a gratification, a physical, material gratification for woman in such self-debasement. Perhaps this is a divine heritage and Myra pretended to Christlike honors. Or that Jesus was a masochist.

For her key, Happy paid her a sneer. Out of obtuseness cruelty came prancing; in the sink of his ignorance mercy was drowned. She closed her eyes, quickly, attempting through speed to stem the hurt at its source. When she opened them again, he was leering! His baleful inspiration seemed inexhaustible. She closed them again and kept them shut, wondering what next device he would have discovered for her torment.

This blinking only confused the man further, and when she saw him again he was only bewildered, looking from her eyes to her expressionless mouth, to the angle she held her head, to the still smoothness of her throat, seeking any clue to explain her behavior. Obviously his first impression had been wrong, but if evidence of a more accurate translation existed, he was too utterly weary to recognize it.

"I don't understand," he whispered, indicating the key with his eyes.

"You look so tired."

"God knows I am."

"We'll *sleep*," she said emphatically.

He took her hand again and kissed it, then turned it over and closed her fingers around the key. "I still don't understand . . . But I have sense enough to know you don't want me."

"It's stupid to make you go where you won't sleep. You're ill. You need rest."

Happy looked quickly at the back of Arnoldi's head. Myra nodded and they moved around the table. The doctor was asleep in his chair.

6

THE MORNING NEWSPAPERS had handled the story with kid gloves. They dared not say, as Happy had, that death had stopped. So far, the evidence indicated only that the mortality rate in North America had sunk lower than the value of stocks and bonds. It might pick up again. Expert opinion was quoted.

Dr. Eric N. Boyer of the Rockefeller Institution said: "The medical profession has labored for centuries with unselfish zeal to prolong life. Each passing year has shown progress. Constant application to our problems, ceaseless investigation and experimentation have gained ascendency for man over one disease after another. Bubonic plague, smallpox, yellow fever, tuberculosis and cancer have given way before the great white light of Science. Man's span of years has been lengthened, old age has been deferred, accidents have been minimized by legislation and safety measures such as the gradual elimination of the grade crossing and, in aeronautics, by the invention of the parachute and the autogiro. New methods and the increased skill resulting from much experience have equipped the surgeon with abilities our fathers could not have imagined. Fatalities through accidents have thus been gradually diminishing (in ratio) for many years.

"To say that old age, poison, the motor car and the gangster's gun have ceased to levy their toll is utterly absurd."

Dr. Herman Wilson of the Yerkes Observatory in Wisconsin was inclined to avoid any inference of culpability: "The stars have been behaving with complete normality. The recent transit of Venus could not possibly affect life on this planet, much less in any one country or on any one continent. This is a problem for your biochemists or your doctors; astronomy has nothing whatever to do with longevity."

Mrs. Amelia Widdecomb-Hunt, of the Mother Church, Christ Scientist, Boston, said:

"It is a demonstration; the most glorious the world has ever known. It will bring perfect understanding to thousands and the Truth shall make them free. This is a great day for Christian Science and I am writing at once to the President, suggesting that June sixth be made a National Holiday in honor of Mary Baker Eddy, whose life of toil has now, at length, borne such rich fruit."

The Pope said:

"Man is conceived in sin. Through penitence and Divine Grace he is granted salvation. If, in His great wisdom, God has decreed that man shall not die, let us praise His name and so live in probity and rectitude that salvation shall attend us on earth as it has formerly done in Heaven."

The President of the Gibraltar Life Insurance Company said:

"My position at the head of this great institution prohibits me from making any statement until the next board meeting. I cannot say what effect the sudden drop in mortality will have on the insurance business in general. The Gibraltar stands, of course, ready to pay all claims of beneficiaries upon presentation of proof of the insured's demise. In the meantime, all premiums must be paid and all contracts with this company fulfilled."

Mr. Lewis Adams, President of the National Association of Atheists, said:

"It's a kick in the pants for the churches. How are they going to scare people into being good now? A great step forward for Freethought and Science. I do not anticipate any general outbreak of crime."

The President said:

"I have appointed a Senatorial committee to investigate the reports that there have been no deaths in North America in twenty-four hours. The findings of this committee will be made public in due course."

From the head of the National Coffin Company:

"This organization has not diminished production. Men have always died."

From the Executive Secretary of the Amalgamated Morticians, Inc.:

"We have not felt the depression yet. It is incomprehensible that the need for skilled morticians and funeral directors should not continue."

Dr. Tucker:

"All nonsense. The next plane crash will burn life from the unfortunates in it. The next ship which sinks will carry hundreds to watery graves. What shall we say has become of the life of a dismembered and decapitated man—if we are not to say death has occurred?"

The warden of Sing Sing:

"It was found impossible to electrocute two white men and one negro last night although each was strapped in the electric chair and subjected to the maximum voltage our equipment can produce, until the flesh of the unfortunate men was most horribly burned. I do not understand it."

7

HAPPY AWOKE before his companion. His start at recognition of Myra roused her and she smiled slowly. "Good morning," she whispered.

"Good morning."

"I think you have broken my arm."

He lifted his weight suddenly. "I'm sorry! Good night! Have I slept on it all night?"

She nodded. "I can't move it. It's dead."

Happy massaged it gently. "We'll wake it up. You shouldn't have let me do that. I was so tired."

"So was I."

They concentrated on her numb arm to conceal their embarrassment.

"We certainly slept; didn't we?" Myra remarked.

"We *did*. It seems a dreadful waste of time—now."

"Please don't," she said. "There, that's better. I must call the hospital."

He watched her leave the bed, watched the limbs and contours of her disappear in the swathing of a negligee, as if he were bidding farewell to hope itself. He was seeing her for the last time. When he left the apartment in a few moments, he would never return.

"Excuse me," she said prettily in the doorway, and went out, tossing her sleep-pressed hair.

"I can tell you before you call," the reporter said, turning his own lank legs over the side of the bed. "Mr. Kent is doing as well as can be expected."

"I want to know for sure."

As she telephoned, Happy dressed, multiplying her question by ten thousand in his mind and projecting the situation a month into the future. He imagined an harassed voice saying: "Of course your husband is just the same. He will never be any better or any worse. He's neither alive nor dead. He's vegetating. We need his bed and would be grateful to you if you would remove him by noon at the latest."

Ah! but remove him where? Would people want a thing like that around the house? Invalids were bad enough, with their demands and their odors. How much worse would one—or perhaps two or three—of these—what were they? "comatants"—how much worse would that be?

Institutions for their housing must arise. As Arnoldi said, man would not bury them while they pulsed. Then a fortune awaited him who first offered a complete service station for the living-dead. "Flats fixed," Happy Suderman murmured to himself. "Change your oil." Sleep had put an entirely different complexion on the face of man's new quandary. Last night it had seemed tragic to him that the cool and solitary comfort of the grave was to be denied mankind, that the long, well-merited, dreamless sleep after the noisy, frantic tail-chase of life was no longer to be had. Refreshed by slumber, enspirited and renewed by Myra's nearness, he saw that the sun was shining—and the spectacle of man unable to die became an amusing prospect. More; if he could get some capital, he would usher in the new era in the best tradition of the mechano-jazz age. He looked at the stubs in his check book and clucked at his $32 balance. "Where in hell can I raise some cash?"

Why Myra returned, he was completely absorbed, holding one shoe in his hand. She started to speak, but it seemed indelicate, somehow out of place, to tell this man her husband was resting "easier". She went on into the bath without a word. Happy finished dressing, going over his friends and acquaintances, seeking a few paltry thousands. He did not find them, but as he smoothed his wrinkled coat, he remembered to call his mother.

"Morning, mom; d'ja read the papers?"

"Happy—tell me!"

"Well—it don't look like we'll be buryin' *you* very soon."

"Happy, talk sense."

"I'm doin' the best I can. No matter what the bigwigs say, nobody's dyin' an' that's *that*."

"Oh, isn't that wonderful? Just think of all the misery poor people will be spared!"

"You like the idea of livin' forever; huh?"

"Don't you?"

"No."

"O-oh—"

"You have any idea how long 'forever' is?"

"We-ell—"

"That's right! It's a hell of a while."

"Can't you explain it to me, son? What's causing it?"

"Nobody knows."

"Well, for heaven sakes! Somebody must be responsible."

"It must be the Big Boss, Himself. Maybe He knows what He's doing. Anyway, I just called you so you wouldn't get panicky. No telling what will happen next."

"Well, until you tell me something more dreadful than just

that I'm not going to die; *I'm* not going to worry."

"That's the stuff, mom. Just be careful not to get hurt and I'll be out to see you one day."

"Don't you get hurt yourself—and when you find out who's doing this, you call me up!"

"I'll call you tomorrow anyway."

"Be a good boy!"

Myra entered the room as Happy's mother said that. "I'll try," he answered, and hung up.

Myra, coiffed and made-up, smiled wanly.

"How's Willard?" Happy asked, thumbing the pages of the telephone book. "Sweeney Sanitarium."

"Better, they say."

"You going right up there?"

"Of course."

"How do you spell Sweeney?"

"S-w—"

At last accounts, Dan Sweeney had been starving nicely in his centrally located sanitarium dedicated to the cure of drink and drug habits. Three or more floors of private rooms, Happy had seen, and framed licenses, diplomas or official engravings of some kind. If the famine had not yet carried Dan off, Happy thought that place would do. "Comatant Solarium," he said, sounding the words for their advertising value. "Keep your loved ones—let's see—perpetual care—"

"What are you talking about?" asked Myra.

"If you'll wait a second—Bryant three-o-seven-six-two— I'll have a bite to eat with you."

"You feel much better this morning, don't you?"

"I never felt better in my life. I'm crazy to see a paper."

"There's one outside. I'll get it. Willard has it delivered every morning."

"Hello, Mr. Sweeney?"

"Yes."

"Dan! This is Happy Suderman."

"Hello, Happy; how are you?"

"Never mind. Do you still run that cure-for-booze place?"

"I got a date with a fellow today. He wants to start a gym here."

"Got any money?"

"Me?"

"No—him."

"Oodles."

"Dan—I'm coming up. I've got the greatest racket ever invented. Stay there—and hold on to your angel. We'll split three ways."

"They won't let you run a house. It's in my lease. The other tenants won't stand for it."

"Nothing like that. Something new."

"There ain't nothin' new, but come up. I haven't seen you in a dog's age."

"An hour."

Myra was scanning the headlines. She turned wide eyes on Happy. "Is—is this what you and the doctor were trying to tell me last night?"

He read over her shoulder.

SCIENCE TRIUMPHS OVER DEATH

UNPRECEDENTED RECORDS SHOWS NO DEATHS ON CONTINENT SINCE NOON YESTERDAY

"That's it."

"You mean—Willard is one of the first of—of these people saved by a—a sort of miracle?"

"One of the first."

"Then he isn't injured; he's really dead? He was—killed, yesterday, but he didn't die; is that it?"

"Don't get excited, Myra . . . Yes, that's it. That's what had me down last night. *You* got me out of it. I've slept it off, but that's it. It appalled me."

She let the paper slide to the floor. Happy watched her closely. She stood rigid, staring at a torn spot on the dirty wallpaper. "All death's horror and pain—without any of its relief. No way to end it. No murder, no suicide; just—that!

Just—as I saw him yesterday. Oh, *no!* No-no-no! That can't
be; Happy!" She whirled on him suddenly in a frenzy. "That
can't be. No God could be so cruel, no devil so—devilish. It
can't be!"

"Myra! Behave yourself! You'll be hysterical if you keep
that up." He grasped her shoulders. "Look here; if that is the
situation, *you* can't change it. Man's been bellyaching about
death ever since he's had life. Now by some damn fool quirk
of physical laws we know nothing about, he's been given
what he thought he wanted. There's nothing to do about it.
Do you understand? You've got to face it with all the courage you've got. Willard's not alone. Ten thousand others
should have died yesterday—and not a damned one of them
did."

Her whole body shook as if in an ague. Her teeth chat-
tered and her eyes begged him—for what? This was the look
Dr. Arnoldi knew so well. This was the questioning, the piti-
fully beseeching gaze of hopeless humanity brought suddenly face to face with the inexplicable. She could listen to
preceptors tell her that she lived on the cooling shell of a ball
of gaseous flame, hurtling through limitless space at the rate
of nineteen miles a second. She could turn her pretty face
from the effulgence of a star-strewn sky, so little awed by it
that an immediate kiss had greater import. But show her
death and she blanched; show her that greater horror, life,
and her senses reeled. "Why?" her eyes asked, as countless
billions of eyes had asked before hers. "Why?"

"Let's go upstairs to Dr. Arnoldi," Happy suggested.
"Let's talk to him."

"No." She withdrew her arm from his grasp. "I don't want
to. I have to go to the hospital."

To sit beside a senseless thing, with bursting heart and
empty dreams. To sit.

"He might regain consciousness," she continued. "I'd
want to be there—so he'd recognize me."

Someone knocked on the door. Happy stepped into the
bedroom as Myra answered. Arnoldi stood there, holding his
old rusty derby in one big hand. "If you are going to the hos-

pital, may I go with you, my dear?"

"Oh, *would* you? Dear doctor, come in. Are you able? Can you go down those stairs?"

"Of course," he grumbled. "I only pretend to be sick."

"Sit down. I'll finish dressing in a moment." She joined Happy. "Go talk to him if you like. It doesn't matter."

"I think it does. I'll wait."

Myra studied him a moment with a wry smile, then took several garments with her into the bath. The doctor's heavy breathing came to Suderman like the panting of some large animal. Myra overturned a glass.

Dr. Arnoldi contemplated the reporter's hat on Myra's table and sighed laboriously. He must apologize to these young people for falling asleep last evening. He was seldom up so late any more. He had so few guests.

She was ready for the street when she came from the smaller room to where the reporter sat, patiently. "You're adorable," he said, rising. "I wish I were going with you."

"Come along. I'm sure Dr. Arnoldi knows you're here. It's stupid to hide."

"He doesn't know I'm here, Myra, and it would look like hell. You mustn't be so bold. You trust people too much."

"What will you do, then; wait until we've gone?"

"Of course."

"Good-bye."

"When shall I see you again?"

She shrugged. "When?"

"Tonight?"

"You'd better call first."

"I will."

"Good-bye."

"I hope he knows you."

. . . "Thanks."

Dr. Arnoldi followed her out and pretended great concern about the adjustment of the automatic lock.

Her escort's girth left only room enough for Myra's narrow hips in the seat of the cab. He sat with his hands cupped over his cane.

"What an odd cane," said Myra. "Isn't it? . . ."

"Um-yes. Yes, I've had it a long time. A billiard cue, sawed off, ferruled and headed with gold."

"Isn't it heavy?"

"I think it is filled with lead, some metal. You see, it is inscribed, in Russian. It was given me by Prince Segor."

"A grateful patient?"

"Yes. He was so proud of his skill at billiards. One of the best in Russia. His right arm was broken when his sleigh turned over one night. I set it. That is all."

"Set it so that it didn't lessen his skill?"

"He played better afterwards."

"Just imagine . . . I wonder if you could do anything for Willard. Will you try?"

Dr. Arnoldi nodded.

They rode several blocks in silence.

"Do you like that young man, doctor? That reporter, Mr. Suderman?"

The corners of Arnoldi's mouth quivered and his brows raised furrows across his smooth forehead. "Yes," he nodded. "I like him. I like everyone."

"Not really?"

"Ye-es—some better than others, of course."

"Don't you dislike anyone? No one at all?"

"I think not . . . Do you like him?"

"Yes. I think he's splendid."

Again there seemed nothing to say. "Did you see a morning paper, doctor?"

"No. I seldom see a paper."

"It's full of this—this thing Mr. Suderman was talking about last night."

Arnoldi nodded. "Yes?"

"Do you understand it, Dr. Arnoldi?"

"No."

"You must understand it better than we do. What is it? What has happened? Is it true that we cannot die, no matter what we do?"

"Did it say that in the papers?"

"Happy says that's what it means."

"Don't you think he might be mistaken?"

"I don't know. Willard lingers on, and all the others. Can't you explain it? How can that be possible?"

"Why should it be impossible? The Egyptians have records of two historic days when the sun rose in the west—and set in the east. At least, they *say* it did."

"Do you believe that?"

"Believe it? Well—perhaps. I think it is an artistic thing to say."

"Artistic?"

"Yes."

"How—'artistic'?"

"It relieves the monotony of the sun legend. It makes history more exciting."

"Perhaps *this* is artistic, then; that dead men shall continue to live. That Willard will never be well, yet never die."

"It may be."

"That Nature is an artist—weary of sameness—"

The doctor turned his head to look into her suffering eyes. "Does it seem a bad joke, to you?"

"It—it seems—very pointless."

"More pointless than always setting in the west; more pointless than always dying?"

She had no answer—and the taxi screeched around a corner alarmingly. "Are you making parables?" she asked, her face turned toward the window.

"I didn't mean to. Perhaps I have."

"Oh, but, doctor, this is so much worse. You must remember—all those agonizing days while *she* wasted before your eyes . . . Forgive me," Myra cried at sight of his tortured features. "I didn't mean to remind you. But—only wait until you see him. Wait until you—you look at—at him."

"If his life is to be prolonged, that will give the surgeons time to make repairs. Perhaps you shall have him—whole again."

Myra brightened a little. "That's true, isn't it?"

"If the surgeons have time—now."

"Time! Oh—I see. So many will need attention. But Willard is one of the first! This just started."

"They will have time for Willard, I think. I hope so, my dear."

His words were so obviously meant to comfort her that Myra touched the soft, rounded back of his hand in gratitude. He was looking out of the cab window.

"This strange circumstance reminds me of a colleague of mine, a Dr. Blucher, a German. He went mad, they said."

"Oh—"

"A very skillful man."

"And he went mad?"

"The court passed that judgment."

"'I can see you don't agree with the court. Was he sent to an asylum?''

"He would have been, but the crowd—the incensed populace—go him first."

"Lynched him?"

"You call it that. It seldom happens in Germany."

"What had he done?"

"He thought of something like this; but it is not a pleasant story. Perhaps I shouldn't tell you."

"It doesn't matter; please do."

8

"HE WAS AN ERRATIC GENIUS. We went to school together. Tall—"

"Did you study medicine in Germany?"

"Yes, my dear."

"—slender, dark, quick, hard; but too brilliant, you see, for his own good. He was impatient. He was wealthy, too; did I say that?"

"No."

"His father had left him independent. He did not need to practice and that, I imagine, increased his impatience. He did not have to keep people sick to make a living, as we are sometimes accused of doing. He was irritated by women who imagined they were ill. Forgive me, my dear."

Myra smiled and patted his hand.

"In a city like Berlin a doctor's chief practice is nervous women. It must be so here in New York, too. But Dr. Blucher would not treat them. He would listen to the stories of their aches and pains, note all their strange symptoms, examine them thoroughly and say: 'Madame, you have wasted my time. There is nothing wrong with you. Please to leave my office and do not bother to come back, for I will be engaged.' He didn't need their husbands' money.

"The next doctor they went to would nod wisely and pretend to find something Dr. Blucher had overlooked. A little sympathy—and the ladies would become steady customers."

"Did you used to do that, doctor?"

"Perhaps—when I was very young.

"But by driving patients away and by curing the few he had in very short order; always avoiding tonsils and simple operations, appendectomies and hernias—he soon had very little to do. He would undertake only the rarest and most fascinating operations. All others he turned over to his neighbor-physicians—who fattened on them. Not once in a month would a case of sufficient interest come to his attention. He had nothing to do.

"His leisure, I am afraid, was his undoing."

The doctor's story was interrupted by their arrival at the hospital. It mattered little, to him, at least. His chief reason, if not the only one, for starting the story of Dr. Blucher had been to divert Myra and to prevent her tears.

The floor nurse was very embarrassed. "Oh—Mrs. Kent; isn't it?"

"Yes. This is Dr. Arnoldi."

"*DOCTOR ARNOLDI?* How-do-you-do? . . . Eh—Mrs. Kent; Dr. Tucker tried to call you."

"Yes?" Why was the woman so upset? What could have happened?

"He—he's had to operate on Mr. Kent—again. We wanted to get hold of you first, but—eh—you must have left your home."

"Oh—is he operating now?"

"Yes! It was our *only* hope."

"Our only hope," Arnoldi repeated without inflection. "Do you know the nature of the operation?"

The nurse bit her lip and pretended to consult a chart on the white metal table. "No-o-o, it doesn't say; merely 'by order of Dr. Tucker'."

"I see."

"I'm sure it will be all right. Dr. Tucker hasn't lost a case in this hospital since he's been on the staff."

"Has he tried losing one—lately?"

Miss Eberstadt straightened in amazement. "Tried *losing* one?"

"Perhaps that takes more skill than Dr. Tucker has."

"Oh—?"

"An adding machine, I'm told, can't make a mistake. When I add, I can. I consider myself superior to the machine, accordingly."

The nurse laughed three inches below her palate and her face was a study in stupefaction.

Myra clasped Arnoldi's arm. "Why should they cut on him? Is there a chance?"

He patted her hand with the cushioned tips of his fingers. "A very good chance. This Tucker is an amazing man, and now—with Nature on his side—it may come out all right. Let us sit down and wait."

Miss Eberstadt watched them enter the visitors' waiting-room, then almost tore the heel off one shoe sliding into the diet kitchen to retail Arnoldi's wild words.

"Tell me, doctor; what are they doing to him? Yesterday they said his entire rib basket had been crushed in, puncturing both lungs and perhaps piercing his heart. What would they be doing, then; lifting those bones?"

"Probably. Probably Tucker is sewing up a rip in a heart. What an opportunity for him. There's nothing the man can't do. His patient will live in spite of him. I'll wager your husband gets well!"

Myra's expression did not change. Willard might get entirely well. Well, well. That's a different story, isn't it, Myra? Willard dead is one thing. Willard only half dead for God knows how many years is still another thing. But Willard hale and hearty and back on the job is something else again. She stared at a crumpled gum-wrapper on the floor, one minute, two minutes, three minutes, without blinking.

Upstairs, downstairs, somewhere, Willard's chest was opened to the morning air, while Tucker—all in a white apron with gauze across his mouth—held a torn heart in one hand, and plied his needle with the other. Myra wondered if he wore a thimble.

Dr. Arnoldi, sitting heavily in a low chair opposite her, rested both his ponderous hands on his odd cane. His small, fathomless eyes stared at the wall over her shoulder.

"How did Dr. Blucher's leisure lead to his insanity, Doctor? You were telling me—"

"Oh, yes, Blucher. Well, he began to experiment. He opened a private sanitarium for mental defectives—in Friedrichsstrasse, the heart of Berlin—and he specialized in spine and brain surgery. He developed some new and very effective techniques. He became quite the master in his field. He used to write to me at that time. I was in Moscow. In his letters he laughed at the stir he was causing in medical circles.

"This really is a very long story, my dear."

"Please go on. I can see the elevator from here. He has to come off that elevator; doesn't he?"

"It is likely."

"Please go ahead."

"In that day, the greatest obstacle to success in the treatment of the insane was the stubborn tendency on the part of the patient to relapse. Perhaps this remains true today. Blucher's secret, I think, died with him."

"He found out how to avoid relapses?"

"Precisely. Before he began his studies, people with sick minds often responded to treatment; sometimes medical, sometimes psychological, sometimes with the knife, but always—in nearly every case—the patients who seemed to be most improved, those who grew saner under treatment of any kind, would lose their grip on what we call sanity and slip back, if not quite to the starting point, at least so far that the doctor had a good part of his long, tedious job to do over again."

Arnoldi's voice droned on, monotonous, flat, with slight inflection. He might have been just a little sorry he had started so long a tale. It was the first time he had ever re-counted it. Only the need of his young friend for amusement, something—anything to keep her mind off her husband and his suffering for a few moments, kept the words coming in some sort of marshaled order.

"Blucher found how to stop that, so that when he had a man or a woman well on the way to recovery, he could arrest their nerves, their brains, their sensations and their thoughts at that point and keep them exactly that way until his at-tempts at cure had progressed again."

"Wasn't that marvelous?!"

"It was a momentous discovery. Mad or not, the medical world lost a great man in him."

"Too bad."

Dr. Arnoldi sighed. "He began by finding out the seat of certain human reactions, the areas of the brain where this is felt, or that. He learned which nerves in the conduit of the spinal column carried certain emotions and sensations to the brain. At least, he said he had.

"I sometimes wonder if he had not fooled himself. It would be a strange refutation of all his work if we should one day find that intelligence is not encased in the cranium."

"Well, it *is;* isn't it?"

"Perhaps. It seems to be; doesn't it? Right behind our eyes?"

"Why, of course!"

"Perhaps it is, then. I don't know."

Myra studied the man with puzzled eyes. A *doctor*—and not sure of that?!

"You may believe it took Dr. Blucher many years to learn these things. The spinal cord is such an unsatisfactory part *to* deal with. Do you imagine it to be something like a complex telephone cable, made up of many small wires? In a sense, it is; but those 'wires' are so fine, so slender that no one had at that time succeeded in separating one or even ten, from all the rest. Separating them, physically, I mean.

"Blucher not only accomplished that, but, in time, learned—or seemed to have learned—which of our impulses were carried over *these* trunk-nerves, which over those."

Myra's interest in Dr. Arnoldi's story had begun to take ascendancy over the opening and closing of the elevator door when that sliding portal suddenly gave out a train of the priests and priestesses of illness and malaise who escorted the offering on its rubber-tired palanquin around a dangerous curve and into a private room. Myra was on her feet, watching the tortuous progress. *That* was Willard. That—under the sheet—exuding strangling ether fumes, that was Willard. She took a step and clutched the doorway for support. Dr. Arnoldi touched her, leaning on his heavy stick.

They waited thus, motionless, until the attendants returned with their empty cart. "Was—" she had to clear her throat, and still her voice sounded like a croak to her, "—was that Mr. Kent?"

"Eh?" Like exasperating automatons in a nightmare, the first two figures looked at her, astonished and taken aback. "Mr. Kent?" One of them turned to those behind. "What was the name of that case?"

"What case?"

"This one."

"This one?"

"Yeah! Kent?"

"Kent?"

"I don't know."

"Do you know, Eloise?"

"Know what?"

"The name of this case."

"Huh-uh."

"Was it Kent?"

"Yeah, I guess it was . . . Yes! Now; I'm sure it was."

Myra watched them filing into the elevator. "Will Dr. Tucker be down soon?"

"Dr. Tucker's in the operating room."

"Yes—but will he be down soon?"

"I don't know. Do you know, Eloise?"

"What?"

"Will Dr. Tucker be down soon?"

"Dr. Tucker?"

"Yes."

"Well, he might."

"Going up!" The door closed on silent bearings.

A nurse with a towel-covered receptacle appeared from nowhere and evaporated. Myra turned and clung to the tottery Arnoldi. "Oh, God," she moaned. "God, God, God!"

"God," the old man breathed, a compassionate echo.

"Visitors are requested not to congregate about the elevators," a soft voice dripped behind them.

Myra's scream pierced walls, ceilings and floors. Sharp as the finest scalpel abovestairs, it shot from her lips, nerve-driven, more powerfully than gunpowder has projected lead.

The corridor filled with white figures.

"What's the matter?"

"What's the matter?"

"What's the matter?"

"What's the matter?"

"Her husband's just been killed."

Who had said that?

Smelling salts, an ounce of whisky, and Myra patted her hair. "I'm *so* sorry," she quavered. "Wasn't that ridiculous?"

Arnoldi was taking her pulse.

"I'm all right now. I'm so ashamed."

"Lie still, my dear. Rest a moment. Try to relax."

"Was it Willard?" she whispered.

Arnoldi nodded. "He's coming out of the ether."

A hum and buzz reached them from the hall. *Dr. Tucker. Dr. Tucker. Dr. Tucker.* The little man entered the room, nervously.

Behold the Lord High Executioner.

"Mrs. Kent?"

Myra tried to sit up. "Yes."

"I have just operated on your husband."

"They told me."

"Yes. He is doing very well; very well indeed. I think, if I were you, I should go home and get some rest."

"Do you think you've cured him, doctor?"

"I am sure he is out of danger."

"Out of what danger?" Arnoldi asked.

"*What* danger?"

"*Yes.*"

"His life is saved."

"We are not so much interested in that. Will he become normal again?"

The wizard's eyes searched the old Russian's for a moment, then a shade of respect appeared. "I have every reason to hope so," he said. "Good day."

9

"Now!" Happy plumped his palm down on Sweeney's desk. "If that is the case—there's a fortune in this building. Forget your gymnasium. Forget your liquor cure. We'll set up the first indoor cemetery for the living-dead. I don't know yet how they behave. Some of 'em may have to be fed and watered. We'll hire doctors to tell us that. I've got just the man, a Russian. We can get him cheap . . . Now, see? We'll go to a furniture factory and have these cribs made to order, with glass fronts, like sectional bookcases. Six feet by two feet. One floor will be wards; the next, private rooms. We'll stick 'em for the private rooms, same as any sanitarium.

"Have pretty gals, see? in uniform. So much for day service; so much for twenty-four hours. We can work out the price scale later.

"We'll patent the cribs; get some advertising agency to name 'em—you know—like Kodak and Vaseline, something that tells what they're for. We'll put 'em on the market and get the undertakers' trade. Do you see it? Every embalmer in America is going to have to turn his mortuary into a—a—a—Haven't either of you fellows got *any* ideas? ... Well, one of these places. What's more—rich people are going to build private outhouses in their yards, mausoleums, vaults—we'll need a trade name for those too. We'll have a book of standard designs for 'em to choose from. We erect 'em—*and* service 'em. They won't be like these concrete things in the cemeteries today. Oh, no! The new keynote is happiness, light, airy gayety. *Keep your dear ones near you always.* We'll build these things like pagodas and pergolas. Taj Mahals, ten thousand dollars; log cabins with spruce and rue, three thousand; bamboo teahouses with wisteria—so much.

"We'll have a traveling staff like the gas company, reading the meters.

"We'll make these cribs for the living-room in period designs, with radios in 'em, clocks, mirrors, anything; to go with the other furniture. Oh, some of 'em will want 'em in the house!

"As I say, we'll have to get a line on how various kinds of comatants act. Probably mangled bodies won't be the same to handle as pneumonia cases. But—that's all the more reason for calling on us. We'll be experts, see?"

"You're a God damn ghoul!" Sweeney ejaculated. "You ain't got no more blood than an oyster; has he?"

The third man had sat through the harangue in hypnotized wonder. As idea after idea had poured from Happy's agile mind, he had scurried, mentally, to keep up. Thump after thump had so shocked his sensibilities and dulled his consciousness that he scarcely realized he was addressed directly and he turned from Sweeney to Suderman and back again without answering.

"Ain't this the most indecent damn thing you ever heard of? Can you beat it?"

"Is it *my* fault?" Happy demanded. "I didn't invent the situation. All I'm doin' is taking advantage of my God-given native intelligence. If we don't do it, somebody else will.

You don't look down on an undertaker for stealing you blind today—or yesterday. Nobody calls storing cadavers in marble-studded parks indecent. What the hell's the difference? All I do is see a coming demand and make plans to supply it. Somebody will; why not us? Look at the fortunes made in the movies, radios, autos. It's the same thing. This is the coming industry. I say, let's get in on the ground floor. Let's us be the Eastmans and Fords of living death. We won't have to handle the bodies ourselves; we can hire it done."

Sweeney puffed a vast cloud of smoke from his lungs. "Jesus what a business to be in!"

"Are you *sure* this—eh—this situation is going to last?" the money-man asked.

"How could I be sure? No, of course I'm not. We weren't sure the old system of life and death was going to go on forever either; we only thought we were.

"It used to be nothing was sure but death and taxes. Chicago hasn't paid any taxes in years and now, by God, you can't die.

"No, I'm not sure of that; am I? All I know is—nobody's dyin'."

"Well, it can't hurt us to be ready."

"That's the spirit. *Now!* Let's get some plans drawn up. Let's get a man in to work out the advertising, and a lawyer to incorporate us."

"And a priest," Sweeney spat, "to bless us!"

"That's part of the racket too! All denominations. The comatant will need spiritual sustenance while he pulses, as well as physical attention."

"No more soul than a cork!" Sweeney declared. "Wouldn't I hate to be you when you d—"

"That one washed out on you, Dan. That's what I was telling Arnoldi. Half the English language has to be rewritten. *You'd hate to be me when I die!* . . . I'd hate to be you when you become a comatant!"

"Say!" the third party interjected. "Are the insurance companies going to pay the families of these poor people?"

"They don't have to."

"But they've got billions of dollars of people's money."

"They'll keep it."

"They can't keep it."

"Who'll stop 'em?"

"Why, a law'll be passed."

"Lots of laws will be passed. Lots of the old ones changed. I see they couldn't kill three fellows at Sing Sing last night. What *is* a 'capital' offense?"

"The gunmen'll run wild."

"I don't know. My guess is the gun factories'll close."

"Suppose there's a war."

"War? What will be the object of war?"

"Object?"

"Yes. If we can't be killed, why will anybody go into battle with us? Will victory go with the largest number of prisoners taken?"

"Well," said the prospective investor with hard finality, "I'm putting up but damned little cash until we see if this thing holds out. People might begin dying again tomorrow; then where'd *I* be?"

"We mustn't be too commercial," Happy mused aloud. "After all, this is a great service to mankind."

"Ringing in *ideals* on us now!" Dan Sweeney mocked. "Professional ethics." From his desk he produced a bottle and glasses. "Let's have a drink."

"What's that?"

"The best rye. My customers won't have anything else."

"Here's to Living Corpses, Incorporated," said Happy, raising his glass.

"There's nothing to kid about," said the money-man. "It either is or it isn't. If it *is,* count me in. If it isn't—let's forget it."

"But we ought to be ready," Happy expostulated. "If it *is*—we ought to be ready." He watched a mole on the man's neck move like a bug as he drank. "These other fellows aren't going to let any grass grow under their feet. The undertakers will be holding mass meetings inside of twenty-four hours. They won't take this sitting down. They have to make a living."

Dan Sweeney made thoughtful circles on his blotter with the bottom of his empty glass. "Ain't there no other way to make money out o' this only by playin' hostler to these comos? I don't like that idea much? As a racket, I mean; as a racket, I just don't like it."

"I don't know," Happy guessed, "probably."

"How?"

"Well, take yourself, for instance, figure out how this is going to change your life—that'll suggest something."

"What'll it suggest? What's the difference? I'm goin' to try just as hard to keep from being a como as I been tryin' to keep from bein' a corpse! What the hell difference does it make?"

"Well, you won't go to *church* any more, will you? You won't go to confession or light candles. You'll quit giving the priest all the dough you've coughed up for years."

"Who will?"

"You will."

"The hell I will! What's this got to do with my Church? How do I know where my soul goes to if I crawl into a glorified bookcase or into a coffin? I don't see how that makes no difference."

"But, Dan, the whole idea of the soul and—and life after death originated with man's observation of the phenomenon of *death*. If that stops, the other stops."

"You're a crazy, God-damn Protestant infidel. How the hell do you know it stops? What stops it? You think purgatory's gonna close 'cause people just don't quite die. You're out o' your head."

"You mean you still believe all that hokum? You'll go right on believing it—no matter what becomes of the world? When billions and billions of these worthless carcasses are stored all over the world and no human being has died in ten years—you'll still believe all that stuff about heaven and hell and purgatory?"

"You damn know it, I will. I'm not takin' any chances."

Happy turned to their companion with a hopeless gesture. "When they *are* sold on that stuff they certainly stay sold."

"We're not getting anywhere," said Shylock. "Maybe you're exaggerating this thing. I don't know he isn't right. What effect is it going to have on my business, for instance?"

"What is your business, Mr. Lamson?"

"Wholesale hardware."

"Wholesale hardware—that's—hammers and files and stuff like that?"

"Yes. Bolts and hinges are our biggest lines."

"Bolts and hinges." Happy studied the ceiling. "Let's see what this *will* do to bolts and hinges . . . Increased market for hinges, of course, because there aren't any on coffins but there will be on these new perpetual beds, or whatever we call 'em . . . But, bolts, now, let me see—"

Dan took another drink.

Lamson tilted his chair back and waited.

Happy finally gave up. "I don't see much change in the bolt industry, not right away. But, look! All industry will be affected soon. There are too many people in the world already, now, without this. More being born every minute. None leaving. In a year that's going to mean revolution. That's all that's wrong with Japan right now. Too many people, not enough land. All right. Look at North America going the same way. And there's no telling when it'll spread. Maybe life's become a contagious disease. Maybe we'll contaminate South America and then Europe and Asia. Anyway—there won't be room for everybody. Our money system and the social order won't stand the strain. The laboring class will use it for an excuse to go Soviet, or something worse. That'll raise hell with the bolt business."

"You mean it will abolish private ownership entirely."

"Well—"

"It will abolish our indoor cemetery too, won't it?"

"But we will have made our pile."

"It will abolish the pile! What good will the money be?"

"Yeah—" Happy admitted grudgingly, "I saw that coming

but I didn't duck quick enough."

"Let me help you," said Lamson. "Evidently you are not a salesman. Obviously, if the state of affairs you suggest should come to pass, I would be a fool to hold on to what capital I have. I might as well plunge it on your comatant cases as to have the reds take it away from me."

Happy grinned. "That's right. I guess you wouldn't give *me* a job selling bolts and hinges. I don't know enough answers."

"It doesn't matter. I'm convinced. You can go ahead with your plans today and if no one dies by six o'clock this evening, we'll have dinner with my lawyer and talk incorporation."

Sweeney drained another glass and rose abruptly. "I'm goin' to see Father Donlevy," he said, and left the room.

Thus Heaven on Earth, Incorporated, came into being. Yes, Heaven on Earth, Incorporated. And, almost at once, a competitive institution which called itself Paradise, Ltd., set up shop only a few blocks away. You can easily imagine the talk that caused. My God! what next? But Happy's outfit had the jump on the other boys and within a week plans were being drawn for a magnificent new building.

Dan Sweeney sat at the feet of his priest, and asked for guidance. "I don't want to go into this, father, unless you say so. Is it right to make money out of this?"

"It seems to be a very worthy enterprise. And you will need a priest in constant attendance to minister to the spiritual needs of your—er—your—clients." Donlevy was looking for a job. Although business had been good all day, given fresh impetus by the momentous news, the fellow-of-the-cloth could see further than his nose and the end of the Church was in sight. The faithful could not be kept in line indefinitely if the mark which had always separated the Here from the Hereafter were erased and the two became one continuous whole. Rome would struggle. Rome would try, but it was doomed. He could stay and struggle and be doomed with it—or he could climb on this new bandwagon and profit accordingly. He fancied the latter course, if the change could be made with a proper gloss. "Yes, my son, a very worthy enterprise. I condone it in the name of the Church; I will visit you and bless your endeavors in the name of the Lord."

"Oh, would you, father?"

"The moment you are ready."

A weight of dread was lifted from Dan Sweeney's narrow shoulders, but the doubts of the Happy-heathen's implanting had still to be resolved. It was a difficult set of questions. Dan hardly knew where to begin. "This is goin' to fill heaven up with a lot o' foreigners; won't it, father? They're still dyin' but we ain't."

"Souls are without nationality or color, my son, and heaven can never be filled."

"Oh, I know that, but—what do you suppose has happened, father? If the doctors don't know, you ought to."

Donlevy was taken aback, but for a moment only. "The Holy See has not issued a statement yet, Dan. I am not at liberty to speak until His Holiness gives us permission."

"But—you *know* all right?"

The priest smiled in kindly indulgence and touched Dan's shoulder. "All I can say is that you may proceed with your plans—within the limits of the teachings of the Church—and I will help you. We will talk about the post of—shall you call it 'Chaplain'?—when your doors are to be opened. I think I should like to enter the work with you."

"*You!* Father?"

"It seems to offer a splendid opportunity to bring consolation to the afflicted. I feel the call."

"Gosh!"

"The doctors will soon determine upon a condition which may come to be accepted as legal death. We will administer extreme unction at that time—for a nominal fee."

"Oh, sure."

"I will myself compose masses for the slumbering ones, if none are forthcoming from the Pope, and those will be delivered periodically."

"For a nominal fee."

"For a fee."

"Suppose some of them recover, though? I don't see how there's going to be any 'legal' death. Suppose a rich man gets to that point and he's declared 'dead' and his property goes to his heirs; say! If he came to again, how would we do then? He couldn't get it *all* back."

"Our law courts will arrange all those matters, Dan. We won't have to worry about that."

"Congress is sure going to have its hands full!"

"Very full indeed. The lawmakers must look to God for guidance."

Dan looked sidewise at his confessor, almost waiting for the laugh, but Donlevy was himself too much disturbed to notice. Mundane considerations, attitudes and respects were all very important; they needed watching, but his long ha-bituated mode of thought was not sufficiently ingrained to prevent the good padre from realizing that this new death was every whit as applicable to his holy self as it was to the Sweeney-sinner. He was thinking of that and looking at Dan when his housekeeper brought a message from the cardinal.

Every Greater New York member of the Catholic clergy was summoned to the Cathedral at midnight on the most ur-gent business of God. Only they who were actually bedrid-den would be excused and it was suggested that miracles be invoked to raise them.

Dan was dismissed with a pass or two at an absent-minded blessing and he stumbled confusedly into the street which seemed more populous than he could remember it. Had the effect of the new order become visible so soon? He scoffed at the thought, but there certainly were a lot of peo-ple out. And they behaved strangely, too. Instead of passing one another, each intent on his own business, all going somewhere, these pedestrians had an ambling, aimless gait. They looked about, not in store windows, not at the traffic, at each other. They seemed to be saying: "Gee! You're alive too; aren't you?"

Scarcely anyone was smiling. A puzzling questing sat in uniform discomfort on every face. Soap-boxers seemed par-ticularly numerous, but Dan did not tarry to listen. Every street corner was a tangle of Sunday-drivers and extras were hawked by a dozen boys to the block. Not even war had been like this. Gesticulating groups filled every doorway. The curb was lined almost as if a parade would pass.

Dan quickened his step. He felt an urgent, crying need for more talk with Happy Suderman. Happy knew more about this affair than God's own emissary on earth. Dan did not know where to find him.

10

ON A SOAP-BOX in Union Square, Sid Lyman brandished a newspaper and screamed at the heavens to lay him low.

"Our day has come, my comrades! We need not wait a moment longer. Strike *now!* You have read it in the papers. They cannot kill us. They cannot imprison us all. Let us take what is ours with the strength of our hands. Follow me!"

The strength of Ole Johnson's hands, rugged, Swedish strength, whisked Sid Lyman off his rostrum and into a waiting auto. The crowd watched him go with beetled brow and growls. Only a few knew that Ole was not a plainclothes man, but those few passed the word quickly and the growls subsided as the car moved away. No attempt was made at a delivery and another speaker was telling them something else from the box just vacated by Sid.

"Listen, all of you!" said this newcomer, "I can speak only a moment." A mounted policemen was even then approaching the crowd. "Do not listen to these harebrained attempts to lead you to destruction, but be alert for the Party movement. It is true that the day is here, but we must act in concert and not waste our strength in petty rioting and plundering. Men will pass handbills among you as you move away. Go peaceably." He stepped down and disappeared in the crowd. The cop was given one of the handbills.

"You know me?" Johnson asked Sid. "You know who I am?" The auto was moving down Broadway.

"Yes! You're the man who keeps the workers sleeping with promises. You are Johnson."

"I am Johnson."

"You are trying to gag me because if *I* started the revolution you would not get the credit."

"You don't know how to start a revolution. Is that the way you'd do it? The corner store was a United Cigar Store. Would you start a revolution by stealing cigarettes?"

"How about Hilman's—a clothing store? Can you think of a better way to start than by taking garments to cover our bodies?"

"Much better, my fine firebrand; much better. We start with the banks."

"The money in the banks belongs to the people."

"We would give it to them. But I did not—invite—you here to tell you our plans until you become a member of the Party. I have taken you off the street because your tongue is dangerous at a time like this."

"Do you think you can stop anything by holding me? I am but a poor mouthpiece of the Cause."

A man sitting beside the driver of the car turned around disgustedly and spoke to the leader of the United Labor Party. "Why don't you smack his mouthpiece shut, Ole? That's the same damned fool who started the trouble last May Day."

"Beat me!" said Sid. "Beat me—and watch my bloody body receive the reverence of the workers through the ages."

Ole wagged his head sadly. "You'll get nothing from the ages, boy. You're just a damned fool. Wait! I'm talking. I left a good speaker back there to quiet those fellows you were frothing up. I've worked too hard and too long to have a monkey like you come along and throw a match in the powder-box. You're going to have your revolution; don't worry about that, but it's going to be conducted under my orders and in systematic fashion; understand?"

"You are a coward," said Sid Lyman shrilly.

The car came to a halt before a tenement on First Avenue and the two men in the front seat got out. Sid's voice rose again like the scream of a tortured violin: "You are a coward! When the workers rise you will be sitting safely in an office, behind a desk, receiving bulletins of their march. I will be in the van of the besiegers, *leading* them. I am not afraid! I am not afraid to suffer. Their bayonets cannot hurt me!"

He was dragged from the automobile without parley or ceremony and hustled up dingy stairs to a room on the second floor, rear. Johnson folded his wide arms across his barrel chest and stood in the middle of the floor. "Get wise to yourself, son. I know what I'm doing. You don't. We're going to carry this thing off without spilling any blood if we can. We're going to take the nation. You'll get your share. Now, be good."

"You can have beer and sandwiches any time you want 'em. The papers will be brought to you. But you gotta stay here until you cool off. A man will be outside this door all the time and you'd break your neck if you tried to go out the window. Sit tight and I'll come back to see you later— maybe tonight. You make up your mind by that time to join the Party and keep your mouth shut and you can go home."

"Betrayed!" Sid yelled. "Betrayed by Judas. You don't know what suffering is! You're in the pay of Privilege! I know you—demagogue!"

The politician turned deliberately to leave, but Sid's ire was boiled over by the scorn of that strong back. He leaped at the man, swinging a puny fist at one large, Swedish ear. Johnson slapped him once, spinning the pants presser into a corner.

"*Socialist!*" the injured one hissed through his tears. It had come to be the vilest epithet one radical could use to another, but Ole, laughing, turned the key on the outside.

Whenever his business permitted, Ole went home for lunch. It made him more fit, he said, fit for the afternoon's battles.

"Hello, mama."

"Hello, Ole."

Mama was not a Swede. She had been an actress of sorts, seduced one lean season into taking a part on the commonwealth plan in a radical propaganda drama at the Cherry

Lane Theatre. Ole had met her there and, in common with thousands of misguided women, she had mistaken physique for masculinity and married him. She let Ole think she enjoyed having him come home for lunch.

"What've we got to eat?" His kisses were broad and moist, as expansive as his manner.

"Steak. Good?"

"Grand."

"Ole, what's this Mrs. Dufresne is telling me about nobody dying? Did you hear anything about it?"

"Everybody's talking about it. Nobody knows anything."

"She's going to bring me her paper."

"I'd have brought one if I'd thought. I don't suppose it amounts to anything. Just coincidence. Nobody's died, it seems, in this country, since noon yesterday."

"Is *that* all? I should think they'd be glad of it."

"They are, I guess. It's unusual, that's all."

"Nowhere in the United States!"

"All North America, the paper says. It *is* mighty strange."

"A lot of people usually die; don't they?"

"Well, don't you be dwelling on it. It probably isn't anything."

Mrs. Johnson realized then that Ole was worried about it. Why? It seemed a particularly jolly change to her. "What's the matter, Ole? You act funny."

"Oh, I don't know. Some nuts are all excited about this stuff they're reading in the papers. I had to shanghai one of 'em to keep him from starting trouble. You know how they get."

"I don't see the connection. What is there to be excited about?"

"Well, this kid has the idea they can't kill him, see? So why shouldn't he take a gang of men to the City Hall and demand the keys to all the bridges?"

"But I thought *you* were going to do that!"

"Yes, darling, but I'm not married to this boy and he doesn't share your opinion of my merit. He thinks that he is the man for the job."

"Well, I like his nerve!"

"There will be others like him, now, if this keeps up. I may have to strike before I'm ready, to prevent some scatter-brain from doing it."

"Don't you let them get ahead of you, Ole. If there's going to be a revolution in this country, *you* be the one to start it. The idea! Who do they think they are?"

"Well, I never did have the idea patented."

"No; but you thought of it! Why! Almost the first thing you ever said to me was: 'Aren't you afraid to be out alone with a revolutionist like me?' Now somebody else comes along—"

"This kid has always been hard to handle. He won't join the Party; has ideas of his own."

"What does *he* want to do?"

"Oh, he wants to start crashing in store windows, rioting and stealing."

"Why! he can't do that!"

"No—but he thinks he can because the police won't be able to kill him or any of his mob."

"Well, they can *shoot* them; can't they?"

"Shooting's no good any more. It just lays you up for a while and—then you get well."

"Through the heart? or the head?"

"It doesn't seem to matter."

Mama Johnson served their luncheon in silence and sat down. She was trying very hard to get this straight. Ole shoveled food mechanically, planning his afternoon. All the work he had done, all the patience he had preached, all the carefully laid plans of the Party due to mature in another three to five years, were brushed aside by the new order, demolished by a whim of Nature. Shutting Sid Lyman in a room could not stem this tide. Sid was just a little previous. In every city, every town, hungry people, discouraged people, even the disciplined leaders, would begin taking what they wanted if life should become or had become indestructible as Sid Lyman sought to establish. The only way out was to seize the government at once and to placate everyone by giving what would otherwise be taken.

"I may not be home until very late tonight, mama," Ole said as he left the house. "If the police come here looking for me, be careful what you say."

"They never get anything out of me, Ole, but you take care of yourself."

"Oh, sure."

He went to Party Headquarters and summoned his local leaders to a caucus. In code telegrams, he warned agitators and organizers everywhere to be alert to quell petty outbreaks and to stand by for his instructions. But Ole's code, like most codes was familiar to the Department of Justice. Alert for danger, in the face of the startling news of the day, that department apprehended Ole and all his minions late that evening and carried them to cells. No blood was spilled.

Mama got sleepy about two o'clock and went to bed.

Sid Lyman had not waited so long. For all his vociferousness, Sid had a stoic strain, and where was a bed—there also was sleep, for Sid.

11

ONE SPEECHLESS HOUR beside her husband was all Myra's nerves could stand. He was no nearer consciousness when she left than he had been upon her arrival. The slender trickle of blood from one corner of his mouth had become almost as much a part of Willard as the mouth itself.

Dr. Arnoldi waited for her, nearly dozing. Tucker had shown so obviously that he resented the Russian's presence that after the briefest look, the big man had left the patient alone with his nurse and his wife. There was nothing he could do. He waited.

"Come, doctor, let us go."

"Is he conscious, my dear?" He pretended to have been awake all the time.

"No; not conscious. The nurse says it may be hours. I must have air."

The elevator boy studied Dr. Arnoldi with the greatest curiosity.

As they passed the business office of the hospital on their way out, a bookkeeping nurse accosted them. "Mrs. Kent?"

"Yes."

"May I speak to you a moment, please?"

They were going to ask for money. Myra knew it. Everything had to be paid for in advance at a hospital.

She had seven dollars. Arnoldi smiled encouragingly as she followed the nurse into the office.

Handling some printed forms of various sizes and colors, referring to them for data, the nurse began. "The compensation company has authorized only a semi-private room for Mr. Kent, Mrs. Kent, and we will be forced to move your husband this afternoon unless you authorize the private room."

"How much is it—where he is now?"

"That room is fourteen dollars a day, ninety-eight dollars a week; in advance, of course."

"Of course."

"The allowance from the compensation company is four dollars."

"That leaves ten—in advance."

"Yes. I wouldn't mention this to you while Mr. Kent is in such a serious condition if we did not need room so badly. Normally, our semi-private rooms have only two beds, three at most, but we have five beds in all of them now, and more coming. So you see—"

"Yes, of course."

"If you'd like him to stay where he is—"

"Oh—no. No—I—I'm afraid I can't. But—isn't—haven't you anything in between? *Six* in a room! That's—almost a ward."

"A ward!" the bookkeeping nurse had a tinkling laugh, like a loose bag half full of beer checks. "There are forty-two beds in our men's ward—and fifty-five in the women's. No, indeed, six patients doesn't make a ward."

"Well, I—I'm afraid you'll have to move him—if you need the room. I can't—I haven't got—ten dollars a day, in advance."

"That's the only way a hospital can operate successfully, Mrs. Kent. Otherwise people never would pay."

"It—it won't harm him—to move him? He'll still get—the same attention?"

"Well, practically."

Dr. Arnoldi identified the cause of the girl's abstraction instantly. "How much do you need, my dear? Perhaps I can arrange it—"

"No. No, thank you, doctor. I couldn't think of it." She and Willard had wondered how the old man lived. Modest as his needs were, some income was necessary to supply them. And he couldn't have much. If he had he would not be living at 408 Canal Street. "They say the care is just the same, practically, where he is going."

"In a ward?"

"They call it a semi-private room. Six beds."

"My purse is yours. I have forty dollars for expenses until the first of the month."

"I couldn't *think* of it. Willard's salary will go on, of course. I remember he told me it would, if anything should happen to him."

"For a period of time."

"I don't know how long."

"Perhaps you should visit the offices of the company."

"I should; shouldn't I?"

"They do not know your circumstances."

"Will you go with me?"

"I will, of course, though I shan't be able to help, I'm afraid. What can I do?"

"You'll be company, darling doctor! I need someone. You can finish your story."

"Oh, of Dr. Blucher. Yes, I can do that."

"I've never done anything alone."

"Do you know the address?"

Myra found it and they set out. "You had just got to the interesting part. Dr. Blucher had discovered the seats of our emotions."

"And our senses; some of them."

"Like sight? and smell?"

"Yes. One of his first experiments was with taste. He fed a patient chocolate and when his mouth was filled with it, by a process which has never been revealed, my classmate arrested the taste of that chocolate, held it at its greatest intensity, so that it was always there."

"Always?"

"Constantly. A letter I have describes the subject's actions in detail. He tried to spit it out, drank water and wine, chewed mint leaves and ate his usual dinner, roast meat, vegetables, fruit. It was all chocolate to the patient."

"How dreadful!"

"That was one of his *first* experiments. His success, they say, unbalanced him."

"Didn't it make the man sick? Nothing but chocolate!"

"Yes. It made him very sick."

"Couldn't the doctor change it? Release it—so the man would be normal again?"

"That worried him," Dr. Arnoldi admitted. "For a long time he could do nothing. Later, he found a way which was sometimes successful."

Myra shuddered. "Go on."

"His experiments grew more elaborate, more refined, as his skill increased. He made one woman patient very cold, almost froze her, then applied his magic, his needle, whatever it was. No quantity of clothing, no blankets or stoves could warm her. She lived a long time like that. His attempts to restore her to normality were fatal. I think he attributed her death to hemorrhage of the brain."

"The monster!"

"And so many more."

"Was it her death that brought him to court?"

"No. He was never charged with her death. I knew of it through his voluminous letters."

"Oh, doctor, you didn't help him? Encourage him?"

"I read his letters."

"And answered them, of course, or he'd have stopped

writing."

"Yes, I answered them."

"Oh!—it's revolting! I never heard of such a fiend!" Myra was trembling, her mouth suffering involuntary contortions.

Arnoldi looked at her, calmly compassionate. "I shouldn't have told you."

"Oh, it's—it's all right. I—I just can't imagine what he wanted to do such horrible things for? Didn't he ever arrest a pleasant sensation?"

"A great many."

"Tell me."

"Perhaps I should not. What brought Dr. Blucher to my mind was this strange phenomenon that has arrested life. There is a similarity. All the body's functions now are secondary to one central fact, the phenomenon of life. Of course—"

"Yes, I know; but do go on about Blucher. You have told me only horrible things. Tell me some sweet ones."

"It may have been no fault of his that most of his subjects were condemned to suffer. He was only groping. He could not find all the nerve centers at one time, all the brain areas."

"Of course not, but, doctor, did his patients submit to these operations willingly? Were their families consulted?"

"I do not know. Probably he deceived them. At first the strange results of his operations must have been attributed to accident. It is almost impossible to predict the outcome of a surgical attempt on an idiot."

"Well, go on. I can stand it. Did some family eventually cause an investigation?"

"The investigation was brought about by the police. Such private sanitariums are not permitted to house or to treat violent or dangerous cases—not in Germany. Probably that is true in America as well. But Dr. Blucher's ministrations sometimes induced violence—and particularly noise.

"To prevent sounds from escaping he had the walls insulated and all doors and windows muffled—built with double sash. Later it became necessary to bar the windows after one man threw himself from the fourth story. The bars excited comment. They were visible from the windows of other buildings. Someone reported them and a search for maniacs and others who should have been in municipal institutions revealed enough to make the authorities suspicious. They watched him and caught him, but not before he had created an hotel full of—prodigies.

"To one man, he handed a letter of preferment, notification of his rise to eminence in his profession. As the fellow's joy was at its height—the doctor pinked him.

"I have thought about Blucher often and—while I was still young enough to be ambitious—I tried to picture his technique. I always came back to long, slender needles—and—the naturalist's moth-case. His subjects have always seemed so many transfixed bugs to me.

"He used other letters. One woman was allowed to read of the death of her two babies by drowning. He caught her just as that false news fully penetrated her mind.

"He burned a man and made his agony permanent although the burns were healed in a few days.

"He sacrificed his mistress to his science; somehow operating, sticking, whatever it was he did, just as she achieved an orgasm."

"He *told* you that?"

Dr. Arnoldi nodded wearily. "Yes. He told me—and the police found her—in a perpetual ecstasy. She died of it."

"After he was dead?"

"Yes. It was a pity. She was very beautiful."

"Oh, how *could* he? How could he?"

"By attaching a great rock to a chain, he so arranged it that a subject should see that rock falling upon him, to crush him. He could not see the chain which prevented the boulder from touching him. In that one horror-stricken moment—Blucher operated.

"He set spiders and rats and snakes on another subject—and made that revulsion permanent. That fellow screamed constantly—and died because he could not sleep."

"He *was* mad!"

"The court said so, but they wished to force him to restore

his patients to something like normality before they imprisoned him. No one else could possibly perform that miracle. It is doubtful if Blucher could. He had destroyed something, paralyzed something, in each case. But he claimed he could do it and the police gave him the opportunity. They had to."

Thorndike and Brodzki, Engineers.

"Doctor—I believe you made it up!"

"Made it up? Invented all this horror? Why?"

"To show me that Willard is—isn't as bad off as he might be—to keep my mind off his suffering."

"No, my dear."

"Because you knew I would never be distracted by a pretty story. It had to be a dreadful one."

A girl in the sumptuous atmosphere of the outer office of Thorndike and Brodzki relayed Myra's name to Henry Thorndike, president. He kept them waiting while a call was hurried through to the hospital so that he might speak intelligently of Willard's condition. The delay permitted Dr. Arnoldi to finish the story of Blucher.

"You are very keen, young lady; very keen, but I am no romancer. I have tried to entertain you, but I did not invent the tale. You would have seen it in the newspapers of that day, if you had been alive. Dr. Blucher was a nine days' wonder.

"A company of citizens, headed by some stalwart relatives of his patients, executed an ambush as the police carried the man from prison to his laboratory to start his work of reconstruction. This was so unusual, so unprecedented in Berlin, that their aim was successful. They took him away from his guards—and tortured him before they killed him."

"How stupid! Before he had *tried* to—to free all those poor people?"

"The mob is like that."

"He deserved it, of course. What did they do to him?"

"Obscene things, all painful. They were greatly aroused."

"But—such ignorance! What became of all his patients? Did they all die?"

"Some, I think, are living still. I have got out of touch

with my European correspondents. I think some of them are still a problem to the doctors of Berlin. No one can help them."

"I shall dream about that terrible man—for days!"

"I shouldn't have told you," said Arnoldi without contrition. "It will trouble my sleep if you have nightmares."

Mr. Thorndike admitted Myra and her clumsy, footsore escort. The engineer was smiling. "Mrs. Kent? I am glad to see you. The nurse says Mr. Kent is resting well and that everything points to a speedy recovery. I can't tell you how *glad* I am."

"This is Dr. Arnoldi."

"Oh, yes."

"Willard was still unconscious when I left him. Did the nurse say he had come out of the ether yet?"

"He—hasn't, but they can tell, these clever nurses; they know. She said he was resting easily."

"He's still bleeding."

"Don't let that alarm you. Should she, doctor? Are you the family physician?" *If he was, he was a pretty old one!*

"In my case the title of 'doctor' is a remnant of courtesy. I have not practiced medicine for many years."

"I see. Well, Mrs. Kent, we have all been very fortunate. It was only an act of God which saved your husband's life— and all those others."

Arnoldi's expression did not change. Myra ignored the man's cheerfulness. The odor of fresh barbering was on Thorndike and the girl contrasted it with the damp gasses Willard encountered below the street level and with the thickness of the hospital room she had just left. "I came to see you about his room," she said, and explained her financial condition.

Although the warmth of his manner subsided perceptibly, Thorndike agreed to pay the extra expense and promised Willard's salary check every week—for four weeks at least. "I shouldn't like to have this generally known, Mrs. Kent," the suave employer said as he patted her shoulder in the door. "The company couldn't afford a private room for every man who stubbed a toe."

"Stubbed a toe! My husband is dead!"

"At the hospital they give me every hope to the contrary. But—I didn't mean to disparage his injury. This is something we are glad to do for you but cannot do for everyone. Surely you understand."

The shoulder pat and the man's tone gave the concession a very intimate touch. Myra acknowledged this with a smile.

"Where shall we send your check?" Thorndike went back to his desk for a pen.

"The same address," she said coolly.

"Of course." He was not put out of countenance but the rebuff was plain. "I'll keep in touch with you regarding his condition." And before they had passed through the door, he found another occasion to pat the roundness of her shoulder.

Myra *jabbed* the "Down" button and looked at Dr. Arnoldi.

Dr. Arnoldi looked at Myra. "Odious," she said with a shudder.

The doctor nodded mechanically, thinking of Happy's hat on her living room table.

12

SECRET MEETINGS were being held all over town; all over a lot of towns, but Happy was engaged with those in New York. It was Board Day with a vengeance—but all behind closed doors. Interviews were impossible and newspaper men were forcibly ejected from conferences they had always attended. The right men at the Rockefeller Institution and Columbia University were *all* "out of the city". Never before, in Happy Suderman's time, had it been so difficult to get expert opinion to quote. He called the Bronx Zoo and learned that mortality had not abated among the lower animals. The mice and rats, killed for the snakes, had given up the ghost with their wonted gusto, and a whelping lioness had trodden one of her litter of three, crushing the life from its body.

Captains of Commerce, however, were not hiding. The cloud over the physicists was not dimming their sun and hay was being made to the tune of merry laughter and ringing cheers.

Telegraph and telephone companies nigh swooned under the burden and the Post Office Department had seen nothing like it since Christmas. Science had nothing to say—yet, but the little man, the forgotten man, the man with the hoe and the ledger pen and the wrench, the saw, trowel, brush, adz, riveter, cleaver, reins, tongs, screwdriver, hammer, pestle, blowtorch, pincers, scissors, rowel, typewriter, hatchet, bellows, spade, lathe, rubber-stamp, awl, swage, oar, crowbar, flute, broom, tedder, scoop, chisel, scuttle, calipers, drill, net diestock, soldering-iron, pliers, mallet, hose, knife, bulb, lever, throttle, punch and niblick; *that* man had more corresponding and communicating to do than ever before within memory.

How's Uncle John?

How's ma?

I saw a guy fall from the eighteenth story of a building—and it didn't kill him!

Katy gave birth to a boy and the doctor was wrong! In spite of everything he's been telling us, both are fine!

The militia fired into the ranks of the union miners who were after the scabs, but nothing happened, A few men were wounded but none were killed and they took the toy-soldiers' rifles away from them!

Fred rocked the boat and spilled us all in the water. We thought we were goners, but—do you know?—after Tiny and May and Fred had gone down eight times they began floating and we finally got them all to shore.

Peleg tried to kill himself while we were at the movies last night. His cancer's been worrying him a lot lately. He turned on the gas. But we got home and saved him. The doctor says it's a wonder because he was breathing the stuff for almost three hours.

We put it in his coffee, just as we planned; enough to kill a horse. It only made him sick.

Happy talked to Myra who waited at the hospital for Willard to throw off the effects of the ether.

"There's no more doubt about it. A train went over an embankment at eight o'clock this morning. Three coaches burned, but there was life in every charred body they recovered. Not an undertaker in town has had a call all day. I was right. It's here."

"Well, Happy, what are they going to *do?*"

"Nobody knows, darling. We'll just have to wait and see. How's Willard?"

"Just the same."

"Are you going to stay there all day?"

"I don't know what else to do. I might as well be here as walking the streets—or pacing the floor at home."

"Go to the movies."

"Oh! I couldn't think of it!"

"Go visit somebody. Where's Dr. Arnoldi?"

"I took him home."

"You have lunch?"

"Yes. I ate here."

"Well, you ought to do something to keep your mind busy. It won't do you any good to dwell on it—or him either."

"I suppose I should."

"Yeah—look—"

"What?"

"Y'want to bum around with me? I'm busy, but I could take you with me. It's something to do."

"I'd be in the way."

"No, you wouldn't."

"I'm afraid I should be."

"Nothing of the kind. Look. I'm going to two hundred Fifth Avenue, to an advertising agency. I'll meet you in the lobby there—in twelve—fifteen minutes. O.K.?"

"O.K."

And the strange, tense, surcharged atmosphere which had impressed Dan Sweeney as he left his confessor, put the mark of its awe on Myra. So thronged were the streets that her taxi devoted nearly an hour to a ten-minute trip. Happy had encountered a like delay.

"What are they looking for, Happy? Just see—everybody's out."

"A lot of them are like you, I guess. They're upset and can't sit still. Look how nervous the cop is."

One Madison Square traffic officer had the jitters. His whistle was not getting the proper respect. A cab driver called him a "lunkhead" and drove away with a dirty laugh. The policeman whirled on the snickering group behind him. Then turned again—and kept on turning. There was always something behind him and he couldn't stand it. He tried quick, darting whirls; sly, gradual, peeping turns. The result was the same. Man's structure is such, with both eyes to the fore, that turn and twist as he will, there is always a point "behind" him. Cops are no exception. It was that, and not the queer peering of his fellow citizens, which unnerved traffic officer No. 4026.

He tried to calm himself. Was he going nuts? Must be the sun was getting him. He had wondered what sunstroke was like. This must be it. Around and around and around. There was *something* back of him, something he couldn't see—and everybody who passed had a crazy, wild look. Jabber, jabber, jabber! All talking about it! Can't die. Can't die. Can't die. "Well, what's going to become of us if we can't die?"

Turn, turn, turn. He signaled weakly to a brother of the club and shield across the street. He was ill. He'd pull his box, report, and go home. What was that? He didn't turn quickly enough. The thing was gone again. Some girls tittered. Officer No. 4026 drew his revolver and began shooting at the sky. Happy and Myra watched two other policemen and a pair of hardy walkers disarm the madman.

"It's beginning to get 'em," said Happy. "Did you see him shoot in the air? Aim like—as if he saw something?"

"He did; didn't he?"

"Maybe *he* did see something."

"What? I didn't. In the air you mean?"

"Yes."

"There was nothing in the air."

"*Me,* I wouldn't say that," said Happy. "I'd stick to the simple fact."

"What."

"I didn't *see* anything. That doesn't mean there was nothing there."

"You mean there might be something in the air—right out here in the street—that he could see and I couldn't?"

Happy nodded seriously. "We have to watch ourselves— now. The old rules don't apply any more. *I* didn't see anything to shoot at. That's all I know."

"Happy! You're scaring me to death."

"Well, I'm *scaring* you."

"God!"

"Don't pray! Somebody's prayed once too often now— and got us all in a hell of a mess."

Myra bit her lip. Happy led her into an express elevator. The faces of their fellow passengers were curiously attentive. Men in the company of other men did not speak. They regarded one another almost as if they saw human beings for the first time, scrutinizing eyes, noses and mouths, as if to say: "Damme, you certainly *look* as if you could die!"

As the car started, swiftly, one fat fellow cast a benign glance all around him. "It don't make a damn bit of difference if this thing falls or not," he said.

Everyone laughed nervously.

"Well, *I* hope it don't," said the dour operator.

In the office where advertising had been invented, Happy explained his needs. "What do you think of that name?" he asked proudly. "Isn't she a lulu? Heaven on Earth, Incorporated! I thought of that."

"Until our research department in Philadelphia investigates the market thoroughly, I'd rather not commit myself. At first glance, I'll admit, it *seems* to be fairly appropriate."

"What are they going to investigate? I want a full-page ad in every paper in town tomorrow. You don't need to investigate anything for us."

"Well, that's a little unusual, Mr. Suderman. This company always investigates a new product very thoroughly before it makes any recommendations."

"You *can't* investigate this. Nobody knows anything about it. It's started overnight. We have to hop on it before some one else does. I represent half a million dollars. We'll be open for business day after tomorrow. All I want you to do is to tell the public about it."

"Before you have been through our Philadelphia plant?!"

"To hell with Philadelphia! Can't you write an ad here in New York?"

"Oh, no! All our work is done in the home office. I'll be glad to take you over there and introduce you to the men who will be working on your account."

"I can't take time to go traveling! I've got a million things to do."

"But, Mr. Suderman, you don't want to launch an advertising campaign until our merchandising department has worked out a set of charts for you."

"Listen, mister. Do you want this business or not?"

"I can't even tell you that until we have investigated your product."

"Our product doesn't *exist* yet. I'm going out now to hire artists to *design* our product."

The agency man laughed at that. When he became serious again, he was tremendously condescending. "I'm afraid we can't do business, then, Mr. Suderman. *This* agency can't very well sell something which doesn't exist. Haw—haw—haw." But when these profound imbeciles saw half a million dollars walking out of their office, the traditions of that agency were put in the background for the time being and a visualizer, a copy-writer and an artist were brought from the City of Brotherly Love to Manhattan. They arrived about dinner-time, and Happy agreed to confer with them after dark.

His next call was at a furniture factory. The head of the designing department was flabbergasted at the first suggestion of Happy's wants. He called the general manager.

Happy repeated the story. A vice president was summoned and finally Suderman had to repeat his plan the fourth time, for the president himself. They looked at Happy as if he were mad, but they knew Lamson, the hardware magnet, and respected his dollars.

"Where do you think these—eh—these comatant cases— ahem—will be kept? Where will people put them?" asked His Nobs, the president.

"That's for us to decide. Nobody has any ideas—any prejudices—yet. We can make it fashionable to put them anywhere we like. I think we should have a catalogue showing designs for any room in the house. For our use at Heaven, we shall need two standard designs. One very elegant, simple but elegant, to be made up individually, on legs, I think, carved legs, for the private rooms, and then a criblike arrangement of shelves, like ship's bunks, you know? Like sectional bookcases, so we can keep twenty or thirty bodies in one room. Those should be finished in white enamel, chromium hardware, very sanitary-looking. See what I mean?"

"Glass?" asked the head designer who was sketching on a piece of paper.

"Yes! Glass doors by all means. We'll have public visiting days at a dollar a head."

"It's revolting," said the vice president who was a little sissy.

"Any more revolting than incubator babies? People pay to see them at Coney Island. What's the difference?"

"The—the women think they're cute."

"How do we know some of our comatants won't be cute? I can imagine some of them developing very entertaining habits. Glass, by all means, and in drawing the styles for use in the home, show them both ways, some with glass, some without. We'll sell them detachable doors so they can hide the contents or disclose it, as the purchasers see fit.

"Now, let yourselves out! Don't let the old coffin influence your designs. Upholster some of them, I guess, and indicate satin linings in others, but don't lean that way. You can get dignity into them without sticking gray plush on the outside."

"How about handles?" asked the practical draughtsman.

"Handles?"

The president was catching the inventive spirit too. "That will depend on the ceremony, won't it, Mr. Suderman? I mean, the ornamental handles on caskets have grown there, as a convenience, because the object is carried. Is it your idea to have these cases delivered into the homes with the bodies in them? With a ritual—pallbearers—and so forth, Mr. Suderman?"

"One man can't think of everything, can he, Mr. Hodges? To tell you the truth, I hadn't got that far. Let's see; if this state comes about in a bed at a man's home, the undertaker would make the transfer with his assistants. Services would be in the parlor. No moving. In our chapel—the same way. But—I guess you'd better make some with handles and some without. Cemeteries are bound to set aside sections for comatants—and some will have to be shipped."

"Some with and some without," the president agreed.

"Some painted; you know? Like bedroom furniture. Some natural woods. Period designs. And make them *wide* so the bodies can be rolled over. I foresee that in some cases that is going to be necessary. The tops and fronts hinged, so that attendants can get in. Most of the comatants will be moved about a great deal, I imagine, because people will remember that 'while there's life, there's hope'. They'll be taking them back and forth to hospitals all the time, trying to revive them."

"Children's sizes, too," the designer made a note.

"Make those especially cheerful. They'll probably be kept in the nurseries of our better homes. For that matter, keep cheer uppermost in your mind as you work. For a few years, most families are going to be delighted to have their loved ones always near them. We have to carry out our name, too; Heaven on Earth, Incorporated."

"Do you suppose comatant children will continue to grow and develop? Under glass?" The furniture designer tapped his teeth with his drawing pencil.

"There's no telling," said Happy. "I more or less expect them to. Time isn't going to stop."

"You can't guarantee that," said the vice president testily. "Anything can happen now."

"Let me congratulate you," said Mr. Hodges, rising and putting his hand in Happy's lap. "I was skeptical when you came in here, but now I see that you have a gold mine. Is your stock all subscribed?"

"I'm afraid so, Mr. Hodges. It's a closed corporation. Just the three of us. Mr. Lamson has ample funds—"

"This is no fun," Myra complained when Happy rejoined her. "If I'm going to sit around outer offices waiting for you all day, I might as well be at the hospital."

"Let's telephone."

Willard's condition had not changed.

"Have dinner with me?"

"I promised Dr. Arnoldi. I'm going to cook."

"Oh, hell! I have to eat with my Heavenly partners."

"I'd better go, then. I have to buy some things."

Happy held her hands and watched her tremulous lips, not yet quiet after so much nervous strain. "Will I see you later?"

A breath of pain touched her eyes, her brow.

"Don't answer," said Happy quickly. He was rapidly growing up. "I'll put you in a cab."

It would be crude and cruel to leave that decision to her. If he was any part of a man he would make up his own mind before demanding that Myra commit herself. What had started harmlessly enough as a matinee of pleasure had become a weighty problem overnight. The girl was fond of him. That much was evident, but, if he was going to take advantage of that attachment, under existing circumstances, he must be sure he was ready to repay her with a like devotion. The previous night had been chaste and not without beauty. Happy knew that if he returned he must do so only because he could not stay away; because his will was subservient to his passion. For tonight, their rest would be troubled and interrupted. There would be no sleep. *If* he went there.

If he went there he must go because he loved her and he must go for the sole purpose of making her love him, not for one afternoon or one night, not now. For *all* time. Not even "until death did them part"—but always. Did he feel any such emotion for this girl? Granted that he could change his mind, later, did he desire her sufficiently to give his protestations the devastating conviction necessary to fool them both? Convincing Myra would be easy enough if he believed himself. Did he? *Was* he being consumed with an inner fire so great that no ordinary human considerations could withstand it?

Then another idea smote Happy with tremendous force. Since comatants were not quite dead, *their* pleasure must be looked to. Heaven on Earth would construct a lagoon, a network of canals through a park of consummate loveliness. All summer long, for a fee, gondoliers would pole the pulsing ones hither and thither to the strains of Venetian songs. Families could come there for outings—and ride a while, get as drunk as they liked, sitting beside papa.

13

CARDINAL RIDELL let his gaze travel slowly around the fringe of the nocturnal gathering of his priests. More than four hundred had answered the summons. "I shall hold the ushers as a body responsible for the presence here of any representative of the press. Let us pray."

Let us pray for the ushers if they've let a reporter in!

"Our Heavenly Father:

"We are met here to raise our united voice in supplication for guidance at a time we need it sorely. To our doors since early morn have come the wives and the fathers and the mothers and the sons of afflicted ones in Thy Church, asking, all the same question: 'What does it mean?'

"We ask Thee, Our Heavenly Father: What does it mean? We implore Thee to tell us in our hearts so that we may answer the sorrowing who stand beside the beds of pain, beside the biers of their loved ones who do not die.

"In all the history of Thy Church, in so far as it is known to us, no such thing has before this come to pass. Thy will be done!

"Bless us with a new intelligence, Our Father; teach us how best to continue in Thy service if this blessing Thou hast sent is to be Thy will on Earth, thenceforward. Enlighten, we pray Thee, the darkness of our minds which have no light save from Thee. Console us with Thy Divine assurance that we may give consolation to these thousands of seekers who look to Thy unworthy ministers for one ray of understanding.

"Show us the way.

"Amen.

"My brothers:

"You have been called together in the hope that one of you can suggest a means of resolving our dilemma. I have been in communication with Rome by cable all the afternoon and tonight I talked to His Holiness, the Pope, by telephone. Although he bids us be of good cheer, he is not able to explain the nature of this strange situation and he asks me to determine if possible who, if any of you, has been praying for this dubious blessing. I have no wish to bring any notoriety to the individual. I shall be happy to have the confession of anyone who feels he may have been guilty, in my apartments, in private. Do not shrink from this obligation to your Church and to all mankind. If there is among you anyone who has by intercession effected so amazing a result, he must be favored beyond all his fellows-of-the-cloth and his prayers should be devoted to the benefit of man under the guidance of the Vicar of Christ on Earth.

"Upon reflection it must be evident to all of you that prolonging the life-span of man indefinitely is scarcely a blessing. After some deliberation, I think I may say that it is almost a sacrilege since it reflects upon Church doctrine, upon ancient Divine decree and the sacred truth of the Scriptures.

"We cannot very well attest that purgatory has been moved to this planet although I can foresee that some such explanation will become believable in the not too distant future if the condition which now seems to be general in North

America continues. Neither can we say that the Lord, God, is punishing this continent, since—even persisting for a generation—the abatement of mortality will appear a boon to many. We cannot admit that the omnipotent Father is *experimenting!*

"Frankly, gentlemen, I am nonplused. Beyond asking if one of you is guilty, and, if so, asking that one to step forward here or to visit me at home, I know not what to say. The Church, in North America, must present a single face to the problem. We must decide what to say and what to do and then we must *all* say and do exactly what we decide. We can expect but little assistance from Rome. This is a local problem although its importance is international—perhaps universal.

"His Holiness will help us if he can, but without a closer view of the situation, he will be unable to advise us through his inability to comprehend the minutiae of our difficulty.

"This may very well be the end. I'm not saying that it is, but it may very well be. I call these matters to your attention. We may be reduced. The Church is eternal and cannot fall, but we who serve it may find ourselves missionaries in our own homes.

"Morals, ethics, rhetoric, the law—all must be changed in cognizance of this vital alteration of man's fate. We cannot be idle. A people which cannot die is certain to lose its concern for an hereafter. And we shall not be able to pretend that this new state of catalepsy is equivalent to death. Science will revive individual cases—and, if such cases have been supposed to have penetrated the veil, they will be asked for particulars. It is a skittish business."

The cardinal referred to some notes. "I have made some appointments, created several committees which I will explain to you. Each committee will elect its chairman from among its own numbers and those chairmen will report to me daily, if you please, until such time as the crisis has been passed.

"The Committee on Doctrine and Exegesis shall be composed of seven; one bishop and six priests." Ridell read the names. "It shall be the duty of this group to study intensively to the end that the teachings of the Church through all these centuries shall not appear ridiculous in the light of the new life. I don't know how you are going to accomplish that, but it must be done.

"It shall be this group's further duty to fashion an explanation, a reconciliation of fact with our doctrine, one we may offer our parishioners, one which His Holiness will approve, one which may be generally adopted by our brothers in other cities in North America. I suggest that you get busy at once.

"The Committee on Law and Government Relations shall also consist of seven; one bishop and six priests." He read these names from his list. "The chairman, when he is elected, will appoint one or two of his committeemen to go at once to Washington and there so to contrive that the temper of Congress and the Senate and the President be known to them. We must learn through these appointees what laws are contemplated, what changes in existing statutes. We must have this knowledge before it is made public, *long* before. This is a delicate and important mission.

"Another subcommittee must be sent to Albany. Another must ingratiate itself with His Honor, the mayor, and with the Board of Aldermen.

"A third committee—" Cardinal Ridell appointed committees until after three o'clock. Father Donlevy drew a berth on the Committee for Temporary Revision of Services and when he admitted that he had been engaged in revising masses all that afternoon, he was unanimously elected chairman.

The cardinal closed the meeting with another short prayer and staggered weakly to his bed. That was all he could do. The burden of all this responsibility was a little too much. He felt let down, abused. The Pope had taken the attitude that the American Arm must work out its own salvation. Lots of people were dying in Italy and all His Holiness could do was pray.

With one apostolic sock in his hand, His Eminence rubbed a toe reflectively. It was all very well to try to strengthen the spirit of that rabble of priests, telling them how noble it was going to be for them to become missionaries in their own parishes, but the prospect of keeping them at it was dismal in the extreme. The cardinal was well on in middle life, by the old standard. He had worked hard to wear the red; he had kissed more feet than he cared to recall.

Lower and lower, his morale was sinking, when a servant appeared with a portable telephone. Mrs. Fitzhugh had called every thirty minutes from one o'clock. Cardinal Ridell rolled a baleful eye at the servant who smiled encouragingly but without any attempt at comment.

"Shall I talk to her?"

"If I may be so bold, Your Eminence, a conversation with Mrs. Fitzhugh has been known to rest you."

"And to tire me at the same time," said the cardinal, reaching for the phone.

The servant bowed at the door and went to rouse the second chauffeur.

"Hello, Fitz, darling."

"Riddy! You're in torment. I can hear it in your voice."

"It's nothing."

"Oh, I know what it is, but you mustn't let it get you. Come and tell me."

"Oh, Fitz, I can't. I have to be up at five. It's nearly four. A wink is all I'm going to get."

"Come wink with me. I shan't importune you."

"Then of course I shan't come."

Mrs. Fitzhugh laughed. "Ah, splendid. I see they haven't hurt you too badly."

"No; I'm not hurt. We shall work it out all right, but I really must be attentive. It takes time and I must be forever thinking. I never think when I'm with you."

"But I'm dying to know what happened. Did they question you afterward?"

"I ran so they couldn't. I dared not suggest it."

"No. Oh, I wish you would come."

"It's impossible, my dear. I'll tell you everything tomorrow. Please don't scold."

"Oh, I shan't scold. I only wanted to comfort you."

"Your voice has done that. I shall sleep—soundly—now—for my hour."

"Good night, Riddy, darling." She sang it.

"Sweet dreams, my pet."

The second chauffeur was sore because he had to undress again. He said some nasty things to the personal servant who resented them. At breakfast, the cardinal noted the discoloration of one of the fellow's eyes. "You have a shiner," said His Eminence.

"Through my zeal to serve you, sir, I met with an accident."

14

HAPPY WAS UP every bit as late as the cardinal, first in conference with Dan Sweeney, the angel, Lamson, the advertising men and lawyers, after that looking for Sid and trying to make up his mind about Myra. Heaven on Earth, Incorporated, was launched with by-laws and articles of incorporation and an election of officers. Happy became president, Sweeney, vice president, and Lamson, treasurer. A bitter female notary who had been in the wholesale hardware business longer than her employer, was elected secretary, and to her was promised thirty shares of stock when it should be printed.

The advertising men were told to get along without sleep until the first campaign was designed and written. About two o'clock these plotters scurried like ants, each to perform his part of the momentous business in hand. Sweeney was pretty drunk. He had contributed nothing but hiccoughs to the conference, nothing but his lease on the building to the corporation. The ideas had all come from Happy Suderman.

The sour secretary, whose name was Ada Werfel, took the minutes of that first meeting with vaulting astonishment. When they parted at the curb, she gripped Happy's hand with a force seldom exerted by a woman. "You're the cat's," she said distinctly. "It's going to be just one bedlam after another, working with you." Aside from perfunctory, routine answers, they were her first words that evening.

"Thanks," Happy said. "You ain't heard no bedlams yet. Wait till you hear me snore."

"Are you suggesting something improper?"

"Happy?" said Dan in mock amazement. "Not *Happy.*"

"Not tonight, anyway," the president excused himself. "I still got a dozen things to do before I snore."

"Some other time, then," said Ada with sarcasm that weighed a ton.

That tickled the ex-reporter halfway to the Canal Street address. He was quiet in the hall. If no light showed under Myra's door, he would go up to Arnoldi's room. It was dreadfully late. One gas jet burned dimly on each floor. Enormous roaches, nearly large enough to saddle, moved only far enough to let him pass. Happy tried to learn if mundane immortality had been extended to that kingdom. His foot left a messy spot on the floor.

He listened at the door of the Kent apartment. It was completely still within. He climbed the screeching stairs to Dr. Arnoldi's home. Apparently he slept, too. Happy turned the knob softly, prompted by no reasoning he could define. The door was unlocked. He tiptoed to the corner of the alcove wherein the old man's bed stood.

Mountainous under the sheet, the doctor faced the wall, breathing evenly. "Suderman?" he asked without turning.

"Yes. How did you know?"

"We expected you all evening." As if what he should see was certain to be unworthy of the tremendous effort required to turn over, the Russian groaned and puffed until he faced his caller.

"Has Myra been here? Did she expect me?"

"She expected you."

"Where is she now?"

"In her apartment, I think. She left here an hour ago."

"Did—did she seem disappointed—because I hadn't come?"

"She was sad all evening. I have tried to entertain her."

(With stories of grave-robbers, likely!)

"Do you suppose she's asleep?"

"She should be, for the sake of her health."

"I won't disturb her."

In the darkness, Arnoldi's smile could not be seen.

"I'll run along. Good night, doctor. Don't you ever lock your door at night?"

"I think I do—sometimes. It doesn't matter."

Happy was compelled to admit that was entirely sound reasoning. He retraced his steps. With his hand on Myra's door-knob, he stopped. Suppose she had left it open! Suppose she had *locked* it! His fingers began to tremble. Either way required a mental adjustment. Did he want to know?

She had been sad all evening. Of course she had. Her husband was suffering in a hospital. Happy stood as still as a carven thing, staring at her door. She needed sleep. He should go home. He needed a clean shirt, for one thing.

Slowly Happy's hand returned to the knob, then he lowered it quickly. More quietly than he had come, he found the street again. If Myra's door were unlocked, Happy did not want to know.

He dozed in a cab to his room in the Village. Sid, of course, was under guard nearly two miles away. Happy called the precinct police station where the pants presser was usually taken.

"We haven't got him, Happy. Why don't you bell him?"

"I think I'll kill him instead." It was out before he thought.

"Oh, yeah?" said the man on the phone.

"Look, Pat," said Suderman, "how is this affecting things? How are hold-ups? Housebreaking?"

"Last night was light. It's a little early to tell tonight. We've only had two calls and one pick-up. I'll tell you what, though; there's an awful lot o' bodies found around. I mean, so far tonight we've had eighteen unconscious men and women. Ain't that funny?"

"What's the matter with 'em?"

"Well, hit-and-run, blackjacks, two were shot. I'll tell you what I think. Ordinarily doctors and druggists—neighbors—

keep that kind o' thing down. And, when they're dead, the coroner's office, some undertaker or a hospital gets 'em before we do. You see what it is, we're getting all the business—and nobody is trying to cover up much."

"None of them dead?"

"Nope."

"And you haven't heard anything about Sid?"

"Nope. I did hear the Federal men took Ole Johnson and a gang of his, though, not long ago."

"I don't think he'd be with them. What was the charge?"

"I don't know. Suspicion of sedition."

"Sid never leaves any *doubt* when he gets through speaking!"

For an hour his roommate sought the witless radical by telephone, unbuttoning his clothes as he waited for connections. Wearied, at last, Happy went to the bath, shaved and changed his linen. Absorbed in considerations he would have been at a loss to name, Mr. Suderman buttoned himself and selected a tie, tied it and took fresh handkerchiefs.

When, on the one occasion that he became conscious of his own actions, he asked himself where he was going and why, it appeared that he was returning to Myra—and because he loved her. Happy admitted the truth to himself when he recalled leaving her knob unturned. There it was, plainly and incontrovertibly. His sentiment, this night, at least, he could never gainsay or retract.

And it was probably equally characteristic of Suderman that as dawn found them, slipping fitfully into twined repose, he should think again of that dimple-brain who had been asleep for hours, and wonder where he was, if not in jail.

The dimple-brain awoke only a few moments after Happy had fallen asleep, and his second waking thought elated him. He would join the Party! *If*—if Ole would make him some sort of executive secretary, give him an office commensurate with his abilities for trouble-making. Since it was broad daylight Sid assumed the morning to be well advanced. He had never owned a watch. He pounded on the door and called loudly to his guard. This was by far the better plan. He would put his proposition up to the big Swede, make an impression by pretending sympathy for their waiting tactics and, when he had won a place of trust, seize the reins and take command. It planned lusciously. Sid hammered the door considerably harder—and yelled.

He would point this out to Ole as an example of the lax manner in which he was obeyed. The stupid guard had gone off and was now probably sound asleep. That seemed a little insulting to the prisoner, as if his importance and his strength were despised.

When he had a desk at Party Headquarters, he would learn all Johnson's plans quickly. If there were stores of guns and other revolutionary machinery, he would locate them—and act.

The man of action repeated his assault on the door, using the one rickety chair the room contained. When it came apart in his hands under the impact without raising his jailer, Sid took thought of escape. If all this racket had brought no one, it was likely he could break the door down. It sounded thin enough.

The panels splintered easily. Chips and chunks of chair and door covered the floor, and Sid stepped through the opening. That would teach them! His exercise had caused his blood to course so vigorously that he fancied himself conqueror of something or other. He swaggered down the narrow hall, alert to rend anyone who should dare attempt to stop him. No one did. The meagerly furnished flat was deserted. A spring lock on the front door opened easily and he stood at the head of a flight of steps at the foot of which was First Avenue, lighted by the newly risen sun.

Sid contemplated the aperture disgustedly. There was freedom. Who wanted to be free? Having devoted an hour to working himself into a state, turning his predicament into a boon, translating misfortune into advantage, Sid tasted liberty and spat it out. But so is the human mind contrived that the simple fact that now he wished not to escape was unbelievable. Without the slightest self-knowledge; without realizing in the least that he vacillated, that each succeeding

emotion in him was a compromise with its predecessor, Sid
acted a pantomime—for the walls, that which passed for a
brain in him contorting itself nimbly in accord with his body
movements.

This was a trap! Ah, self-esteem! He flattened himself
against the wall. Somewhere an eye watched through a
chink! He recoiled from the stair. One step down, one more
step toward the street—and he'd have been shot! Sid edged
slowly back—back toward the door he had only then demolished. Thus he outwitted them. He crawled through the jagged hole he had made with the chair—and smiled wisely.
Now his guard would appear, probably carrying a gun. "It's a
good thing for you you didn't try to go down them steps!"
the guard would say. Sid waited for him, planning a witty
retort. He felt entirely master of the situation. Never before
had life been so complete. He had demonstrated not only that
he could escape if he chose, but his superior cunning as
well—by not escaping. He adjusted his features to receive
the ass who had been set to watch him. Careless, insouciant,
he lit a cigarette. "Take me to Ole Johnson," he practiced. "I
have a proposition to make him." One revolutionary leader
to another.

No one appeared. Sid's cigarette was smoked—and no
one appeared. He sat on the edge of the bed, deflating. Were
they going to keep him waiting all day? Anyway, where was
his breakfast?!

Sid estimated an hour had elapsed since he finished
smashing the door. He *wouldn't* believe he was at liberty to
go out if he chose. Dwelling upon the thought of breakfast,
however, nerved him for ignominy. His pockets produced
sixty cents. Stealthily, he went again to the head of the
stairs—and looked down. Like a cat on doubtful footing, he
tested each step before trusting it with his weight. Nothing
arrested his descent.

In a rage of chagrin, he walked to the corner beanery and
flung himself down on a stool. The man who had been left to
watch him the day before was dunking a doughnut and reading the morning paper. He looked up. "Hello!" he said. "Get

out?"

"Of course I got out. Were you gonna leave me there to starve?"

"I was bringin' your breakfast up to you."

"Well, I'll eat it here."

"O.K."

"You're a fine guy to leave in charge of a prisoner. Why don't you get a job at the Tombs?"

The man grinned. "They don't hire nobody but cops."

"Where's Johnson? I want to see him."

"He's in jail."

Sid almost fell off the stool.

"In jail?"

"They got eight of the officers last night." The man moved the folded newspaper along the counter toward Sid.

"So—that's why you let me get out."

"No. I didn't think you was awake. Dja have a skeleton key?"

"No. I broke the door down."

"Broke the door down!"

"*Yes!*"

"Aw, for the love o' God; what you do that for?"

"Well, why not? Ole Johnson has no right to keep me a prisoner."

"I know, but—Jeez, we'll have to *pay* for that."

"That makes no difference to me."

"Ole'll be sore."

"What do I care. He's in jail now."

"Yeah, but he'll get out right away. You better get out o' here before the landlord sees it."

Sid Lyman began to fume. "You mean you're going to let me go?"

"What the hell do I want with you?"

Sid had no answer.

"You think *I'm* gonna feed you?"

"Well, somebody has to if I'm a prisoner."

"You ain't a prisoner; you escaped."

"Now, listen!" Sid was beginning to worry about his

status. "Suppose I went back upstairs to my cell!"

"Go ahead. If the landlord comes around, he'll make you pay for the door."

"He will like hell—"

An excited man burst in. "Say! That guy got away! I was just up there—"

"This is him."

"Huh?"

"Sure. He escaped."

"Are you Sid Lyman?"

"I am."

"Well, look." He turned to the guard. "Ole got word out not to let him go. We got to keep everything quiet until Ole gets out."

Sid decided to run; and—man of action—he did. He bolted through the door, still chewing. The owner of the lunchroom joined the baying pursuit, but they were outdistanced by the pants presser, whose feet seemed aeronautic.

15

EVAN FITZHUGH greeted his wife with a kiss as polite as his rise from the breakfast table at her entrance, as considerate and as habitual as his folding and discarding of his morning paper. Evan had told her at their wooing that he was not the sort of man who read the papers at table with his wife and he had remembered it—all those years. Wince, the butler, said his good mornings and draped his mistress' napkin across her lap as Evan finished seating her. The movements of all three persons at this rite had not varied more than seven-eighths of an inch, or four-fifths of a minute for nearly sixteen years.

Mrs. Fitzhugh quirked the corners of her mouth sadly up as she looked at the third place laid at the sunny table. She shook her head delicately at Wince and blinked once before looking down, as if the tear he could not see was very near the surface—for all that. "His Eminence is not breakfasting with us, Wince. You may remove his plate."

Her husband's face represented exactly the proper degree of sympathy, kindly interest and curiosity. He even patted the back of her fragile, blue-veined hand. "Ah, this strange new life. The paper is full of it. John must be having a *very* difficult time."

Fitz adjusted her head at the end of her neck, not unlike a swan in her movements, tilting her chin slightly upward to remove any suggestion of sag in the flesh of her throat, then she spoke. This tic of hers was thoroughly familiar to Evan and to all Mrs. Fitzhugh's intimates. They liked it. They respected it. Evan likened it to an overture in the theater. It prevented interruptions. It was a long warning that the lady was about to give birth to a word. "I talked to him by telephone at five this morning." Her voice had the timbre of a low flute, thin and resonant at once, by *Tardus mustelinus,* out of Barrymore, altogether in keeping with her features and coloring. "Those little seculars are such a bore. He was addressing them."

"Poor John," the husband said.

"He didn't seem too worried, only very tired."

Mr. Fitzhugh looked longingly at the inverted newspaper. "There is some reason for alarm," he admitted. "The President has summoned the editors of the *World Almanac* to Washington."

"Oh."

"A conclave of engineers is meeting at the City Hall to discuss New York's water supply."

"Summer, too."

"Yes."

"Perhaps we should go to Europe."

"Perhaps we should. A bill was proposed in Congress to stop immigration entirely until the crisis has been passed."

"May I see the paper, please?"

Evan handed it to her resignedly. The statisticians had taken over the front page.

U. S. POPULATION WILL
MORE THAN DOUBLE IN TEN YEARS
PRESENT RATE OF INCREASE 15,388 PER DAY
Prospect Viewed with Alarm

If no one dies, and that possibility became still more nearly a reality yesterday when not a single death was reported anywhere in the United States, Canada or Mexico, the population of the United States of America alone will be 259,580,677 in 1944. These astounding figures were made public last night—

The swanlike Fitz looked across the table at her spouse. "It's rather harrowing; isn't it?"

"One wonders, sometimes—" said Evan, rising.

"Doesn't one?" she murmured.

10,766,633,742 POUNDS OF BREAD
CONSUMED LAST YEAR
BAKERS CAN TRIPLE PRODUCTION IN SIXTY DAYS
"IF WE CAN GET THE WHEAT"

Mrs. Fitzhugh blinked her patrician lids very rapidly. "Will you be going to business, Evan?"

"I had thought I would. Would you prefer to have me stay home?"

"Oh, no; no. John will be over directly . . . Do you imagine the—the bakers will be able to—*get* the wheat?"

"The wheat?"

"For bread."

"Oh! I rather think they will. They always have."

"Yes."

"I think so."

"Be rather dreadful if they couldn't."

"Rather."

"Did you read it all?"

"Eh, that? No, I hadn't finished."

"One billion, seventy-nine million, eight hundred thirteen

thousand bushels; well! That sounds like enough, doesn't it?"

"Exportation will be restricted, likely. I wouldn't worry about going hungry, my dear."

" 'Beef Shortage Predicted in Three Years'."

"Not really."

"Here!"

"Hm."

"It seems to me they should be able to do something about it in three years."

"Oh, they *will*." Evan was reading over his wife's shoulder. "See there." He pointed.

"NO FAMINES POSSIBLE," SAY EXPERTS
ARABLE LAND SUFFICIENT TO FEED
TEN TIMES PRESENT POPULATION

"Oh—eating!" said Fitz, as if the thought disgusted her.

The head of their small family pressed his lips to the austerity of her brow and left the cardinal's consort to her own interpretations of the figures with which the paper abounded.

Evan Fitzhugh was a dealer in rare books and autographs, a very wealthy man and as charming as a benign monarch once he was away from the Swan. In her presence he differed little from any other occasional piece, blending with the bric-a-brac like umber in a tapestry. *He* had been the Catholic, the lady embracing his religion at their wedding and his cardinal shortly after. "I never do anything by halves," she had told him a score of times. "If I forswear Luther for you, I will take the Church to my heart." Thus forestalled, there was nothing Evan could say when that brilliant red bib came to swing from the back of his slipper-chair. He had been warned and he had done nothing about it. Besides, he liked John Ridell. If the graying locks over his eyes were to be parted by a headdress of another's choosing, let a fellow of taste and discretion do the work and do it well. Evan never had to complain of John.

But—alone, that is, apart from her and in his place of

business, Evan became a different man. It was, "*Good* morning, Marceline," to his secretary, and, "*Good* morning, Mr. McDougall" to his manager, "Up betimes, *aren't* we! What's in that precious morning mail?"

"You old darling," the comely mistress of his bookish affairs said with a shake of her head, "you wouldn't change if the heavens fell. Asking *today* what's in the mail!"

"Why not today?"

"Why not today, indeed," said the lank and lorn McDougall, wiping a shelf with a greaseless dust cloth. "You know very well."

"You must not let this upset you, my children." McDougall was fifty-four. "Lead exemplary lives; never touch the electric light while you are in the bath; look both ways before stepping off the curb—and on your three-hundredth birthdays I shall present you both with a genuine holograph of Charlemagne!"

"It means revolution," said McDougall.

"Then we'll quell it. Meanwhile, let's sell books. Has Quimby seen those items from Washington's library? I thought not. I'll take them at noon. Marceline, my dear, please to call the Honorable Stafford Quimby and say that he is lunching with me and with George Washington—at the club." He applied himself to his mail.

The second letter Mr. Fitzhugh opened was signed by Henry Thorndike, president of Thorndike and Brodzki, Engineers.

DEAR MR. FITZHUGH:

An incident strange to me occurred today in my office and I should like you to tell me what you think of it. As you may have read in the newspapers, several of our employees met with a serious accident two days ago. This morning I was visited by the wife of one of those men and on her arm was an old fellow, a tall, heavy man, not too well kept, who called himself "Dr. Arnoldi".

Do you remember "Dr. Arnoldi" in *Breaking Point* by Michael Artzibaschev? This chap is that character to the life! He *looks* like him, speaks like him, moves like him. It is he, incarnate. I write to learn, if you can tell me, whether you bookmen have any knowledge of the novelist's drawing that portrait from life. Have you ever heard of a living "Dr. Arnoldi"? Was there such a person in Russia? Is there any way to learn?

I am more than curious because *Breaking Point* has for years been my favorite Russian novel and the character of Arnoldi has remained clearly in my mind as one of the most remarkable and memorable of all fiction's people. If he is alive and *was* alive when Artzibaschev wrote the book, I should like to know his history—in fact—I *shall* know it, if I have to brave the Soviet to dig it up in person.

What makes his appearance doubly remarkable at this time, is the series of apparent miracles which have been saving people from death. The book, you will remember, is a saga of suicide. Death stalks its pages. Of the score of villagers one meets there, Arnoldi alone, of the interesting ones, remains alive at the finish and *he* is not "alive".

"Why don't you shoot yourself, doctor?" Tchish asks him—and Arnoldi answers: "Why should I shoot myself? I've been dead for a long time as it is!"

It seems *most* extraordinary to me that that man, that doctor, should appear in my office on the day when—if we believe the papers—it first becomes impossible to die. I have not a drop of superstitious blood in my whole body, but there is something uncanny in this circumstance.

I said practically nothing to this doctor, asked him no questions. I was afraid of being disappointed. I couldn't bear to hear him grunt that he had never heard of such a man as Artzibaschev. I decided, if possible to get some facts first. Tell me what you know. If you have no data, start looking it up for me. Let the Russian press be searched—from 1908 to 1915—at my expense, of course.

Meanwhile, find ten more copies of *Breaking Point,* I want them for gifts.

Cordially,

HENRY THORNDIKE.

Evan scratched his left horn and took up the next letter.

Due to the death of my father, I wish to dispose of his collection of autographs which include—

The bookseller sat up straight and smiled. Due to the "death" of her father! A ray of hope. People could die. This man had. But the letter had come a long way and its inditement antedated The Change. When Mr. Fitzhugh realized that joy had swollen his heart at the tidings of a death, he crossed himself hurriedly, then tried to undo it again. *For,* he had been right to warm to those words. In a short time it would be man's *aim* to die. The positive proof of animation caused absolutely to cease forever would be cause of rejoicing, thanksgiving and celebration! Bonfires in the street! Fireworks and parades! Confetti and music and feasting— perhaps a prize for successful murders.

Evan looked from shelf to shelf of the books in his store. Lucky ancients! There was no recalling them. Or—*was* there? Had anybody thought to investigate the condition of the "dead"? Had authority exhumed any corpses to see how matters stood below the sod? He looked nervously at Marceline. He mustn't let these faithful employees realize that he was going crazy too. He had to maintain his calm cheerfulness, to set an example for them, to keep up their morale.

Newsboys screamed a new extra past the door and McDougall and the girl both started guiltily. Evan made a face of scorn. "You mustn't let the hysteria of the day affect you like that," he instructed his secretary. "How can you be so frivolous in the presence of all this calm wisdom?" He indicated their stock. "Is Plutarch astonished? Did you see Seneca start at that boy's voice? Did Beaumont and Fletcher pale—or Dr. Johnson blush? . . . Go get one of those papers, Mr. McDougall, please, but go calmly."

That extra was as unique as any other event of those strange times. It was an *advertising* extra, issued at the behest of the advertisers who could not wait for the regular editions of the daily papers to let be known their need for men.

Men Wanted! Women Wanted! Employment of every sort

offered. Who could drive a car, sell a stove, lay a brick? Pharmacists begged for licensed men and offered apprentices rare opportunities. Packing houses, railroads, transfer companies, construction companies, wreckers, mines and mills and factories all sought broad and willing backs, skilled and unskilled hands. Candy factories, canneries, breweries and vintners joined the bakers in their attempt to triple production in sixty days.

"Boom! Boom! Boom!" said the United States, and Canada and Mexico echoed the sound. The doom-sayers were silenced. To hell with posterity! Grab a wheel and turn it. Today is here; use it! Fortune awaits *you* in Alaskan forests and mines, in Canadian wheat fields, in Mexican oil lands.

Detroit and Indianapolis begged mechanics to come there. Wages soared.

McDougall, Marceline and Fitzhugh turned the pages of this strange extra and reckoned the boom in terms of autograph prices. "It's too bad *we* can't triple production," Evan mourned. "Button Gwinnett and Napoleon—The market's going to be there. We are out of gear with the times."

"You ought to be ashamed of yourself," said Marceline. "It's being out of gear with the times that keeps mellow souls like you in this business."

Evan gave her his most kingly smile for that pleasantry. "You're right, my dear, but don't you see that we shall be out of business in a very short time? The demand for our goods will increase in the same ratio it always has, perhaps faster. With new fortunes being made every hour and the population increasing thus—we shall be out of stock in a few years, no matter how high we price our wares. And the principal source of supply has dried up. Collectors have ceased to die. No libraries will come back to market."

"The thing to do is buy now!" McDougall discovered. "We should have an ad in that extra."

"We *shall* have one in the next issue!" Fitzhugh clapped his employee on the shoulder. "We shall stave off the end as long as possible. Take this down, Marceline: Highest cash prices paid—"

16

A TORRENT was in the breasts of Myra and Happy, an anguish in their heads. They did not speak. It was to their credit
that words were despised that morning. What could either
say?

It had come about as both had desired it should. They had
spent some part of the night in each other's arms. They
should, then, be gratified. Somehow they were not.

She left the bed without a tenderness for him. It was
Willard's bed. Happy pretended not to waken. She took her
rigid features to the bath and the sound of the water itself
was a spiteful gushing. As the tub filled, she made eyes of
loathing at her face in the glass. Myra loathed herself in
Willard's shaving mirror. She started to brush her teeth, then
realized—by the shortness of the handle—that she held
Willard's brush. She started to exchange it for her own, then
resolutely lathered it with Pebeco. After what had passed in
the night, that was the least she could do.

The tub was not full. Myra thought she could call the hospital before it ran over.

Happy heard her coming and closed his eyes again. So far,
he had been unable to plumb his desolation. Why *should* he
feel like a child-beater? He could remember plainly that his
thoughts had been lofty and his feelings positively noble as
he mounted Myra's stairs only a few hours back. Was the
aura of that dead man, yes, that *dead* man, to prevent them
from enjoying the full fruition of a love he was certain was
genuine, sincere and—and—eh—beautiful? Myra had
wanted him. She had sat at her window, waiting, all night
long. She had seen him come—and go. She had loved him
for coming, then, again, for going, crying herself to sleep in
the chair where he had found her. A transport eclipsing all
other pleasures she had ever felt welcomed him when he
wakened her with a kiss. Happy tossed fretfully over in bed.
He felt like a cad but could find no reason for it.

Myra was connected with Willard's nurse. "The bleeding

has stopped, but he isn't conscious yet."

"What time will Dr. Tucker be there?"

"That's hard to say, Mrs. Kent. Dr. Tucker is so busy now. I could call you when he does come."

"Will you do that, please?"

As she passed again through the room where Happy tossed, she said: "The bleeding has stopped," and proceeded into the bath.

It annoyed Happy that she should lock the door after her. She certainly had no rudeness to fear from him. Probably Myra had acted entirely from habit.

The paper was Suderman's next concern and he donned Willard's dressing-gown—in case anyone was passing in the hall. The unfamiliar texture of the cloth irritated him and he flung the robe off with a "damn" of disgust and found the paper nudely, regardless of the neighbors. The statistics and their purport held Happy's attention until Myra entered from the bath, fully clothed. There was no pretense in her stunned amazement at sight of her lover, reading the morning paper in the middle of the room and in nothing else.

"Well!" she said—and Happy turned, blushing to the roots of his hair.

"I—I was waiting for you—" he mumbled feebly.

"I *see you* were."

"—to finish with the tub."

"You might have put something on!" She picked Willard's robe from the floor where Happy had thrown it and held it toward him, averting her expressionless face.

He took the garment, tossed it on the bed with the paper and strode into the bath, slamming the door.

Myra made the bed.

In a few moments, over the roar of the water, Happy Suderman's unmelodious voice rose defiantly.

> "Oh, believe me, if all those endearing
>   young charms,
> That I gaze on so fondly today."

He stopped singing suddenly. The *neighbors!* And he wasn't entirely sure of the words after that, anyway.

When he reappeared and started dressing, Myra excused herself. "I'm going up to Dr. Arnoldi's. Do you mind?"

Those few bars of song had partially revived Happy's spirits. He pouted and cocked one eye at her.

"You wouldn't make a poor old man a cup of coffee, would you?"

Myra had not yet had the relief of song. His improved humor was not sufficiently infectious to enliven her. "Oh, of course I will."

Dashed, he caught her arm as she went toward the kitchenette. "Don't bother. Thanks just the same. I've got to run, anyway. I'll get it on the corner."

She looked a long time in his eyes.

"That will be better," he said, releasing her. "On second thought, I'd rather."

Myra remained motionless as he resumed his dressing. Finally, standing so long, silently, became embarrassing. Happy had got as far as his necktie. "There's no use fooling ourselves, Happy. We both feel it."

Suderman gave no sign that he heard, but his arms going into his coat, jerked stiffly.

"Don't we?"

"You do—at least."

"So do you."

"Well, it's this place! I told you you were too good for this dump. You don't belong here."

"I belong here as long as he needs me, Happy. As long as there is the slightest hope."

"I understand," he said.

Mrs. Kent turned slowly and left him, closing the front door softly and thoughtfully ascending the steps to Dr. Arnoldi's room. She found the old man washing his breakfast dishes in the sink. He left off abruptly and dried his hands, unable to stifle entirely a small resentment at being discovered in that menial task. His enormous, tottery frame was given added height by her smallness. "How is he?" the doctor asked.

The momentary confusion into which the pronoun threw her, amused Myra. One *he* was recovering his self-composure belowstairs, the other had ceased to bleed, but her answer was entirely proper. "Just the same. The bleeding has stopped."

Probably because he has no more blood, thought Arnoldi, but he smiled at the news. "Good!" he said. "Have you had breakfast?"

"Yes," she lied, knowing he would urge food upon her if she replied otherwise.

"And a good night's sleep?"

She smiled wanly.

"Perhaps you will take a nap today. You cannot remain well without sleep. It's deplorable, I know, but there it is." He sat down with a weary sigh.

Myra put one hand on his ponderous shoulder and studied his smooth old actor's face.

"What do you see?" he asked.

"You want me to flatter you."

"I do not. Please pardon me for contradicting you, but I do not wish to be flattered and I should discount your smallest praise."

Myra laughed and went to his sink, adjusting the sleeves of her dress.

"Now, don't do that!"

"I will! Sit still. I want a glass of tea."

"But not the dishes! Please?"

She ignored him, setting a kettle to boil and finishing the duty he had relinquished at her entrance.

Arnoldi's pleasantries were almost as laborious as his body movements. "Now I shall have to call on you, after Willard returns and wash your dishes for you. Will you let me?"

"Of course not."

She was finished in a trice and sat with her tea and a scone when Happy kicked the door with his toe. His hands were full. Coffee and pastry and toast from the restaurant.

"Oh," said Happy as he saw Myra swallow.

"Pleasant fellow," said Dr. Arnoldi. "What news?"

"None, I'm afraid. Have *you* eaten?"

"An hour ago."

"All the more for me!" He drew up a chair and opened his purchases. "Doctor, I want to employ you."

"And you said there was no news."

"I mean it."

"Still more important."

"I want you to come and meet my partners in a new enterprise, Heaven on Earth, Incorporated."

"You can no longer surprise me, Mr. Suderman. Whenever I see you I know that what you are going to say is calculated to shock."

"Not at all. I'll tell you about it . . . Won't you have one of these rolls?"

Myra took one, fearing to hurt him.

Happy explained the nature of Heaven on Earth between bites. "And we want you for medical adviser, to tell us for sure when there's no more hope."

Dr. Arnoldi chuckled. "You have picked out an *easy* job for me!"

"Will you do it?"

"No."

"Why not?"

"I am not able."

"We'll fit up a suite of rooms in Heaven, give you servants and as many assistants as you want."

"No."

"Set your own figure."

"That has nothing to do with it."

"We'll give you anything you ask."

"But I *can't.* I shouldn't know when hope had ceased! You ask something that is impossible."

"All you have to do is sign the papers when we tell you. You needn't move from your chair."

"*That* appeals to me."

Myra had sat through Happy's discourse in silent, awe-struck amazement. Suddenly she rose. "Excuse me," she said and left the room.

"What has she been talking about?" Suderman asked at once. "Tell me what she said."

Arnoldi shook his massive head slowly. "I can't do that, my friend, although our conversation has been harmless enough."

"Did she mention me?"

"I think not. I don't remember."

"I don't know what I'm going to do about her, doctor."

"Must you do something?"

Happy nodded. "We love each other very much."

"There will be no more waiting for husbands to get cold, now; will there?"

"That wasn't entirely called for!" In his anger, Happy rose and began pacing the floor.

Dr. Arnoldi sighed heavily. "I meant no offense," he said without emphasis, a simple statement of fact.

"Am I to blame because I met her on the day her precious Willard was to get hurt? Does that blind me to her beauty or make me less sensitive to her charm? I *love* her, I tell you, regardless of how many husbands she has or what the state of their health happens to be."

Dr. Arnoldi began clearing the little table. "What do you want me to do about it?"

"Only make her philosophic. Let her see that she owes no devotion to a dead thing. You saw him. You know he will never leave his bed. Help her bear that—and I will help her to forget it."

"Are you in such a hurry?"

"Hurry? No. I'm willing to wait. I'll wait as long as she likes—but she hates me now."

"A moment ago you said she loved you."

"She did. I'm sure she did, until last night."

"You *were* in a hurry then. Last night!"

"It wasn't that. It was the night that changed her. She loved me then. This morning she can't bear to look at me."

"Ah—" said Dr. Arnoldi with complete understanding.

"Do you think it's only a wave of remorse? Will she get over it?"

The Russian put his cigarette machine and his canisters of tobacco on the table and prepared for a morning of work. "I don't know, my friend. You have come to a poor oracle for advice on the subject of a woman's heart. I know so little about them."

"But, you know Myra. She is your friend. She confides in you."

"She hasn't mentioned you—beyond asking my opinion yesterday."

"She asked your opinion?"

"Yes."

"Of me?"

"Yes."

". . . Well, well, what did you tell her?"

"I said I liked you."

"Is that all? That's not an opinion."

"I suppose not, but that's what I told her."

"What did she say?"

"That she liked you, too."

"Is that all?"

"That's all I remember."

"She might have said that about the ash man!"

"Yes. She might."

"I don't think you do like me, doctor. You don't approve. Was Willard such a very good friend of yours?"

"I scarcely knew him."

"Didn't you visit each other, evenings? Play cards, perhaps?"

"Once or twice we spent the evening together . . . He didn't approve of me."

"Oh? What didn't he like?"

The little pile of long cigarettes was mounting under Arnoldi's thick fingers. "I don't know. Perhaps I was too radical for him."

"Radical? You?"

"Perhaps."

"But you aren't radical! Do you mean politically?"

"I was only guessing." The doctor's tired smile was turned on Happy for a moment.

"I wish I had known this Willard. I'd know better how to act."

Arnoldi said nothing.

"You see? I've driven her away from you now. She was sitting here talking to you. When I came in she ran away."

"You chased her away with your comatants. Having one in her own family makes her sensitive on that subject."

"That's going to be horrible. Imagine living in a place like this with a comatant in the room—always."

Dr. Arnoldi looked around at his own walls, bare except for several shelves of well-worn Russian books and a rack of dishes and pans curtained with faded cretonne. "I haven't room for one . . . What a calamity it would be for my family if I should fall into that state—if I had a family."

"She'll have to have a case to keep him in."

"You'll send her one, of course."

Happy saw more amusement in the doctor's small eyes, hiding under his fat, bulging brows, than he had ever seen there before. "Of course. But I shall have moved her by that time. I'm not going to let her go on living here."

"Cigarette?" asked Dr. Arnoldi.

Happy lit one.

"Then I shall be alone again." The old man spoke solemnly but with no effort to arouse sympathy.

"I wish you'd come with me and talk about this job I offered you. There'd be no work attached to it. You'd be your own boss."

"But what would you pay me for if I did no work? Why do you want *me?*"

"We need a man who is not too ambitious. Someone who can keep his own counsel, someone with imagination. An ordinary doctor will not do. Young men would be forever experimenting, trying to raise our 'dead'. You wouldn't. You could prescribe the proper care—Oh, you're perfect for the place."

"I fail to see it. I think I prefer the quiet here."

"But you'd be so much more comfortable! At least come and discuss it with my partners."

"I dislike to go out, Suderman. I dislike it."

"You don't mean to say you're happy *here!*"

"Happy? No. I ceased to look for happiness, many, many years ago."

"But you're uncomfortable, and when I take Myra away, you'll be alone. You have nothing in common with the rest of your neighbors. You think it over. I've got to run along now. Buying furniture."

"Chasing your tail! Come back and play chess with me tonight."

"I'll try, doctor. I have so many things to do—"

"Oh—later, then. I thought we'd talk. It isn't important."

"I'll try."

The doctor watched the door close with his usual, meaningless sigh. Alone again. He had made thirty cigarettes as the young man talked. Suderman reminded him of someone. Who was it? Dcheniev? Naumov? No, no one in the village. He gave up trying to think of that and smiled at the madness of the proposal that *he,* old and worn-out, take the position in this novel industry which the *new* life had caused to spring up. They didn't want him. Somebody had said "doctor" and Happy, only out of his presence a few hours, had thought first of him. All nonsense. His sight was failing, as his feet had. Infirmity was beginning at both ends as well as in the middle. Dead! Indeed, he had been dead a *long* time. And they wanted him to wear his shroud about an office, saying what they told him to say—for money. What would he do with their money? With their servants? It had been years since he had had a servant. One would annoy him with his stupidity now. He was better off alone, at peace, without their money. He had enough for his needs.

That tapping would be Myra, returned, now that her impatient lover had gone. "Come in," he said, dropping the sweet shreds of fine tobacco in the hopper of his little machine. "You are quite safe," he said, smiling. "He has gone to buy furniture."

"What kind of furniture?"

"I don't know. He said just furniture."

"Oh, doctor, what am I to do about him?"

"He asked me the same thing about you. Do you young people take me for the god of love? What do I know?"

"I think he loves me."

"He thinks so too."

"Don't *you?*" Umbrage—at an inflection!

"I?" He closed his eyes to sigh better. "I am no judge of the affairs of the heart. He makes himself very miserable if that is evidence."

"I *know* he does."

"And *you.* You aren't very cheerful."

"Cheerful!"

"Well—do you love him?"

"Oh, I wish I hadn't started talking about it. I don't know. I thought I did—but I can't, I must not." She walked to the window behind him.

More nonsense. A man and a woman crying out in their anguish, beating their breasts and belaboring their consciences for a figment two lesser animals would have avoided by the simplest of actions without reasoning. Ah, that power of reasoning! It was the tormentor. *I love. I do not love. We die. We do not die.* Through reasoning, every circumstance and its opposite made man miserable.

"I shouldn't worry about it," Dr. Arnoldi said without turning. "You are sure to know in time. Why try to decide just now? Wait a little."

"You don't understand, doctor. Happy—Happy—"

He could not help her. She would find the words. This suffering would be real for only a moment.

Some one else applied for admittance. Myra struck a scowling, defensive attitude. If that were Happy Suderman, he had returned to trap her.

It was Sid. He entered, cringing, his eyes raised to his icon, but not his head. "I have come again," he said.

Dr. Arnoldi exhaled a lungful of smoke that colored the

atmosphere of the room. "I see you have," he answered boredly. "You're the one who wants me to speak."

"Yes, doctor." Then Sid saw Myra. "Oh! I thought—I didn't know anyone was here."

"Yes, someone is here." He made no move to introduce his guests.

"I'll come back later," said Sid, backing away. "I'm sorry."

"What is it you want?" Arnoldi asked, annoyed by the fellow's scraping. "There's no use asking me to speak, you know."

"I'll come back later. I have been imprisoned. I have suffered too."

"Who else has suffered? What do you mean?"

"You must have suffered, in Russia, under the knout."

Dr. Arnoldi made a futile gesture of disgust with his hand. "Nothing of the kind. Go away and save yourself the trouble of coming back. I am seldom discourteous, but you take me for something I am not—and your pleading disgusts me. I have nothing to tell—the workingman."

"Didn't my friend, Mr. Suderman, speak for me? Didn't he tell you I had quit my job?"

"Is Mr. Suderman a friend of yours?"

"A very good friend. We have lived together for nearly four years."

"Oh, the pants presser!" said Myra.

The doctor questioned her with his eyes.

"He said you kept him awake all night," said the girl.

"The dog! Is that all? Just made light of me."

"He said you were a radical."

"I am!" Sid's voice rose thinly.

"Your ranks will be thinned, now, I think," Arnoldi said with an odd smile.

"Thinned?"

"There will be so much work to do."

"More work! *More* work. But we won't do it! We—won't—do it."

"I hear you," said the doctor.

"That's why I was imprisoned," Sid explained, swaggering. "I was inciting the mob to fury."

"What for?" the old man asked.

"To *strike!* To strike before Privilege strikes. To throw off our chains. They cannot kill us now."

"Shshsh." Dr. Arnoldi tried to quiet him. "I do not wish to argue with you. If you want the country, take it, but leave *me* in peace."

"You are a sloth!" Sid accused. "You are not rich, but you are fat, and that's almost as bad. Do you know that thousands of babies are hungry today? They went to bed hungry last night; they'll go to bed hungry again tonight! While you loll in slothful ease and do nothing for them. *You* who have known the knout—and the lash—you, a Russian who has seen the revolution."

"Knout—knout? I was never beaten."

"You saw your fellows beaten! You were spared because of your learning, but what about all those others? They had no education to save them. You were saved—to heal their wounds. You were valuable."

Dr. Arnoldi sighed. "I wish you would go away, little man. I can't do anything for you."

"Happy has taught you to laugh at me, but you'll see! *You'll* see."

The thick, heavy lids lowered slowly and raised again. "You are very obstinate, little man. Please go away now."

"Where is Suderman?"

"I don't know."

"*You'll* know," Sid sneered at Myra. "You're the one who's too good for this environment." He snorted. "Where's Happy?"

"He's gone—about his business. I don't know where."

"Did he spend the night here? He wasn't home."

"I'm sure I don't know," said Myra, walking toward the door. Arnoldi's eyes pleaded with her to stay.

"He's quit the newspaper. I called there."

"He's gone to Heaven," said Dr. Arnoldi softly. "Do you know where that is?"

"Heaven! How do you mean, heaven? I thought you were smart."

"We all make mistakes," the doctor murmured.

"How do you mean? He isn't dead!"

"No," the doctor answered. "It's his new employment. He's president. I don't know where it is. Did he tell you?" His small eyes appealed to Myra for an address to which he might send this private scourge which had descended upon him.

"It's Dan Sweeney's place. Do you know—"

"Sweeney's? The booze cure? Is that called Heaven now?"

"I think so."

Sid sneered again at them both, but his step toward the door was a relief. "So you won't talk to the workers? Our problems don't interest you?"

Dr. Arnoldi only stared. He did not even touch his cigarette machine or the tobacco lest a movement call Sid Lyman back or evoke a new tirade.

"All right, Dr. Arnoldi, when the torch is applied to all this civilization you think is so fine and equitable, *then* we'll see if you'll talk." He indulged in one more snort before slamming the door.

"Why—doctor!" said Myra, when she found her tongue. "Isn't his mind deranged?"

"I think not," said her friend. "Not really. He was here once before."

"Well, *I* think he's dangerous."

"He hopes he is."

"Don't you?"

"I don't know. His is really a mild case compared to some I have seen back home. They used to meet at midnight, before the revolution. Long ago they were called nihilists. They'll have their day here too, I suppose. This is a heavy blow to them."

"You mean—"

It was obvious that he did. "Yes. Thousands will desert their sacred cause to become rich. It will delay them."

Myra remembered her telephone and went away to listen for its ring.

17

ALLARDICE TUCKER, M.D., took God's intervention as a personal affront. He had been getting along pretty damned well without all this help. He didn't mind, now and then, a *little* lift. With Bamberger, now, it had come in handy, but why ruin a fellow's reputation by conferring the same Divine Blessing on every little old pill dispenser on the continent? Tucker didn't believe in the efficacy of prayer but he couldn't help casting a dirty look or two aloft as he made his rounds the third day of the miracle. The zest and zip and tang were gone from surgery. Anybody could trephine now. A pocket knife and a darning needle were the only instruments needed and if they weren't too clean it didn't matter much. Your patient got a little sicker, that was all.

What was left for a man of his genius? Must he learn an entirely new trade? What? After playing with Life and Death as if they were cubs of some dangerous beast which would devour him for carelessness, to what could he turn for excitement? Without the grave to trifle with, what thrilling hazard was left? He didn't mind being noble within reason. It gave him a pleasant glow to alleviate suffering, but the kick had lain in outwitting man's greatest and strongest adversary, the old Grim Reaper.

He could go to Europe, of course. It would be something to make a stir in Vienna, but that was begging the issue. He wasn't the only good surgeon in America. What were the others going to do? They couldn't all go to Vienna.

Dr. Allardice Tucker admitted that he was not the only accomplished surgeon in North America, but he was by all odds the best. If he changed his profession, such was his constituency, he would accept no lower station in the ranks of his foster-work. "I can place myself at the top of any line of endeavor that has ever interested Man. I have this power, this capacity. But what, now that medicine and surgery require no more intelligence than working for Henry Ford,

what art or science remains of sufficient moment to excite
me to the necessary application?"

To sweep the cleanest street?

To shave the softest chin?

To paint the livest portrait?

To build the tallest spire?

What were the future prospects of these trades? Suppose
he mastered the intricacies of architecture as it was known.
Would not the new order change the needs of mankind,
evolving a house and a temple and a forum no man could
imagine? Wherein lay the satisfaction of edifice designing?
To inspire vulgar stares? Was that the pinnacle of achievement in that field? The Empire State Building, Eiffel Tower,
the Parthenon and the pyramids! The badge, the medal, the
token for supremacy at this business of setting up stones
must bear a peasant's head, there graven, eyes bulking and
mouth agape.

Tucker dallied on the street. There was no hurry. No
man's distress was mortal and without that imminence his
feet were loath to move. Never again would that fine shock
of a midnight bell call all his faculties into vibrant, tingling
life. He need never hurry again. With a smile he remembered
his first croup case at dawn. The baby's first unlabored
breath and his discovery that he still wore the coat of his
pink pajamas had come simultaneously. Gone, gone, gone
were those half-clad dashes through the night, those breath-
less hopes that his Buick would be swifter than Pluto's char-
iot. Tucker tarried outside a door.

Which way romance? Was not the risk of life the essence
of adventure? Smuggling, flying, dueling, diving, racing,
sailing, climbing, warring. There was no use living if one
could not die. Gambling? He might take up card-sharpery.
Montaigne reserved that thrill only for men too old for any
other.

Little Allardice had dabbled with colors. Some talent had
shown. But on the third day of the miracle, the joys of painting well seemed meager indeed to the doctor.

"Allardice Tucker, the celebrated portrait painter, has

been commissioned—" He tested the sound of it.

"The wizard of the gaming tables, M. Tucker, is again among us and no man's purse is safe."

"Ho-hum," said Dr. Tucker, and he passed through the door.

That day a man had been decapitated in a machine shop. Tucker fitted the pipes and cords together and sewed up the skin of the neck. "Put a cast on it," he said despondently, "and keep his bowels open."

He was due at the West End Hospital at noon at the latest. He did not appear. The staff had not arrived so quickly at Dr. Tucker's desolate conclusions. It still took its work seriously. When two o'clock came and they had no word, the girl was instructed to call and to keep on calling until the wizard was located. They found him at last, in the boiler room, dealing blackjack to the engineer and three elevator boys. He put on his coat sulkily and followed the interne from room to room.

"Keep them all out of pain," he said when he left. "Nature will do the rest."

Myra had gone to the hospital in her impatience by that time. She confronted the surgeon in a corridor. "Tell me, doctor. Will he ever be normal again?"

The beauty of her face in suffering made Tucker think again of painting. He studied her to see if he could find the subtle colors which gave her pain reality to beholders. He squinted at the lines she would not naturally have about her mouth. He focused on the lights in her eyes. How the devil could a painter catch that?

"It's very doubtful. At first I thought it was just his heart and lungs. He'd have got over that, after I lifted his ribs, but—there seems to be something else. I don't know what. We'll keep him under observation."

To be sure, if he stayed in the medical racket, there were two problems worthy of his consideration. First, the nature of this protracted animation; second, a means of inflicting death. Just like any other disease. These were the questions doctors had partially resolved regarding smallpox, typhoid, malaria and itch—some itches. Cause, course, crisis and cure! Well, Death was the cure for Life but; who could ad-minister it? "I'll bet a dollar I can kill a man!" Allardice said to himself.

That consideration engaged his mind through dinner to the exclusion of portrait painting or gambling. He took the night train to Albany, determined to obtain a commission from the State of New York, to set out purposely to kill. He would make them give him a convict for a subject.

Tucker left New York City a welter of confusion. The Board of Health was up a tree. City equipment and personnel could not handle the situation after the fourth day. Mortuaries were crowding, hospitals were jammed, the Army had been asked for cots and medical units were setting up house-keeping in armories all over town.

Mattress factories worked three shifts a day and goose feathers were at a premium. Army and Navy stores and sporting goods houses were out of cots and sleeping bags. *Tents* were sold like chewing gum; yes, in cellophane.

The good fathers of New York City had provided well for future sewage disposal, so that no immediate anxiety was felt in that quarter. Smaller communities had been planned less intelligently—or had been planned not at all—and typhoid and scarlet fever joined hands with the surgeons in creating monsters to roam the thoroughfares. For, all recovered, no matter how sadly disfigured, and baldness, lop-ear, purblind-ness, drool-tongue and hare-lip defaced whole townships. Thousands suffered softening of already loose-jelled brains but the salvaging of the Divine Spark was still praised in those early days.

Protestant churches set their congregations to praying in relays and Almighty God was subjected to such a barrage of supplication as He had never before known.

Up at the prison, the warden saw his opportunity to avoid executions. He had always hated them. Had, in fact, written books against capital punishment. Now, he couldn't kill the unfortunates, and his death-cell block began to resemble an hotel in a town where both Elks and Shriners have decided to convene the same week.

And what a ribald crew they became. Liberty seemed to have lost its meaning temporarily. None of them called for reprieves or commutations. Some fatalistic, inexplicable quirk in their mental set-up made it meet and desirable to stay just as they were, as long as the law liked. Those rooms adjoining the hot-spot came to resemble a picnic grounds. They kidded with the guards and laughed and joked and sang. Here, if anywhere on earth, the change was appreciated. But the problem facing the authorities was their housing.

From twelve condemned men living there one day, their number increased to thirty in a month, which constituted a record. Most of these convictions were for kidnapping for ransom. Life everlasting had caught the administration in the very middle of this catch-the-kidnappers! frenzy.

Thirty more tractable, jolly, easy-going human beings never had been gathered together in any other one spot. They said, "Yes, sir, Mr. Guard," and "No, sir, Mr. Guard," and "Is there anything we can do for you, sir?" until the turnkeys blushed for their own bad manners.

The crowded and immoral conditions under which these men were living became the news of the day, one day, and humane societies and some churches petitioned the governor to do something. The governor realized his responsibility keenly and went into the silence for inspiration. Many public figures were turning to astrology and spirit-control for advice in those days; many more than usual, although they had always been the chief support of half the clairvoyants in the capitals.

Before making a public pronouncement, it was suggested that other attempts be made to effect the execution of some of these men. States in which hanging had been the means of despatching undesirables reported no better luck and those in which formerly lethal chambers filled with poison gas had been the end-all for miscreants now found that their hitherto fatal fumes only made the men violently ill.

Drastic measures seemed the only solution to the dilemma and in the face of all the evidence that leaden pellets no longer caused death, a firing squad was suborned to do the men in.

Dr. Tucker, whose greatest misfortune (practically his *only* misfortune) was his outward resemblance to Adolf Hitler, had constituted himself a lobby of one with no other purpose than to demonstrate his ability to do what they could not. Just at that period, the life of a public servant was such a bed of nettles that public benefactors were mistaken by them for enemies and enemies for good friends. It was not astonishing, all things considered, that the doctor's petition did not reach the hands of authority until a week after his arrival in Albany, that is, on the day following his meeting with the governor.

Tucker, disgusted with the delay and the several affronts to his swollen ego, waylaid the governor's party in the rotunda one night. When one of the plainclothes men stuck his elbow in Tucker's stomach with a "One side!", the doctor kicked the fellow's left shin and screamed, "Do you know who I am? . . . I am Dr. Allardice Tucker from New York City and I know I can kill people!" There were all his eggs in one basket.

The newspaper men trailed the party to the governor's home and waited four hours for the little fellow to come out. He beamed on their flashlights and reported his success. The post of Special Adviser to the Executioner had been created and Dr. Tucker was on his way to Sing Sing with the taxpayer's money backing his proposed experiments.

"What's the secret, Dr. Tucker? How are you going to do it?"

"Maceration," said the wizard simply, "maceration."

18

THE BED of an officeholder always had been nettlesome, still seekers after the distinction of reclining there were ever numerous. The losers of all the most recent elections made light of the new problems imposed on their successful rivals by suspended mortality. They even increased the aggravation wherever possible, to build up campaign issues for the Fall.

The first big fight was with the insurance companies, a fight which almost attained the proportions of a war. It was colored considerably, given a comic turn and high-lighted, by the inability of the insurance companies to agree among themselves. Obviously, legislation affecting any one company must affect all, yet they could not come to terms on that one major issue: *Shall "total disability" be read into policies covering only death?*

"If we don't pay claims on that basis," the stentorian voice of one board chairman declared, "why on earth should the assured pay premiums? *Why?*"

His helpers helped him: "They won't!"

"On the other hand," the opposition argued, "if we do pay such claims, all the policyholders who have been paying for the added protection of a total disability clause *will demand a refund.*"

"Let them demand. How are they going to collect?"

"If we don't refund, *they* will lapse. I think the actuaries should furnish us with a detailed report on the probable loss both ways."

"That's not all," the chairman continued, "that's not all. If we don't pay these claims, how are we going to write any new business?"

"I don't see how we are going to write any new life business whether we pay total disability claims or not," a timid member said plaintively. "It looks like the doom of life business to me."

"The public will want death insurance now," said the crusty president.

A keen member squinted both eyes and drummed on the heavy mahogany table with his stubby fingers. "Put your actuaries on that," he said. "And see if Lloyd's will take such a case on an inhabitant of this continent—today."

The chairman sent his secretary to cable Lloyd's at once.

The opposition was reasonable. "I wouldn't object to paying this new type of claim if the chance for fraud weren't so great. It isn't the money, you know."

"And they'd recover later. Lots of them will. Then where would we be?"

"Well, if we don't make up our own minds pretty damned soon, it will be made up for us."

And when a board of directors finally decided upon a course of action, it coincided in no way with the decision of the board which had met upstairs above them or another two blocks down the street.

New business and cash receipts fell off alarmingly, before any decision had been reached.

Inundated with letters from their constituents, congressmen and senators turned their attention to the right of the matter.

Myra was urged to file a claim by Mr. Thorndike. The situation at 408 Canal had changed. Happy was so engrossed with the development of Heaven on Earth that he was known to Myra and Dr. Arnoldi only by memory, through the newspapers, and over the telephone. The doctor bore it well.

FOREVER
Near Thee!

The headline of Happy's first advertisement burned its letters into Myra Kent's brain as she read it over Dr. Arnoldi's shoulder.

The shadows of the tomb and the silence of the grave are banished. Rejoice! The veil no longer separates, the scythe of Time no longer severs. Rejoice.

Heaven has come to Earth!

When the ravages of disease, the cruel hand of accident, the inexorable march of age deprive your loved ones of their wonted vigor, place them here, at rest, where you may visit them in privacy and witness the tender care they enjoy.

Heaven on Earth, Incorporated,
2206 West 44,

New York City.

Prospect 9102   Physicians and nurses
          9103   in attendance all of
          9104   the 24 hours.
          9105

Heaven (nonsectarian) on Earth, Incorporated, is the natural successor to the mortician, undertaker, embalmer; the cemetery and crematory. A booklet fully describing all the services placed at your disposal here is yours for the asking. A postcard will bring "Forever Near Thee", 116 pages, beautifully illustrated, to your home or office.

Send no money!

The illustration accompanying this text showed a voluptuous girl in a bathtub. "That," one of the experts from Philadelphia had said, "is necessary. You can't sell anything without sex appeal."

The hospital had not yet asked Myra to take her husband home when she read that. It did not apply to her. When Dr. Tucker came back from Albany he would operate again, and Willard would be up and around. She was sure of it. She kept assuring herself she was sure of it and all but lost her mind wrestling with conscience, because she dreaded to see Willard walking around again, unless he was walking away from her, out of her life forever.

It did not apply to her! *Forever Near Thee!* That didn't mean Willard and Myra Kent. It meant Happy and Myra, that's what it meant, but that was wrong. That was shallow and small and detestable in her. If only she had never *seen* that man! He was doing his share. He was staying away. She had driven him away.

The chill confusion, the spasmodic iciness of that morning—three days before—when they had found themselves together in Willard's bed, still convulsed her reason and gripped her heart. Sultry June, sunny and dry, yet, Myra was *cold* with that memory.

Loyalty, perfidy; passion, devotion contested and writhed in contesting for her self-respect, her honor, her life, for what is sometimes called a woman's "soul". Pity Myra. Pity lovers. Pity those who vow. For constancy is a dreadful thing.

Dr. Arnoldi's small eyes, expressionless for the moment, moved over the contours of the lady in the tub and then found his companion's chalky face. He sighed for his monkish years, sighed briefly in token of respect for a loss but dimly comprehended. He had been always apart from life. It was considerably more than phrase-making to say he had been dead for years. When had he been alive? At school in Berlin, a prostitute had laughed at his nakedness. He had never uncovered again. Not until Maria Pavlovna had come back to the village to die had the tenderest sentiment touched him and he had not recognized it then. The phlegmatic celibate turned from the picture of youth in her bath without recalling the gentle melancholy of those hours he had sat beside the actress as life slipped regretfully from her pale form, her wax-like fingers. He recalled nothing.

"I think you are anemic, my dear," said Dr. Arnoldi.

"I know I am," Myra answered.

"You should start at once on a diet. Raw liver and spinach."

"*Raw* liver!"

"It is unpleasant."

Myra made a face and sat down trembling. "Ugh! I couldn't."

"Your blood pressure can't be over seventy. You must take care of yourself."

"I don't know why I should . . . Was that my phone?" Her quick little feet scarcely touched the steps.

Could she come to the hospital at once?

"What's happened? Can't you tell me?"

Nothing alarming. The directors were being forced to remove some of the patients. Dr. Jocelyn would like to discuss it with her.

It had come. Myra stared vacantly across the poor room and out the window. Willard was to come home to pulse. Instead of the piano they had planned to put between the window and the door, in that corner, she would set her husband there. Happy would give her a case to keep him in.

An insane giggle sounded in her head and someone rapped, politely. Someone asked with knuckles to be forgiven for that interruption. It was Mr. Henry Thorndike, still smelling—or smelling again—of the barber shop. Myra giggled again.

"I've brought you your check," he said. "I thought you might be needing it."

Did she need a check? "Oh, yes," she said. "Thank you."

He looked past her into the shabby room. Wasn't she going to invite him in?

Myra took the envelope and struggled to suppress another mad snicker. Here he was! Lewd man! Rude man! Fool! She hadn't enough to worry about with a cataleptic husband and a base love she dared neither take nor leave. *He* had to come around with his fine stench of panetelas and bay rum. What did he take her for?

"You could have mailed it just as well," said Mrs. Kent.

"I wanted to see you again. Is there anything I can do?"

You can go away. "No, I'm all right. Mr.—Mr. Kent is coming home. I'm—I'm going to the hospital now to see about it."

"My car's downstairs! I'll run you over there."

It would be too much trouble. It would be no trouble at all.

"I've got to run upstairs a moment. Excuse me, please?"

"Does your friend, the doctor, live up there?"

"Yes."

"Do you mind—?"

Why should she mind?

Dr. Arnoldi showed no surprise at Mr. Thorndike's presence. He nodded to the engineer who stood in the background.

"I've got to bring him home. They called. They need the room. No one knows when Dr. Tucker will be back."

"They need the room." Arnoldi repeated. "They need the

room already."

"I'm going to call Happy. He'll know what to do."

"If you prefer to have Mr. Kent left at the hospital, I'm sure I can arrange it," Thorndike volunteered. "They can't need one room as badly as that."

"One room?' said Arnoldi. "They need a vacant city."

"Don't you think I ought to call Happy?"

"He'll want to take him to Heaven," said the doctor.

Of course! Myra's heart leapt and a tint of rose came in her cheeks. Take him to "Heaven on Earth". That's what the place was for.

But, when Happy proposed that, she balked. It was too obvious, too cruelly apparent that she was getting rid of him, putting him out of sight, shirking her duty.

"I can't, Happy; but—if—if you'll send—one of your cases—" she began to sob uncontrollably, "—one of those things you're making, down to the house, I'll—I'll be ever so grateful."

"Myra!" Suderman called loudly. "Myra, darling! Don't cry like that. My God, don't take on so. It'll be all right. I'll send one. Please stop crying. Oh, I love you so, darling. Please stop."

"I-I-I'm—stopping."

Happy dared not take the case to her himself. He sent a uniformed interne and a nurse. This was part of the service. The nurse had instructions to remain.

Henry Thorndike's money was spurned at the West End Receiving Hospital. Dr. Jocelyn was very sorry, but there seemed to be no help for it. The local chapter of the Medical Association had approved a time limit for hospital treatment. The Board of Aldermen was in special session to make this restriction a city ordinance. Ground was being broken for an annex. Every unrented house and many apartments were being used for patients awaiting their turn. "It isn't a question of money. Many on the waiting list will be unable to pay a cent. They must be attended."

Thorndike's limousine followed close behind the ambulance. Myra thanked the rich man for his kindness.

A street crowd gathered before 408 Canal to see what a comatant looked like.

"Hey, mister," yelled a little guinea, "turn d' sheet down an' let's see 'im."

"Hurry," said Thorndike, guiding Myra and poking a way through the jam with his stick.

Happy Suderman's emissaries from Heaven (not necessarily "angels") helped the ambulance attendants roll Willard into his new home. Their stretcher folded, one scratched his thatch of red straw and screwed up his face in comic awe. It was his first mission of exactly this kind. The future appalled him. He blinked at the Heavenly couch and watched the body breathing evenly the other side of the glass door. It was a moment requiring speech. He sought in his small purse of words for a group that would honor him.

"Well—?" said his assistant.

The red-head swallowed hard. "Hmmph," he said. "It—it won't be long now!"

The interne and the ambulance surgeon had a long talk, the gist of which was retold to the nurse. "Two ounces of whole milk diluted with warm water, morning and night. Two ounces of strong barley water at noon. Lime water and syrup of figs once a week if necessary. Kidneys every five hours, bowels at ten every morning. You won't have any trouble. If you do, just call me."

The pretty nurse smiled encouragingly at Myra. The buzz of her neighbors' voices just outside her door had an ominous vibrance—almost as if they would hiss and hum like that forever.

Mr. Thorndike blinked. "You can't stay *here*," he said. "This is no place for you."

Myra closed her eyes. *She was too good for her surroundings.* Happy had told her that. "Where am I to go?"

"The most salubrious thing would be travel."

"I can't afford to be salubrious. I have no means."

The engineer looked meaningly at the nurse. "Mr. Kent's insurance should permit you a vacation at least."

"Will they pay it? He isn't dead."

"They'll pay it. You come to my office tomorrow morning and I'll go with you. I'll send a car."

"The one downstairs?"

"Or another. Does it make any difference?"

"Send that one. It's a Cadillac."

"Do you like Cadillacs?"

"I've been told I have Cadillac eyes." But she was looking another way so that *he* could not check that point, and her voice was bitter as gall.

Mr. Thorndike postponed anything else he had to say concerning travel, or Myra Kent's taste in automobiles until such time as no nurse should be there to hear. And, how about these comatants, for the matter of that? Couldn't they hear? He took the lady's hand in what was meant for a fatherly grasp. "I want to speak to Dr. Arnoldi, my dear, then I must run along. If there is anything I can do, day or night, please call me. I'm in the book—and I'll leave instructions that you are to be connected."

Myra smiled up at him faintly. Not such a bad egg. He had carried her to the hospital and back without monkey business. Perhaps she was overly suspicious. Maybe she had grounds for a suit against him and didn't know it. This generous, helpful attitude would be the natural maneuver to forestall that. Myra let him go, puzzling about his interest in the doctor. It was interest in the doctor that had brought Happy to her door.

The ladies who lived in 408 had finally mustered courage enough to ask. Why should they not? Who was she with all her airs? *Might they see her husband?*

For the first time in her life, there was something hard in the expression around Myra's mouth. She stood at bay in a corner, watching them file past the showcase. They spoke to each other in guttural languages and touched her with commiserating hands.

"Too pad," they insisted. It was just "too pad". Women she had never seen before, with infants balanced on their hips or held by grimy hands, filed in, passed the case and spoke to her, until the slim legs which had never felt exactly like that before bent under negligible weight and dropped her quietly to the floor.

It was all the nurse could do to get rid of the mob then and shut the door. Every woman there knew what to do in this emergency and they'd have done it if the nurse had not had ghetto experience. She drove them with cuffs and a vicious tongue, locked them out and put Myra on the bed. Half an hour later she was talking to Happy on the phone.

"She's sleeping *now.* I gave her a bromide. But she's twice as sick as her husband. She needs care."

"Get Dr. Arnoldi, top floor, rear—and I'll be right over."

Thorndike had not yet left. He was basking in his own good fortune at finding this amazing man when the nurse interfered. The doctor, with Mr. Thorndike to back his prescription, ordered an immediate change of surroundings.

"I have a place at Rye."

"Just the thing," said Arnoldi firmly, more firmly than Myra had ever heard him speak before. "Take her there. Nurse; pack her things. I'll write out a diet."

"I wish you'd come too, doctor. Don't you feel a—a responsibility for your patient?"

Myra protested weakly. "I can't go."

"You're going," said Dr. Arnoldi, "at once."

"And you?" Thorndike persisted.

"No," said the old man gruffly. "Thank you very much, it is impossible." He sat at the table and tried to write without trembling.

"How—'impossible'?"

"My practice," the Russian said sarcastically. "I cannot neglect my practice."

When Happy arrived they were gone. The great, hulking figure of the old physician hid the chair which supported it. The nurse stood at the window looking down at the dusky street, her back to her companion. Willard, of course, was where he was.

"Sociable pair!" said Happy, going straight to the bedroom. "Has he insulted you, Gracie?"

"No-o—"

"Where is she?!"

The story was told.

"Uh-huh-uh-huh. That's swell. She'll get on her feet up there. Good!" He was looking at Willard's case in the dark corner of the room. "I'm glad I came down here. Never would have thought of it otherwise. Doctor, see that?"

"What?"

"Too dark, see? I'm going to wire them for neon lights."

19

HERE AND THERE, funerals were attempted. Some few heathens sought to bury their comatants. The processions were stopped and the bodies examined. They pulsed. Then it was found that in all the multifarious statutes regulating man's association with man, there was none specifically forbidding living interment. The only legal stricture on the act was very indirect, the misdemeanor of burying without a permit or— somewhat more serious—of assuming death without a doctor's certificate.

Some of the bodies were shreds and snatches, fragmentary in the extreme, but arrests were made and the otherwise upright citizens branded with horrible names.

Real estate agents petitioned the lawmakers to do something about the trouble they were having. Along with old shoes and broken wind instruments found in closets of vacated houses, comatants were being discovered in alarmingly increasing numbers. It was hurting business. You couldn't expect a client to keep the proper pitch of enthusiasm for a house when, upon walking into the master's suite, you stumbled over the recent master or one of his family—breathing, it is true, but spectacles often enough, for all they were alive!

It became illegal to dig a hole. Abandoning useless or objectionable members of one's family was made punishable by imprisonment of not more than five years.

Abuses and inhumanities never before dreamed of became so prevalent that the existing agencies for law enforcement were utterly unable to cope with them. "Murder" became ridiculously simple. One merely kicked the object of one's hatred down some steep stairs, telephoned a doctor, and stopped feeding the unconscious man, woman or child. By the time the doctor arrived, three or four days later, the deed was done. The patient was too weak to speak, often still unconscious. If medicine was prescribed, it was never bought, and no proof of culpability could be established.

Court dockets were nearly as full as the doctors' calendars at the end of that first month. The jails were bursting and the municipal coffers were empty. County farms and state asylums had to ration the inmates—and finally the attendants—because they couldn't afford to feed them.

New taxes were imposed at every session of every legislative body, but no one paid them. "To hell with it. They haven't got room in the pen!"

Riots and brawls and assaults with "deadly" weapons wore the police to a shadow. Banditry and robbery, although enormously increased, were responsible for but a fraction of the bludgeoning. The chief cause of the acceleration of all but fatal blows, struck with meat cleavers, lead pipe, wrenches, canes, clubs or anything which came to hand, was the shortening of the national temper, nay, the continental temper. With nerves on edge, turned so by the strangeness of incident and the tenseness of the atmosphere, insult—real, fancied or assumed—was almost never taken without swift reprisal. The veneer of civilization peeled from the mammal, man, and private debate was seldom terminated bloodlessly. Nor was there any important or generally concerted effort to reestablish the *code duello*. Upon the utterance of a disparagement, the fur flew, and the stronger or best-armed walked off, leaving the vanquished where he fell.

Rookie cops who took the trouble to arrest the winners of such encounters were laughed at by their superiors and reprimanded for wasting their time.

This new order finally altered the dress of North Americans and folk with known enemies never ventured abroad without short, tough, leathern sleeves, sometimes studded with metal—and the jagged upper half of a broken bottle.

Disfigurement of the face was the first object of the quarrelsome, since scars and deformities were so often the mark brought from the hospital by the living dead.

Originally objects of the greatest curiosity, these *miraclants* (fem., miraclante) shortly became so numerous and often so monstrous in appearance that normal men and women turned from them in aversion. The *miraclant* differed from the *comatant* in that he had regained ambulatory and some measure of mental powers after the best efforts of Fate had failed to carry him off. The first few thousand of these creatures plied a prosperous begging trade, but alms diminished as their numbers increased and the public heart became inured to their revolting appearance.

Whipping post and rack were revived as punishments for certain crimes since these correctives could be administered in the open. Vacant lots and fields near cities sprouted stocks and the prisoners there were fed by their relatives and friends or not at all.

Medical students became doctors almost overnight. Grades of forty per cent were declared "passing" and the degree of M.D. was obtainable in eight months. Interneship was reduced in compulsory duration to thirty days and the brood of practitioners thus produced was as numerous and as objectionable as had been the friars of another day.

Some time later national conscription was necessary to recruit medical students but at first the schools were crowded. That law, like a thousand others, had to be *evolved.* Nothing was done in haste. Nobody would believe the condition was going to last.

The lieutenant governor, with the example of Alexander the Great and the Great Roosevelt before his mind's eye, sought to sever a Gordian knot. "What we *should* do," he told the state's chief executive, "is rush a bill through substituting this new comalike state for death. One bill would do it . . . *Let it be understood that, until further notice, in all statutes appertaining to or using the word 'death' or 'demise,' 'murder' etc., etc., the new and now commonly accepted state of coma shall be substituted or used inter-*

changeably."

"Do you think so?"

"What else are you going to do? That fellow Tucker can't kill a man."

"I don't know . . . There'd be opposition to such a bill."

"Who'd oppose it?"

"Well, somebody's opposed to every bill. The insurance companies would be the strongest, but the automobile associations would fight it too. It would turn half the accidents into manslaughter. The liquor interests; New York City; Tammany. Why, we'd have half the world against us. It would never pass."

"Well, something like that has to be done or the law will go to pieces."

The governor smoothed his hair over the temples. "I don't see that it makes much difference whether it does or not— now. We won't have any need for law in a *few* years. The whole machine of civilization will break down. We aren't geared for this."

"But we'll have to have laws no matter what happens."

The older man shook his head slowly. "You don't get it yet. You don't feel it. In fifty years law will be a farce. Any attempt at order will be stamped out by billions of milling feet, feet that can't die. Mere existence will be the reward only the strongest can achieve. This civilization will crumble like an eggshell. Our standards of living will sink and be obliterated. The arts will no longer be practiced. Nothing that is not directly connected with brute appetites will be given any attention."

"It's up to us to stop that if we can. That's what we're here for."

"You're in a very heroic mood tonight, Carter. Very heroic."

"Well, you're certainly fatalistic enough!" The lieutenant resented his superior's complaisance.

"I don't see what we are to do about it. I try never to fool myself. The old system was tottering before this happened. Democracy was doomed. Capitalism was on the way out.

The—eh—cataclysm has merely been hastened by the repeal of a physical law. Institutions, whether of government or commerce, which have been built by chance—as all ours have, you know—just the result of several centuries of blundering—cannot stand when man completely outgrows them."

"How can man outgrow the need for government?"

"Your manner is insolent and irritating. I don't know that I shall tell you."

It was difficult for the ambitious, younger politician to apologize, he felt so strongly on the subject, but he had to be more polite or leave the house, so he bowed.

"Simply by becoming so numerous that he can no longer be watched. It isn't the need for government he will have outgrown, but authority itself. We have outgrown private ownership—since the World War. The only reason it has not been abolished lies in the balance of organized power. You don't fancy for a moment the voice of the people put me in this chair or you in that one—do you?"

"I'm afraid I've been harboring some such boyish notion; yes."

"I'm glad you see your mistake."

"I'm not sure that I do."

"Then you will never hold public office again—unless you are reelected to your present post, time after time. You are as far as you will go—"

"We're all as far as we're ever going, according to your prediction."

"That is probable too."

The lieutenant governor rose abruptly. "Well, I'm not going to take it like a whipped dog! I'm going to *do* something."

"I've never seen you exactly like this."

"I've never felt exactly like this. I didn't know that my chief was a—a—a Bolshevik! What do you think the people would say if you spoke your radical views in public? Do you think you'd be governor of the state if the voters had ever heard you talk as you've talked to me tonight?"

"I'm sure I should not."

"Why! You're—you're no better than a hypocrite!"

"I'm afraid that's what I am, Carter! I'm *sure* that's what I am."

"It may be funny to you. It isn't to me. I could have you impeached for some of the things you've said. You're a—a radical, an enemy of your country."

"Young man, you are entirely too excitable!"

"I'm leaving. I'm leaving right now. Good night!"

"Good night," said the governor.

When the hot-head was gone, the old man tried to read. The pages made very little sense. Despite his pretended calm, the critical situation organized government must face—and soon—had been on his mind for many days. The young fool had enough Galahad in him to start trouble. It had been the height of folly to speak plainly before him. The legislature was like a powder magazine, ready to blow the city of Albany including his honorable person into oblivion at the first spark.

He'd like to report that Dr. Tucker had been successful. That would quiet them. *That* would quiet everyone. He tried vainly to get the special assistant to the executioner on the telephone. Dr. Tucker had gone to his laboratory and could not be disturbed. He had made it very plain that the success of an experiment depended upon his complete isolation.

The governor called for his car and sent word to the airport that he would fly to Ossining at once. The pilot put him down only a few minutes from the prison gates in record time.

He was recognized and gates swung awesomely to admit him. Courtesy bade him greet the warden first. The good man had been asleep for hours. Too impatient to wait, the governor shook the fellow's pajama sleeve. "Don't dress. I've come to see Tucker. He seems to have something encouraging on tonight."

"Encouraging?"

"He hopes to succeed before morning."

"Succeed in killing—one of my boys! Little Johnny Ledger—"

"We'll waive that, warden. Do you want to come with me?"

"No, thank you. If my duty called me into that butcher shop—I should resign!"

"Butcher shop?"

"Yes, sir! I've been told, although I have never been there. He cut up one poor boy so fine—actually put him through a meat grinder! Oh, sir, it should be stopped. I beg your pardon, governor, but that should not be allowed."

"What happened? Didn't that kill him?"

"They say—" the warden bit his lip and swallowed hard to keep back his tears. "They say—that—that the pile of—of human hamburger—went up and down, up and down, up and down, like that!"

"Wheew!"

"Yes, sir. You see? It's horrible."

"But, warden, something's got to be done. Death *must* be effected some way. It's necessary."

"Necessary!"

"Excuse me. I haven't time to discuss it with you. We all know your views, but you'll have to change them. You will, in time."

Two guards accompanied the governor to a low building apart from the rest, a building without windows and only one wide, steel door.

"The governor is here."

"The *governor* is here."

"The governor."

It took several minutes to get that door open. It grudged admittance to all. Two more doors had to be unlocked, unbarred, before he reached the abattoir.

In the most completely fitted operating room money could equip, under the whitest and most brilliant illumination electricity could produce, Dr. Tucker and six assistants surrounded a body on a table. The governor could see only the feet and ankles of "little Johnny Ledger", the creature on which they worked. The men were silent, unhurried, intent upon their task. No one heeded the new arrival.

A porcelain tub, an enormous dish as large as a bath, stood close to the operating group. A specially constructed gas burner was set under this tub ready to light. A rubber hose connected the burner with an outlet.

Several gallon jugs of a light yellow liquid were near the tub, out of danger of collision with the feet of the surgeons.

The governor moved around to the foot of the operating table, fascinated by the spectacle. Sickening slightly, yet held in his place by a power too strong to be denied, the old man watched the skillful knives and saws.

One assistant quickly wiped the operating table clean and rolled it aside.

"Hello, governor," said Tucker without stopping his work. Another man poured another gallon of the yellow substance into the tub.

"What is that?" the governor asked.

"Sulphuric acid. Everybody out," said Tucker, taking a wooden scoop full of a white powder from a cask and sprinkling it over his hellish broth.

"And that?" asked the governor.

"Nitrate of soda. Get out of here, please." More nitrate was put in the tub.

Dr. Tucker was the last to leave the room. He watched the caldron start to boil and dared not stay for the fumes which were already rising. But as he turned away and ran out, his eyes were dull and heavy with disappointment.

"Let that boil for six hours," he directed, "then shut off the gas outside, ventilate the room and call me.

"Did you want to see me, governor?"

"I—why—yes," the executive's throat and mouth were dry.

"Come over to my diggings and have some coffee. I'm tired."

"I should think you would be."

"That's no good, even if it works, you know," said the doctor. "It costs too much."

"How much?"

They were walking across the prison grounds in darkness

that was sliced by the revolving spotlight in a turret.

"Apiece?"

"Yes."

"Well, you'd have to absorb the original cost of producing the surgical unit. How many men do you kill a year?"

"In normal times—a dozen to fifteen. Now, for the sake of argument, say sixty. That's four times as many."

The searchlight found them and played over their features until one of their attendant guards bid it begone with a signal.

"Sixty." Dr. Tucker shook his head. "See there! It would take a long time to pay for itself executing only sixty a year. It takes forty dollars worth of sulphuric acid. Of course, if you could write off the original investment, the overhead could be cut down. Two men could attend to the dissecting. Three is really all you need. I have those others for other experiments."

They entered a bungalow through a white, arched trellis over which vines clambered. "It doesn't matter *how* much it costs, Tucker. We've got to be able to kill men. I smell coffee."

A trusty in a butler's white jacket served the two men steaming and odoriferous cups. A plate of sandwiches was offered. They fell to heartily. The servant retired. "Is he a prisoner?" the governor asked.

"Yes. He's a lifer."

"Does—does he *sleep* here?"

"In the back."

"Aren't you nervous?"

"Why should I be? I had nothing to do with sending him here. He doesn't know what I'm doing."

"Suppose he found it out?"

"What can he do to me?"

"Well, he can beat you up! *Mar* you pretty badly."

"If I think he's found out why I'm here, I'll ask you to pardon him."

They chatted an hour, then the governor flew back to *his* job. The results of the acid cookery were to be reported the moment the outcome was known. Early next morning, word came. The doctor's disappointment was so great that he could not think of telephoning Albany. He sent a telegram.

FOUND JOHN LEDGER SCRATCHING HIMSELF STOP KINDLY ACCEPT MY RESIGNATION.

Tucker.

20

SID LYMAN, the peripatetic economist and ex-pants presser, found Father Donlevy a willing partner at cogitative dialogue. Between extreme unctions, they sat in the main office of "Heaven on Earth" and waged an endless debate. Like roustabouts on a bench at the door of a livery stable— yesterday, or on the shady side of the depot—even when no train was expected, this team held forth contentiously on single-tax and reciprocity, gold and moral standards, until Ada Werfel, who really had work to do, was driven well-nigh mad. Her ears, very pretty ones, although hidden by day— were further tortured by Sid's newest pose which required him to ape the merest rumor of the conduct of his life by Demosthenes. This quaintness, for the moment, demanded that he carry a handful of pebbles in his mouth while he talked, giving every utterance and almost every breath a bubbly, spattery, overtone.

Miss Werfel, who never minced a word, had adopted a name for Sid almost on sight. She never called him anything else. It was: *That* Sonofabitch!—as if everyone in the office was of a stripe, *sinister,* but that *he,* of them all, was *That* one. This was not a profanity in Ada but clairvoyance.

The morning the stones first came into the office, Ada was wrestling with her first Heavenly trial balance. There was a matter of some eight dollars and sixty-three cents for which she was searching her columns. Over the head-high partition she heard Father Donlevy, fresh from matins for the Privates. That always took him until ten. "Good morning, Sid. God bless you."

"Goo' 'rning Fa'r; Go' 'less you."

"What has That Sonofabitch got in his mouth?" Miss Werfel demanded aloud.

Father Donlevy looked at the young man in alarm. "Toothache?" he asked.

"Noo," Sid slobbered. "Gravel."

"Gravel?"

"Makes impediment," Sid meant to say. It sounded like an off-stage noise. "Demosthenes walked by the sea. Stones in his mouth. Made him great orator."

The priest understood. Ada stuck her head around the door and stared hard at Sid. "Swallow something?" she asked without friendliness.

"Noo," he said loftily.

"You sound like you'd been eating pennies."

Sid let the artificial impediment run into his palm, moistly, and arched his neck for a tremendous squelch. "You wouldn't understand. These are stones."

"Well, I've heard of people having 'em in their bladder, but I never knew they came in the mouth before." Miss Werfel retired.

The fad persisted for a week, then Sid became Socratic. He was composing a speech so cleverly contrived that it should be all questions. This speech he would deliver in Labor Temple. Each question admitted of a simple, obvious answer. His audience would fill in the *yeses* and *noes* quickly between sentences, each in his own mind, as Sid paused for breath. "It's a stunt, see?" he told Donlevy. "It'll get a lot of publicity. The entire social system devastated by a question mark."

"Right now the entire social system *is* a question mark," said the priest. "It will be interesting, if you do it."

"If I *do* it! It's practically finished. Well—it's started. Listen: Ladies and Gentlemen: What have you done that you should bear the burden of all the world's toil? By what right do the overlords of creation squeeze you and milk you dry of energy and of life? Who are these men who sit on their fat money bags and make you fetch and carry as they will? What god gives them the right to—?

"See what I mean? It's a pipe."

"Pipe down!" said Ada Werfel, and when they got too loud, she complained to Happy.

Mr. Suderman was a poor one to complain to just then. His heart was in the hielands of Rye and his worldliness put the most painful interpretation possible on that circumstance. Myra had gone after the dough! And why not! Why shouldn't she? Four years of starvation, living in dumps, a poor man's slave, had dammed up enough cravings for soft and rich and sweet things to dissipate a small fortune. What could he offer her—when the law was finally passed and she was declared a widow in fact? All he had was prospects; prospects in the reformed coffin industry! Every time she saw him she would remember that. Nobody enjoyed shaking hands with an embalmer.

Happy did not doubt that Myra loved him. Happy believed that she had no such tender passion for Mr. Henry Thorndike. Yet his confidence brought him no peace. Only by throwing himself whole-heartedly into the development and perfection of Heaven's service could he forget her.

In a sense, of course, Happy was right. The pursuit of money had carried Myra to Rye. That had been in her mind when she allowed the rich man and Dr. Arnoldi to persuade her to go. "I won't have to sleep in this roomful of memories—and I'll be on hand to go with Mr. Thorndike to the office of the insurance company." No money beyond Willard's insurance occurred to her. She was not making plans of any kind for the future. She did not know or did not reason that any legal definition of "death" incumbent upon an insurance company would or should or could render her a widow. Myra was in such a turmoil that only the advantage of getting away from 408 Canal Street was in her mind.

Happy, who probably never in his life had correctly interpreted a woman's acts, took her vacation sullenly and would not call her on the telephone regardless of Dr. Arnoldi's urging. The doctor's "urging" was temperate, of course, but

Happy should have recognized its wisdom and its sincerity.

He was having a time of it to keep his hands off the French hand-set on his shiny new desk when Ada Werfel came in with her complaint about Sid and Father Donlevy.

"Prezzy," she called him. That was the Werfel diminutive for "president"—"Prezzy! *That* Sonafabitch makes so much noise I can't work."

Happy rose, glad for an opportunity to relieve himself of poison gases. "I've told him a dozen times to stay away from here!" He charged into the outer-office-but-one. "Listen, you squirt—"

Father Donlevy happened to have been speaking at the moment so that Happy had to recant, apologize and explain. "I understand perfectly," said the extremely unctuous padre.

"Scram! See? And don't come back. You give me a pain in the puss. Go get a job. If you had the initiative of a midge you could be rich in ten days. Look at me!"

"I been looking at you for years. It still makes me sick."

"Then what do you come around here for? Beat it. This is a place of business."

Father Donlevy took Sid's part. "Oh, Mr. Suderman, we were just discussing miracles. Mr. Lyman and I find each other's company highly diverting."

The irate employer beetled a brow at the ecclesiast. "You got all your morning chores done?"

"My 'chores'? I've said mass for fifty-two individuals!"

"They must have been damned short ones. How about old Skeezicks, Whatsisname? His wife's paying for *two* masses."

"I am aware of that."

"Did you say 'em both?"

"I did."

"Well, if you want to divert yourself with that halfwit you'll have to go where Ada can't hear you. She's got work to do . . . And for Christ's sake spit that sand out o' your mouth or swallow it or something, Jesus!"

Sid vibrated to his feet and lost a pebble in his vehemence, but Happy walked away without troubling to decode his burbles.

When he could speak again, Sid bade the priest follow him. He knew where they could talk. Dr. Arnoldi received them with little pleasure. He was eating brandied cherries and angel food cake. He set two small plates for his guests and invited their participation.

"To show you how uninformed the American clergy is, doctor, this man had never heard of you," said Demosthenes' ape.

"Does that seem strange to you? Will you have vodka, father?"

"I have never tasted vodka."

"There! You see?"

Arnoldi measured three glasses of his drink from a decanter on the table.

"Happy drove us out," said Sid when neither of his companions contributed any conversation. "He's nuts about his bookkeeper—and she can't work because of my regimen."

"Regimen?"

"His stones," Donlevy explained. "We were debating upon miracles. My friend finds them incompatible with his materialistic philosophy. He wishes to call the handwriting on the wall trickery, the walking on the water chicane, the modern healing at shrines of which we have many—hysteria. This vodka is a pleasant drink."

Dr. Arnoldi nodded graciously and turned to Sid. "And how do you explain scourges and pestilences? Do you doubt that they are manifestations of Jehovah too? And stigmata?"

"Surely *you* don't!"

The priest looked at Dr. Arnoldi suspiciously. He would have preferred to stick to miracles.

"No, I don't," said the Russian.

"Miracles either!" Sid was certain.

Dr. Arnoldi flavored his vodka with a spoonful of the cherries' liquor.

"Miracles, doctor?" the priest insisted. "I should like to hear your opinion of miracles."

"I have no opinion of miracles. More cherries?"

"Oh, you must have formed some sort of opinion. Surely

nothing but the Will of God could have rescued us from the grave."

"That's a smoke-screen," said Sid, helping himself to the vodka. "The Will of God is a smokescreen."

Father Donlevy tried flavoring his drink with a spoonful of the cherry juice and brandy. He smiled companionably at the doctor, as if to say: "I contend with this godless chipper only when there is no first-class intelligence around. Please do not judge me by his stupidity merely because it was he who brought me here. Now that I am in the presence of a *mind*—see how I can ignore him!" It escaped Donlevy that he was giving Arnoldi mental stature almost entirely on Sid's recommendation, since the doctor had neither exhibited nor pretended to startling attributes.

"Just a smoke-screen," Sid mumbled. "You priests been hiding behind that for centuries."

"As a medical man, doctor, how do you explain this cessation of physical death?"

Sid laughed shrilly. "You think you can get anything out of him? Watch this: Tell us about the street fighting in Russia, doctor. You saw it. Tell us."

Dr. Arnoldi poured vodka into his own glass and pushed the bottle toward the priest. As the alcohol permeated his sluggish system, his hands became steadier. "There is nothing to tell," he said wearily. "They fought."

"They fought!" Sid roared with laughter. "Get that, father! 'They fought'! Ho-ho-ho."

"That's quite understandable," Father Donlevy frowned. "The picture of that carnage is ugly, its memory painful. Dr. Arnoldi wishes to forget it."

"Oh, I have forgotten it. Long ago," the Russian said listlessly. "It was all very clumsy. Please help yourself to the cake."

Sid took courage from the vodka and through its influence imagined that he was tormenting the old man. "Is it true, doctor, that the Countess Prsybeski was raped by ten men in front of the post office?"

"I don't know."

"Ten days," the priest mourned to the vodka as it rose in his glass. "Ten days that shook the world."

"But they won't compare with the days that are coming," Sid threatened, his voice rising now, his words stubbing their toes on his gravel. "We'll see how the fine ladies take it *here* when ten men enjoy them on the post office steps! We'll see; the damned swine!" He slopped vodka on the table as he replenished his glass.

"It was in front of a bakery—not the post office," said Arnoldi slowly.

The priest drank off his liquor at a single gulp to sustain himself through this horror. "Dreadful!" he ejaculated. "Dreadful!"

"What's dreadful about it?" the young radical demanded. "They got nothing they didn't have coming. The knout was wrested from their hands—for the first time in history—they felt the sting of their own lash—and here they will feel it too!" He had risen, clutching the table for support.

"Raping!" said the priest.

Arnoldi munched a cherry.

"I'm going to practice my speech," Sid Lyman announced. "Listen."

The double encumbrance of pebbles and strong drink made him wholly unintelligible. Father Donlevy dozed. Dr. Arnoldi continued to fill and to empty his glass with the precision of a metronome. Sid rambled with bleary eyes through a thousand questions to the comrades. If this boy should become a comatant, thought the doctor, his voice would go on forever, mumbling nothings of perpetual unrest in his ornamented case.

Suddenly a frantic, high-pitched squawk caused Arnoldi to look up. Sid had swallowed his gravel. His mouth worked hopelessly, like that of a dying fish. His eyes were glazed and horror-stricken. That one raucous explosion had roused Father Donlevy. He stood, only half awake, and as Sid pitched to the floor, he asked: "Where is your bath, doctor?"

"Three doors down the hall," said Arnoldi. The priest had difficulty with the knob. He giggled.

Sid's head had encountered the back of his chair as he fell, cutting his scalp.

With a prodigious sigh—"Ho—haw—hum—" Dr. Arnoldi pushed back his chair and leaned over the fallen orator without rising. "I wonder if I should interfere with this miracle," he debated. "Surely this is the Will of God."

Sid was having a convulsion. The doctor watched him attentively. He was strangling, certainly. One of his ambitious stones had lodged in his windpipe. Legs and arms thrashed. The table careened and Arnoldi grabbed for the vodka and the cherries.

A furtive sound like a shuffling, snuffling animal looking for its home came through the door to the hall. It went away. A moment later there was a groaning cry and the rolling bump of a drunken body descending stairs footlessly took its place.

"Ho—haw—hum—" said Dr. Arnoldi, rising and crossing painfully to the door. Father Donlevy sat on the landing, halfway to Myra's apartment, holding his head in his hands. "Are you hurt?" the doctor asked.

Willard Kent's nurse looked up the stair-well. "Hello, doctor. What's going on?"

"The Will of Allah," said Arnoldi a little thickly. "Would you mind helping me a moment?"

"Not at all." She was running toward him.

"I have guests," the doctor explained.

"I see you have."

Together they carried the vicar of the Vicar of Christ on Earth up the dirty stairs. "I'm all right," he assured them. "I'll be all right in a minute."

They threw him to his own recovery devices on the bed and turned to Sid, weakly fighting for air.

They mauled and pummeled Sid a long time before he coughed, sending a shower of gravel over the floor.

21

PUBLIC HYSTERIA filled the churches. The righteous multi-

plied their rectitude by the sum of their awe and their fear—
and fist-fights over pews were not uncommon. Like bush-
men, the votaries prostrated themselves before the inexplicable. Cardinal Ridell and Father Donlevy had been premature
with their fear. A guilty conscience, you may remember,
needs no accusing. Lions, lizards and wilder asses would be
moving into the churches later. Their premise was right, but
they had the speed of thought wrongly computed. And their
estimate of governmental participation was way off. The
cardinal had foreseen new laws, but he had not reckoned for
war. It came very suddenly.

War came just in time to prevent revolution, for Ole Johnson had got out of prison with the first batch released to
make room for more serious offenders. They had no case
against Ole. Sending him home saved them money. The
moment he was out, however, he started making a case for
them and if the flag hadn't been wagged out about then with
fifes and drums and bugles playing, the post office steps
would have served for raping and Sid Lyman would have
had street fighting of his own to watch.

The United States started it by shipping a boatload of ce-
lestials back to Nippon. The authorities found the task of
separating Chinese from Japanese too vexatious, so pooled
them. There were over two thousand Chinese and an even
dozen Japs on that ship. By the time they reached Kobe, they
were a fighting unit with only twelve officers.

Parley was held in the bay between the United States gunboat convoy and the commander of the fleet of Japanese vessels which refused with aimed ordnance to permit the landing of these men. Kobe would not even receive its own sons.
Japan was afraid of the North American Plague. The authorities were very polite, but get the hell out.

They tried China. No admittance! Uncle Sam did not like
this dose of his own medicine. The merchant captain was
advised by Washington to land his cargo under the protection
of the gunboat convoy, regardless of consequences. There
was no time for diplomatic exchanges and—in Washington—no diplomats if there had been time.

The President thought the yellow men were bluffing.
Congress thought so too. They were not. The bluejackets
went over-side, rifles ready, and the boats of the merchant
began plying the noisome harbor, loaded with men come
home. One withering blast of fire came from the warehouse
windows and roofs of the Bund. The contraband screamed.
The marines looked at their sergeant in consternation. He
nodded and winked at them. It had been arranged. If this
happened, the ships would speak.

All that target practice—

A broadside from four gunboats almost silenced the de-
fenders. More bluejackets left the ships, *laughing.*

It all happened so fast.

A Japanese squadron arrived and fired without warning.
The Pacific fleet was on its way to the relief of the four gunboats.

The cargo the Chinese dreaded was landed. The will of
Washington had been carried out. Nearly half of them were
laid like cord-wood on the wharf. The wounded marines received treatment under fire. The battle lasted eight days. Two
of the United States gunboats and the merchant had sunk in
the harbor, the other two slipping out with a cargo of half-
dead which made the decks to run with blood.

Pulsing marines floated between the junks and the sam-
pans. The piles of yellow bodies delivered at such cost expanded and contracted and expanded and contracted as the
breathing of their integers became concerted. Not more than
fifty Orientals and perhaps six marines escaped without
wounds. That was enough! The virus of the North American
Plague was implanted. It spread all over Asia.

Every nation closed its doors. "We like you and we'd like
to do business with you," they said, "but we don't like this
Life-everlasting, so, please stay home."

Tell the United States a thing like that! Every foreign-born
inhabitant was ordered to his home instanter, and it came to
pass that Nationalism all over the globe, which had been
weakening at the onslaught of the miracle, achieved new
heights of intensity, new depths of stupidity. Walls rose be-

tween countries and border lines became inviolable. A new provincialism, marked by the distinctions of each nation's manner of dealing with its comatants, hurried the world back over the course it had come so painfully from the Dark Ages.

War has always filled Christian churches, and with the outbreak of hostilities attendance at places of worship was doubled. Science was in ill-repute. This was the lesson. Golden text and sermon subject came from the lesson man was receiving at God's hands. As the cardinal put it to Fitz: "We've never had a guarantee from Him that the old system was going on forever."

"It's highly disconcerting," said the Swan. "I had never given death a thought, no, truly, I had not, not even in the confessional, until this happened. Now it's impossible to think of anything else. Wherever one turns, one sees evidence of this change."

"I see by the papers that automobile speed has been reduced to ten miles per hour, to eliminate accidents, you know. New cars are to be made so that that is their maximum speed."

"And no building under ten stories in New York, for fear of wasting the land." It was indeed an accomplishment to remain languorous through such a discussion. Mrs. Fitzhugh managed it. Her languor was permanent, indelible, as much a part of her as the waxen fingers which melted in Ridell's palm, as the swan's neck which His Eminence proceeded to kiss.

"No matter how old we grow, Fitz," he murmured near the petal-lobe of her ear, "you will remain charming."

"I wonder," she breathed into the thinning silver of his hair.

"Always," he said stoutly. "To the wonder and amazement of mankind, while beauties turn to crones and movie stars decline behind their wrinkles, you will remain forever as you are at this moment, graceful and slender and pale; I know it." With the slow and deliberate movement he employed in the holiest rituals, John lifted one side of her sheer negligee and gazed reverently at her right breast which partook of the calla in coloring, as—indeed—did Fitzhugh's whole body. "You are three parts flower," he said, in his mind likening the orange tint of her nipple to the stamen of some exotic bloom.

"My priest-poet," she whispered in his fine hair. "I wish I could remain flowerlike—always."

"You don't believe me?"

"That I shan't decay?"

"Yes."

She saw that it would hurt him to insist on rationality. The sensitive lips, of no great size nor brilliant color, trembled into a smile, voluble through its delicacy. She veiled her violet eyes with lids almost transparent. "I believe you, John."

He covered her breast without touching it and stretched like a man replete. "I'm sorry you can't witness my afternoon's work," he said, rising. "The ambassadors of Japan and China, on their way home, are stopping for a word with me. I know you'd enjoy it."

"Of course I would."

"I'll have it taken down, and I'll describe it fully. They speak English, I'm told, very well."

"What do they want?"

The cardinal took his red bib from the back of Evan's slipper-chair. "They want our missionaries recalled; all of them; and they are right. Back they come."

"What will His Holiness say to that?"

"I don't know. I'm past caring. With things as they are I cannot allow white men and women to stay there, subjected to perpetual torture."

"Some will insist on staying."

"Then they'll become saints, my dear, but without my sanction. That will be a novelty, eh? We're backtracking! Those who remain will become saints and if we ever recover their pulsing remains, we shall have miracles again, by the dozen. A living saint in Manhattan! Ah, *that* will be worthwhile."

"We're back-tracking. Men's suits have armored sleeves and breasts. Martyrs will be healing—here. There will be pilgrimages!"

"But we shan't go *all* the way back."

"What's to stop us?"

Cardinal Ridell winked broadly at the Swan. "We shall attempt to have the miracle that of effecting death—if it can be arranged. Good Catholics will bring their aged from homes a thousand miles away, that sight of Saint Thomas of Wang-Ho may them."

Mrs. Fitzhugh's flowerlike feet sought her dainty mules at the bedside. "John, dear! You are *so* clever. I should never have thought of that."

She told Evan of this stroke His Eminence planned and basked in the reflected glory of her husband's appreciation. "Splendid; splendid," he kept repeating, "but—but how does John know these new saints can pause death?"

A very unswanlike gulp was Evan's first answer, then she made him another: "John is very wise, my dear. I sometimes think he is inspired."

"It's too bad John isn't in Washington. They're having a dreadful time."

"The war?"

"Well, that—and insurance! That insurance business is certainly in a tangle. Montague, New Jersey, had the floor four hours. He wants a time limit set on the Piccard bill, so that policies will be paid after coma has persisted a month without change."

"Isn't that fair?"

"Oh, Glazer of California shot it full of holes. It's subject to abuses. Suppose I had a stroke tonight—and the doctor said I was a goner; you'd put me in 'Heaven on Earth' for a month—"

"No, Evan," said his wife gently. "I should never part with you. This is your home. Here you would lay."

Evan craned benignly to see around the flowers on the dinner table. "Myrtle!" he said with feeling. "Why, Myrtle!"

Fitz shot him a devoted glance, flirted her brows aloft just once—as if she could not help speaking thus plainly no matter what people might think of her for it—and applied her knife and fork to her viand.

"I don't know when anything has touched me so much," said Evan. "I should like to stay here, you know. Especially since I won't be—quite dead."

"Surely you knew—"

Both Fitzhughs ate several silent bites. It was a beautiful moment, a precious moment. When its poignancy had passed, the Swan spoke: "You were speaking about the insurance debate—"

"Oh, yes. Well, if anyone were inclined to cheat the companies, he would merely make no effort to cure or revive the insured person until the period agreed upon had expired, then *every* effort would be made. In many cases, the comatant would come out with his life and his insurance money too.

"There'd be no way of getting it back. They're considering escrow and trust angles now.

"Another thing—I don't know who proposed this measure—it has been suggested that once a person has remained in a coma thirty or sixty or ninety days, they be declared legally dead and no effort of any kind ever be made to revive them.

"That raised a great rumpus. They called each other names, barbarians and murderers."

"Barbarians. We're back-tracking, Evan. We've leapt back to feudal times in a few weeks. Where will we be in a year? In ten?"

"One hundred," said Evan.

"And we *will* be here—to see it."

"It looks that way."

"We'll be here—at least—whether we can—see—or not."

"It looks that way."

Reminiscently, "Dreadful changes will occur in us, of course. We'll—decay."

Evan was conscious that he should notice something. He made himself very attentive to his wife's words. "We'll get very old," he hazarded.

"All of us."

But, that was true, of course. Why was she dwelling on it? The woman of it, of course, mourning the loss of youth and beauty. Evan became melancholy, too. It was going to be pitiful, lingering on and on, losing first one faculty, then another. They who avoided accident and disease and aged, merely, would be least fortunate of all. Unsightly burdens, too stubborn to lie down! One hundred, two hundred years! No wonder Myrtle was appalled. He must say something to cheer her, he was the stronger, the male; he had less to lose. The prospect was not so bitter for him. He had never been beautiful. Something comforting. Something John might say. Or Casanova. He ran over some Keats in his mind, some Swinburne.

The Swan had given up hope and returned to her plate.

"We—we'll grow old together, Myrtle."

The eyes of Fitz dwelt on him kindly for this boon he offered. "Yes, Evan, together."

Dubious at first, her reception of his speech made him think it had come off quite well. It was like paying her back for the sweet thing she had said earlier in the meal. What had that been—now? Something that had pleased him greatly at the time!

"England has positively closed the doors of India. Cargoes are to be landed only by natives of the port cities and the work to be done under military supervision."

"Think of that," said Fitz, thinking of something else.

"They seem content that the virus of longevity can be transmitted only by human contact. For good and sufficient reason, they choose to ignore that it might arrive in commodities."

His wife's bland nod told Evan she had not been listening and would not interest herself if he went on. He relapsed. The cardinal was a hard man to follow.

After dinner, Mrs. Fitzhugh went to the piano and played softly for her own amusement. Evan retired to his library where Wince brought a second cup of coffee. "Thank you, Wince."

"Thank you, sir."

"Will you be going out, Wince? Say—at about eleven?"

"A newspaper, sir?"

"I wish you would."

"Yes, sir. On the radio, just now, in cook's room, it was announced that a round-up is being made of all swamis. They're fortune tellers, aren't they, Mr. Fitzhugh?"

"Well, not exactly, Wince. Some swamis practice divination and many use crystal globes, to aid concentration, I think, but I'm afraid they'd resent being called 'fortune tellers'—as a class, I mean."

"Yes, sir. I've always thought they were fortune tellers."

"They're all Hindus, one kind or another. What is the government going to do, deport them?"

"Yes, sir. So they said."

"That means war with England, Wince."

"England too? We shall soon be at war with all the world, shan't we, sir? I see that peremptory notes have been sent to Russia and Italy."

"We shall become a great maritime power again, at all events. There's method in this madness. Every corpse we leave abroad is one less to care for here."

"Yes, sir. It seems a bit hard on the Johnnies we leave in the water though, doesn't it. Do you know if these foreigners fish them out?"

"Some, I imagine."

"It's a pretty pass, sir, a pretty pass."

"A pretty pass indeed, Wince. You won't forget the paper?"

"No, sir."

"And—if—if any more announcements such as that come over the radio, run in and tell me. It won't disturb me."

"Very good, sir."

The wistful appeal of a French lullaby stole up the main stair and into the library. Evan listened a moment, smiling, pensive. He could see her, clearly in memory, as clearly as if he had been in the room with her. Her chin would be raised a little, her fragile fingers moving—so. Her violet eyes—ah! all that would never change. No matter how old they got together, those charms would remain always the same. Evan closed the door quietly and took up a book.

22

BACK-TRACKING to barbarism! How the senators yelled! "This infamous proposal, that no effort shall be made to repair the injured and heal the sick must have scorched the tongue and withered the mind of the man who uttered it. Within our grasp now is the supreme science. By the proper application of our knowledge acquired through the years, disease will be driven from the face of the earth and ere long all pain of the flesh will follow disease to oblivion. Not try?! Not *treat* our comatants? The gentleman from wherever the gentleman is from is mad."

But the longer they talked, the further away Willard's insurance money seemed to Myra to be. She stayed on at Rye from sheer dread. Dread of that box in the corner of her living-room. Her living-room. Not her dying room. Her living-room. She stayed on for dread of that and for dread of seeing Happy. She wanted to see him. For all she was worth, she wanted to see him, but she dreaded it.

In the seclusion of Henry Thorndike's costly residence at Rye—where she had not until yet been called upon to defend her virtue, not even with a single wile—Myra appraised Happy Suderman and found him without character. How many other girls, yes, married women, had he embraced mid-afternoon, so easily, so confidently, while their husbands were at work? She was fair enough to give herself no more quarter than she gave Happy, but, finding herself despicable, what was there to do about it? She had embraced a moment not a man. It was sneaking of her to do it—and the color or shape of the moment which had seemed so unique and breath-taking had changed with the passage of time so that she could hardly remember how she had come to regard it as glamorous or romantic—but it was done. It was just her luck to have the solar system go awry the same afternoon! All those other women—she was sure they were legion—had enjoyed Happy or their moment and then gone on about their business. With some of them, doubtless, the event was now a sweet stab of pain, to refer to dull evenings at home. Others had forgotten it entirely and—damn it—some of them, in *all* likelihood, still entertained him. Not she! Nothing so peaceful could happen to her. She could date her infidelity unerringly until the end of time. Miracle Day!

It meant nothing to him. Worthless! He had his clownish business to keep him absorbed. Never gave her a thought. If he did, he'd call. Dr. Arnoldi would have told him where she had gone. She had taken the trouble to telegraph the telephone number to her neighbor so that he could call her if Willard needed her. Suppose he did misunderstand her flight, her residence in Mr. Thorndike's house. She didn't understand it herself. There was nothing wrong in it. Mr. Thorndike was a perfect gentleman. That was what Myra couldn't understand. She was more or less waiting for an advance at which she could take offense for an excuse to go home. Mr. Thorndike did not come out to Rye every day. Often he stayed at his club or elsewhere in town. He kept one servant at his apartment all summer. There was no reasonable reason for leaving. As Henry had pointed out, she could do nothing for Willard's comfort. She was receiving his salary weekly. Henry would be glad to take her in to the theater any time she cared to go and the cars were at her disposal for shopping through the day.

Was she afraid of scandal? Did she dread the hateful tongue of gossip? Myra had pretended that that certainly was a consideration, but she had sniffed at it to herself. Who, pray, would talk about her?

As the second week of her stay drew to a close, Myra decided that Happy would not call because he thought she was practically living with Mr. Thorndike. It was preposterous, of course, the man was old enough to be her father. What kept the millionaire from making love to her she could not imagine. Finally, she realized that his reserve was insulting and determined to go home. All he did was talk about Dr. Arnoldi—as if the old Russian had been the cause of his visit to

408 Canal! It had been he Happy had sought there. What did they all want with him? Myra acknowledged that she would like to see him again, moving so slowly, never flustered, never upset, never surprised. Not even the miracle had surprised him. Dr. Arnoldi had acted as if he had been expecting nothing less for months.

Well, if Mr. Thorndike was not sufficiently interested to so much as attempt to kiss her, and she wanted to see the doctor, and Happy had a bad opinion of her and Willard *might* be aware of her absence—she had better go home.

There had been a small yachting party on the Sound and when Henry bade her good night that Sunday evening she told him she was leaving. "I have a feeling he—misses me. Nobody knows how much—they—they hear, lying there, day and night, like that. No one knows how active their minds are. I worry about it. I have to go back."

"Of course," her host agreed pleasantly, "I can't urge you to stay if you feel that way. Why not have your husband brought out here? There's plenty of room."

"Oh, no, Mr. Thorndike, I couldn't think of it." It was a tough proposition to avoid. There were so few rational reasons for rejecting the invitation.

Henry insisted on threshing it out and as she talked Myra was forced into a palpable ignobility to have her way. "Don't you understand, Mr. Thorndike? I just want to be with him—alone."

Her former employer-in-law was impressed. "I understand," he said solemnly, "but it isn't good for you. Let me move you, at least. Don't stay there."

Cadillacs—Cadillacs—Cadillacs.

"Oh, that's so sweet of you! So generous—"

"Let me go back, first, and see how things are."

Things were just the same—except that the nurse was now most insufferably bored. Nothing had happened since Father Donlevy had fallen down the stairs—absolutely nothing. Gracie did not recognize Myra.

She kept her foot against the inside of the door lest the caller be working her way through college.

"I'm Mrs. Kent."

"And so what?"

"I live here."

"Oh—Mrs. Kent! Oh, excuse me." They laughed about it afterwards.

Myra looked at Willard fearlessly. "How has he been?"

"Just like that. He hasn't moved, except when I moved him."

The thing in the case did not seem to be Willard at all. Her husband was more real to her at a distance than he was when she could see his face. Yet, that was Willard's face. It was exactly as if he lay there asleep, except that it did not matter. A man was asleep in a fancy box with a glass lid. Just any man.

"I'm going upstairs," said Myra, "to see the doctor." She wondered why the nurse grinned at that.

Her old friend struggled to his feet, smiling in welcome. "There ' You've come back."

"Yes. Did you think I wouldn't?"

"Oh—"

She did not really expect an answer.

"Admit you've missed me!"

"I have."

"Good."

"You look better. You seem cheerful."

"Your prescription."

"Mine?"

"You made me go."

"Oh—did I? Yes. I remember now. I urged you. Well! I shouldn't do it again. Now that I know how much I miss you, I shall be utterly selfish another time—even at the cost of your health. Will you have beer?"

"Yes!" she said quickly—almost dramatically. The old, familiar sound of the invitation was warming, gratifying. "I'll get it." And doing that was a source of satisfaction. Perhaps Happy was right and she did not belong here, but it was good to come home all the same.

Dr. Arnoldi acted a little ashamed of his own enthusiasm.

He sniffed broadly, wrinkling his big onion of a nose and turning his back to her before sitting down.

"What you been doing all this time? Have you had much company?" Myra poured beer for both of them.

"I have been doing nothing, my dear."

She waited a second, sipping her beer, to see if he would go on. "Company?"

"Lots. I am becoming quite notorious. There was something in the papers and almost every day someone comes." He winked one lid slowly at her, lowering and raising it like a small awning. "They think I'm a philosopher."

"Don't you think you are?"

Arnoldi thought a moment, concentrating on his home brew which had raised perspiration on the sides of the tumbler from the five-and-ten cent store. "Perhaps," he said.

"Of course you are," said Myra. "Like Omar."

"Like Omar?"

"You know Omar."

"Am I like him?"

"You're exactly what I have always thought Omar looked like; exactly. What do they say, these people? Where's the paper? Did Happy put it in?"

"When he saw that I was not flattered, he denied it. I don't know."

"Haven't you got the clipping?"

Dr. Arnoldi saw at once that he should have had the clipping. His admission that he had not was a little shamefaced.

"Well, I never!" said Myra. "When was it in?"

"About a week ago, I think. A man brought it in. He wanted to see the learned Dr. Arnoldi." The old fellow chuckled at memory of the man with the paper. "He seemed to be a brilliant fellow."

"Too much, eh?"

"He was a great talker. He stayed two hours."

"Who was it? Some well-known person?"

"I—I don't remember his name. He left a card, I think."

"Doctor! He was probably somebody important. Maybe they want you to go to Washington and help the President with the miracle."

"He didn't say so."

"Well, what *did* he say? He could have made a dozen leading remarks and, modest as you are, you'd never notice them."

"I think I'd have known if he had wanted me to go to Washington."

"Others too, you say! You're a fine one—not keeping the paper."

"I don't know that the paper was ever left here."

"And you wouldn't send down to the corner for one! Where's the man's card? I'll bet he wanted to make your fortune for you."

"Pure romance."

"You'd be surprised if it turned out to be a true story."

"But—I don't want my fortune made. I have everything I want; more than I deserve, now that you are back."

Myra stirred her beer with a forefinger and licked the foam from it. "Where's his card?"

It did no good to find it. The name was unfamiliar and there was no address. "Just the same, I'll bet he was important. I'm going to speak to Happy about you." Like a tot threatening her grandfather.

"You speak to Happy about *you*—and leave me out of it. I don't mind having people come here to see me. I'm not unsociable. But neither of you can draw me back into Life. It's too late. I'm not interested." He spoke entirely without passion but his meaning could not be mistaken.

"Has he spoken about me? Mentioned me?"

"Many times. Hasn't he called you?"

"No."

"But you've seen him?"

"No."

"Yet you criticize my conduct?"

"That's different. It wasn't until just a few minute ago that I really felt Willard—was dead. After all, I have some honor."

"Perhaps that is my affliction too," said Dr. Arnoldi

softly.

"Do you think honor is an affliction?"

The doctor smiled at her seriousness. "I don't know, my dear. I was only trying to live up to my reputation as a philosopher. Don't you think that remark was worthy of Omar?" He began chuckling.

Myra emptied her glass and rose. "What?" she asked.

"A Russian Omar strikes me as an almost impossible combination. It's such a long way from the steppes to Persia."

"Well, Omar wasn't the only philosopher who ever lived. Pick out a cold one to be like." She walked to the door. "I'm going to call Happy, but I'll be back, don't worry. I'm coming back to have this out with you."

"I'll be right here," said Arnoldi, "thinking of a good cold philosopher to be like."

Myra sat at the telephone so she could watch Willard breathe as she talked. That would be the acid test. If she could do that, her husband was dead. She could see Willard, but she could not see Ada Werfel, relieving the telephone operator for a moment at "Heaven on Earth". "Who is calling Mr. Suderman, please?"

"Myra Kent."

"Oh! Just a moment, please . . . Get set, Happy."

"What is it?"

"It's your coma-widow and I don't mind telling you that I'm listening in."

Myra could not hear this, of course.

"Myra!?"

"Yes, Myra."

"Put her on! Put her on!"

"Happy! Don't you make a date with her."

"Oh, no, nothing like that. Come on, connect us."

"I'll *dis*connect you the minute you get mushy."

"Ada—didn't I tell you that was all over? Come on, let me talk to her. I'll show you."

"I don't trust you out of sight."

"*Will* you—"

"Here she is!"

"Hello, Myra!"

"Happy! It's like telephoning God to try to get you."

"Well, that's the idea."

"How have you been?" Now that they were talking it was difficult to think what to say.

"Fine! And you?"

"Fine, thanks."

"Glad to hear it."

"I—I just got home."

"Yes? Dr. Arnoldi said you'd been away."

Oh, of course that would be his attitude. She might have known it. Old *friends!* Glad to hear she was doing so well. See her around somewhere in two or three years! "I want to see you, Happy."

"Oh—well, aaah—well, I'm in every day."

"Happy!" Her voice was full of hurt. He was carrying the thing too far. Hadn't she been through enough? She was staring at Willard without seeing him.

"Well, Myra?"

"What is it, Happy? What has happened?"

"Nothing. What do you mean?"

"Oh, it's that I want to see you about. You've got everything twisted. Do you imagine—" *I can forget that you laughed at me and walked away the first time we ever met? That you lay in my arms tenderly—and slept! That you came back at dawn, adoring me? Do you imagine I can forget that?* But—perhaps he had forgotten! "—have you forgotten—everything, Happy?"

Bitter Ada Werfel pulled the plug.

"God damn it!" said Happy, grabbing his hat. As he went through the outer office he yelled at Ada who bore down on him with her own hat in her hand. "You're fired! Pay yourself and get out."

"Fired am I? I'll fire you! Where are you going?"

"That's my business."

"I'm going with you. Besides, you can't fire the secretary of a corporation without a meeting of the board of directors.

Come on, let's go see her. I've been dying to have a look at that woman."

"Ada—I'll break your neck!"

The entire office force was watching and listening with a silly grin spread from ear to inclusive ear.

"I'll scratch her eyes out!"

"*Miss* Werfel! This is a place of peace and quiet—a place of rest. There are visitors here and you are making a spectacle of yourself. Have you no regard for the interests of Heaven? How long will people leave their loved ones here if they are treated to such a display of discord and insane jealousy among the executives? Go back to your work and let me alone."

"Go back to your own work."

Happy went out, but he could not slam the door because Ada had caught hold of it. She got in his taxi with him and boiled all the way to 408 Canal. They shouted and yelled at each other, regardless of curious stares. Finally the driver turned around. "Why don't you clip her on the chin, mister? Nobody cares anymore." Happy calculated the distance his fist would have to travel.

"Do you expect to hold me like this? You're out of your mind. I wouldn't have anything more to do with you now if there was no such person as Myra Kent in the world. Can you get that through your thick skull?"

"You'll have to do with me just as long as I say. My mark's on you, Happy Suderman! Did you think you were fooling with a *dove* when you came to my nest? You're in the talons of a hawk, Happy. I'm a hawk."

"Go ahead and hawk. I'll have you put in jail."

"Ho! *What* jail?"

"I'll have you deported."

"You'll do nothing—and very damned little of that!"

"We'll see." A plan had formed in Happy's mind.

At 408 he led the way up the stairs, all the way *up*. He knocked at Dr. Arnoldi's door. "Come in," said the thick voice of the doctor. Ada, like a shadow, slid through the door at Happy's heels.

Evan Fitzhugh was helping the fat man dispose of a bottle of beer. Introductions kept Happy's furtive looks about the room from being noticeable.

"Sit down, my friends. Mr. Fitzhugh had read about me and wishes to know if I am alive."

"That's a silly question now-days," said Happy. "Everybody's alive." He saw what he thought was a key on the edge of a shelf near the door.

"But the doctor insists he is dead," said Evan, beaming at Bitter Ada. "That's a novel pose, don't you think?"

"I'd resent that 'pose' if I were you, doctor," and Happy's fingers closed around the key. With silent supplications to the gods that the thing fit this lock, and heedless that he was being addressed, Happy darted through the door and held it against the girl's tugging—until the tumblers shot the bolt home.

Evan rose excitedly and looked from the door to the impassive face of Dr. Arnoldi.

"You son-of-a-bitch!" screamed Ada and she began to kick the door.

"He's locked us in," Evan announced.

The doctor looked over the rim of his upturned glass at the virago. She ran to the window and looked at the hopelessness of escape that way. Grim of eye and rigid of mouth, she seized a chair and started to lift it over her head.

"Oh, please don't break my door," said the doctor calmly. "He'll be back directly."

"Most extraordinary," Evan murmured. "Most extraordinary."

"Where does she live?" Ada demanded, relinquishing the chair to the autograph dealer. "Does she live in this building?"

"I don't know," said Dr. Arnoldi. "Who?"

"Myra Kent's who. Does she?"

"No!" said the doctor. "Would you like a glass of beer?"

"I'd like to wring his neck, but I'll take a glass of beer."

"That's sensible," said her host.

Suddenly all the fire and strength and tiger-fury were gone

from the lean form of the harassed girl. A perfect flood of tears and a sob of desperate recognition of the inevitable accompanied her to the doctor's bed where she threw herself face-down, kicking.

Evan made curious eyes at the Russian. Mr. Henry Thorndike had told him to be prepared for surprises, but this hour came under the head of shocks. Furthermore, *he* was locked in. The bookman did not like that. Although he had watched Ada fight with the knob only a moment before, Evan tried it. "It's locked," he said.

Dr. Arnoldi nodded. "Yes, but I wouldn't worry about it. I don't *think* he's an incendiary."

"I hope not," said Evan, and he would have gone on—if the doctor had not stopped him with a shake of his head.

"I knew all those people very well," said Arnoldi. "Tchish, Treniev, Krause, all of them. Nelly. I've been thinking of them—since the 'miracle' as the newspapers call it. I've wondered what Naumov would say about this boresome prospect."

"Would you say that most of the suicides in your village were the result of Naumov's random talking?"

"I really don't know," said the doctor, "but perpetual life would have amused him greatly. The classic 'open door' locked tight! I can see his face—"

Ada's sobs had subsided a little. She raised herself on her elbows. "Where's my beer?" she sniffed.

23

BELOWSTAIRS, Gracie, the nurse, watched Happy and Myra meet. Attuned but half an octave beyond her own psychic requirements, she vibrated in accord with only such visible aspects of their embrace as were familiar to her in fact or through meager dreams. Gracie, thus hampered, could not appreciate the nice arrangement of the time in the encounter, beautifully regulated by some invisible stage manager. She did not know that they stood silently regarding one another *exactly* the required number of seconds to bring about a spontaneous, mutual, dynamic propulsion *toward.* She could not see, and the principals did not need to see, the director's baton suspended to time that pause. If they had stood a second, nay, half-a-second, longer, an artificiality would have entered the scene. If one had moved half-a-second sooner, that one would have seemed the aggressor. Precisely long enough to know, they held each other's eyes, speaking there the awe they felt for what was in their breasts—then rushed, with a rhythmic, a leashed rushing, into arms which so contrived themselves that no thrashing or bumping incommoded them or bruised with clumsiness the delicacy of that first tender contact. It was really a classic meeting despite the base natures involved and the inglorious environment; a meeting any Hollywood director would have been proud to call his. That they achieved this grace and smoothness without rehearsal was no tribute to the strength or veracity of their yearnings. Afflicted souls every whit as sincere as these have bumped noses and clashed teeth and scratched necks with impetuous nails—time without number. That they blended thus easily and gently and thus built up, stemlike and tapering, to the blossom of that kiss of reunion is without cosmic significance and is remarkable chiefly because it befell that way and no other. Gracie, then, was none the loser for being unable to appreciate such a fine show to the fullest and only certain pictorial elements would have been lost if the team had chosen to express themselves by butting like goats instead of dancing, nay, flowing together like persons in a play.

"Here's a quarter, Gracie; go see yourself a movie." Happy gave her a ten-dollar bill. He did not even glance at the awful corner behind him and turned Myra's body so deftly the other way that she was aware only of the pleasing pressure.

They sat on the bed when Gracie had gone and fitted short sentences about the future into the small chinks and infinitesimal apertures between kisses and those other endearments which occupy the lips.

"Are you sure he'll come back?" asked Evan several

hours later. "I had a luncheon appointment. You're sure, are you? Because he looked a little mad to me."

Ada sneered with characteristic Werfel violence. "Let him go," she said. "My mark's on him."

"Your mark?" the Swan's husband was being initiated into new mysteries of womankind.

"I mark them," the bookkeeper swaggered. "They love it."

Evan raised fluttering brows in Arnoldi's direction, but the doctor had no elucidation ready.

"My life was very calm here," said Dr. Arnoldi without complaint, "until *he* came to see me one day. He is a very active young man."

"He's too damned active!" Ada contributed. "I ought to put him in one of his own cases."

"He'd be no good to you there," said Arnoldi.

Ada grinned. "I could crawl in with him when I want to. You don't know the—ah—idiosyncrasies of these comatants like I do."

"My word!" said Evan.

Ada's "mark", whatever its nature, was not nearly so indelible as her ego prompted her to believe. If it had ever been on Happy, it was not visible to Myra. So absorbed was she, however, in a branding and ear-clipping of her own that it could have escaped her notice that day. So absorbed was she. So absorbed were they, both of them, that the door to Willard's living-room was left ajar when thoughtful delicacy would have closed it.

Willard had only to turn his head to see that he must be dead. He did not turn.

And thus was ushered in an entirely new order on the earth. Madness increased amazingly and attempted suicide— at first only epidemic—became a world-wide phobia. The money system, crude as it had been before, was supplanted by a scrip nostrum backed by the printing press.

War debts became an issue in all the countless new wars and the factor deciding victory in the battles was invariably the number of men left on a foreign shore, regardless of their physical condition. France emptied her homes for incurables and landed them in droves by night on the defenseless coast of Carolina. Georgetown and Charleston awoke one morning to find the stronger of these spectres peering in at their windows hungrily.

All the abortive and stillborn attempts at world disarmament and economic stabilization were forgotten in the press of frantic effort for national isolation. Treaties with Canada and Mexico united North America, since the cause of each was represented to be identical, and special measures provided for amplification of the coast defense.

The round-up of aliens was continued and as fast as ships could be filled, these and—eventually—condemned men were taken for a ride to their homes. The condemned were put off at any land the ships' commanders elected, it was certain to be hostile soil since no foreign nation was friendly, but the most scrupulous care was exercised in returning Russians to Russia and Italians to the boot.

With the arrival of the French incurables, a doughty regiment including syphilitics, lepers and some captive Nazis, the new warfare took on the excitement of a football game in Southern California. As many of these as would hold together were piled back on the decks of freighters and returned to France with Uncle Sam's compliments. If a nigger orphanage got mixed up in the shipment, the War Department showed no official record of it and the Gascons who discovered the black babies among the other offal caught the spirit of fun and accused their infirm compatriots of highjinks down in Caroline!

Back-tracking to barbarism! There was no "shipping" at the end of the tenth miraculous year, so it was no menace to vessels to dump whole shiploads of bodies mid-ocean. Responsibility for starting the practice was never accurately placed, but popular opinion gave England the palm, most particularly London because there overcrowded conditions had become unbearable. The bodies were white so it couldn't have been Japan. Having the upper hand in China permitted the Nipponese to expand in that direction anyway.

Whoever started it, the balance of the beleaguered world

was quick to take it up and navy reports often included mention of "floating island of human bodies sighted two points to port in latitude so and so. 'Island' about three miles across and six long. Men and women walked like lumberjacks on log-jams on this bobbing 'terrain'. Their signals for help were ignored."

There was no "shipping" in the modern sense. Transoceanic passenger lines had but a single source of revenue, fees from the government for comatants, aliens, criminals and other objectionable matter delivered. The smaller lines had all folded and a middle-size ocean liner could be picked up anywhere around the Battery for the price of a meal at a good hotel.

Feeble and sporadic attempts to move mail internationally ceased in the fifteenth year of the miracle because by that time treachery had become so commonly the order of the day that ships—no matter how innocent of human contraband— were not trusted within miles of any shore.

Hardy merchants, remembering the traditions of the sea, the colorful history of argosies, armadas, pirates and privateering, seized the opportunity to assist humanity along the path back to chaos and sent out laden vessels with scant hope of ever seeing hull, crew or cargo again. There were not many of these, but they were a romantic lot, meeting in radio offices, communally maintained for this purpose to listen-in for news of their ships.

For a laugh, one day, a bluff old member of this party, a descendant of ships' masters and maritime men for a score of generations, appeared at their morning session carrying an enormous, brass-bound telescope such as watchers for sails had used on housetops and high cliffs for two centuries. This conceit so pleased the crowd that next day other members came wearing or bearing this or that article from their own sea-chests, long stored. In two weeks, without a blush, this group of adults had adopted uniforms and when they sat around the loud-speaker, hanging hungrily on every burst of static, they held their telescopes athwart their knees—like the old, stale trade-winds they were.

With the appearance of scrip, with the inundation of the continent by tons of engraved paper, came the bravo. The guardian henchmen of Prohibition days gave solvent Americans the idea. They liked it. There was considerable that was childlike in most of this back-tracking. They liked the idea of surrounding themselves with bodyguards to protect their purses and persons from the rabble and the law as well. And on this vanity the profession of bravo fattened. Armorers returned. Steel corselets came into general use and to conceal them or to show them to best advantage, as the wearers listed, the costume of everyday took on an added hue and fancy. Twixt leathern sleeve and steel breastplate, all manner of innovations were introduced. The codpiece and shinguard followed soon after.

From the upper half of a broken bottle the sweet steel, hundred-tined *hasher* was developed, a weapon of great utility. It blinded, gouged, cut, mangled, disfigured, slit, crushed, maimed, bled, cracked, minced, pained, scarred, scratched, punctured *and* hashed—in a strong and cunning hand. It swung in a guard at your gentleman's waist, encrusted, as to handle and less abrasive parts, with engravings, precious metals and jewels. It was strictly a gentleman's weapon. No self-respecting bravo *hashed.* A knife for throats and a peculiar, short pistol with a soft-headed cartridge were his arms. His defense lay in being first to attack.

From attempting to regulate the affairs of man by legislation, the people's servants were graduated to the higher endeavor of attempting to keep most of the laws in rough conformity with popular usage and custom. This was no radical departure from the older practice, but the startling changes made the nincompoop nature of their service more apparent. When public treasuries ran completely dry and the tax collector had taken the Vice President's place as national clown, senators and representatives ambled to their homes, jobless. Government thus disappeared in the most natural way, like a parade that has passed without a calliope. The paymaster had nothing for them and Sid Lyman's pet anathema "Privilege" laughed at the idea of continuing its contributions. "What the hell for?" asked former franchise seekers. "We have to hire and equip our own police. Yours are no good." For the administrative branch had been starved out too.

City streets swarmed with police magistrates with their hands extended for a crust, their toes wiggling skyward through what had once been shoes.

Fire departments subsisted by passing the hat in the larger cities. Small towns reverted to the old volunteer system.

The last public institution to suffer from lack of funds in the United States was the schools. Grimly, the middle class held on to popular education as if their devotion to its principles would restore order. Surely knowledge was the touchstone. Science and Religion had both failed, but wisdom, learning, the stuff in books, whatever it was, philosophy, maybe, metaphysics, that wouldn't fail. *Thought* would lead them out of the wilderness of their dilemma. The public schools would lead their children out. It was their children they must save (kill?). The hope of the future lay in their tiny brains.

The teachers were quartered on the community—as they had been at the birth of Diedrich Knickerbocker—and, as lawlessness spread, they adopted a habit to distinguish them from laymen who might have money about their persons. Their habit was a scanty white jumper, a cassock—in fact, which could be drawn on quickly over anything else one happened to be wearing. The cowl and the rosary had lost their power to awe, but the white cassock of the teacher was respected for several years. To get raped or even played with, the prettiest young tutor had to leave her jumper at home.

Any other woman, regardless of age or pulchritude, could almost count on success if she chose the locale of her nocturnal promenade with any sense at all. Naturally, rumor could not always be relied upon and old maids continued to exaggerate. If a crone with a broken nose and store teeth claimed to have had her pleasure in a street known to be frequented only by gallants, her tale could be taken with a grain of salt, but if she were honest enough to call the name of the bridge under which she had encountered some ape, the chances were she spoke the truth and the ape could count on steady employment merely by remaining in that neighborhood.

Prostitution went the way of the Senate, dwindling, failing, starving to extinction. Woman was stripped of pretense exactly as government had been. Those who honestly wished to remain virtuous, as the saying had so quaintly run before the miracle, stayed indoors and received no callers. They had none but the impotent to receive in a short time and, since that was what they asked for, they must have been perfectly happy.

The Red Cross and the Salvation Army joined ranks and became a private military organization supported by popular subscription. This outfit took over the remains of the United States Navy and continued the comic-valentine wars, calling each delivery of men and women to foreign shores a "sanitary" measure. Thus the world-wide conflict became known as the Sanitary War and it was waged relentlessly by the Red Cross-Salvation Army of North America and no less relentlessly by the same organization in Germany, France, Spain and all European countries.

Naval battles were common and token of surrender was the abandonment of cargo to the mercy of the waves. An entire literature of harrowing experiences grew out of the naval engagements of the Sanitary War. When the cargo was comatant or decrepit, chucking it overboard was easy. When it was miraclant or otherwise sturdy, it resented the abrupt injunction to join the polyps and instances of successful rebellion of cargo were not unknown.

When the crew succeeded in divesting a vanquished ship or flotilla of the human encumbrances for the possession of which it had been attacked, the flagships of opposing fleets saluted with colors and both proceeded in good order to withdraw from the new-formed island. The commotion in the water was of long or short duration according to the disposition, temperament and physical condition of the integers in the mass. The shock of submersion sometimes revived comatants of months' recumbency. No one ever drowned. With rare exceptions, the folk thus marooned upon the desert of themselves drifted, floated or swam toward nuclei which were subsequently merged by the action of the water or the intelligence of the rational survivors. In the course of time several such islands, left, originally, in different seas, might drift together and unite, the stronger island absorbing the weaker, as a morphological vesicle might absorb a zooid, as in polyzoans. Thus vast carpets of human beings floated from zone to zone and none could estimate the depth of their pile.

The dethroned physicists who dared no longer appear in public unmasked for the raucous laughter which greeted them, who lived in constant dread of only one last straw, i.e., that some witless oaf should somewhere succeed in lifting himself by his own bootstraps, came hat-in-hand to the Red Cross-Salvation Army and timidly asked leave to put observers aboard their vessels so that notes might be taken on the behavior of these islands.

Some monographs on the subject finally appeared and one was especially noteworthy. This one island, and the writer had creditable, sworn witnesses, rose forty feet above the level of the sea at several central points, the elevations being pyramids, honeycombed pyramids of comatant bodies. Living, active humans crawled in and out of the cells of the comb, as if these pyramids were somewhat hollow. The inference was that they were *houses* erected by the visible dwellers there and that life, of a sort, was going on, perhaps developing in that place. It was estimated that to support these edifices, the depth of the island below the level of the sea must be even greater than the height above. Further cogitation, by law of probability only, since it was impossible to investigate closely, revealed the likelihood that the supporting foundation was changed periodically, constantly—in fact, or that man, forced to live under water, was developing the ability to do so. The author stopped himself there although the possibilities for elaboration on that contingency were infinite and enticing.

The age of these islands could be estimated by their odor which was dreadful.

One story was told of a man who, left with several hundreds of others to work out his destiny in mid-ocean, swam *away* from the clustering bodies and followed the homing ship for miles. Several members of the crew watched this heterodox fellow from the poop through their glasses for four hours. He had not ceased to swim in all that time and, since the tub they were on in this particular case had no great speed, they were able to keep him in sight until the sun set.

The captain was told of the incident and he ordered the speed of the vessel reduced to a minimum for steerageway, and a watch was posted. No one expected to see the swimmer again, but dawn revealed that he had cut the distance between himself and the ship in two. This commanding officer was the same one who had laid-to in the China Sea to retrieve a tired Icelandic tern. The determination of the soloist impressed him as the sight of that bird had. He ordered the ship about and in half an hour, the man was brought dripping before him. "What's the idea?" asked the skipper. "You trying to work on our sympathies?"

"I don't want your sympathy!" the man cried. "But I demand justice. Why should *I* be condemned to stay forever with those Socialists? There isn't a real radical in the lot of them! I demand justice for the workingman, for the wage slave, for the downtrodden masses. Who are those oily pigs who sit so sleekly on their money bags and condemn me to *float* the rest of my life? Who gives them the right—?" The thin quavering tremolo of Sid Lyman was cut short by the hard palm of the first mate at a signal from the captain.

"Throw him back," said the skipper with a wry face. "Throw him back."

24

TWENTY YEARS after the miracle, the once celebrated Dr. Allardice Tucker sniveled through the door of Evan Fitzhugh's autograph emporium and book store. He shuffled up to the white-bearded McDougall who was doing absolutely nothing with his rump resting against an empty bookshelf. "I am an artist," Tucker began, "see?" He took three or four long-handled, camel's-hair brushes from his pocket. "I am a portrait painter."

"Oh, yes," McDougall croaked.

"Could you spare me a dime for a cup of coffee?"

McDougall looked at Marceline, aslump in a chair, studying her nails. She looked up, sniffed and shrugged. "A dime—" she said without committing herself.

McDougall began to empty his pockets and to make a pile of the scrip that came forth. It grew in a brilliant green and gold pile, spilling on the floor and covering a square foot of shelf space. Tucker helped him count it. "Four hundred thousand, eighteen dollars and fifty cents. Let's see—that's—eh—that's thirty, thirty-five cents, about . . . Sorry, mister. That's all I've got to last me."

The one-time genius of the scalpel put his brushes back in his pocket sadly. "I wouldn't have asked it—if I'd known. Are you the proprietor?"

Evan had hobbled in with a steel box under his arm as the two men had been counting the money. "He's the proprietor," said McDougall, inclining his head toward Mr. Fitzhugh. "Talk to him."

Tucker cleared his dry throat painfully. "He says you're the proprietor."

Evan looked the stringy little man over suspiciously and handed his steel box to Marceline. "Lock this in the safe, please, Marceline. He wouldn't buy it. He doesn't believe it is genuine. Now, what can I do for you?"

"I am a portrait painter," said Dr. Tucker, again withdrawing the evidence from his coat. "Down on my luck and hungry. Could you spare me some change for a sandwich and a cup of coffee? Do you know of anyone in need of a portrait? Any of your rich clients?"

That made Evan laugh. "My rich clients! Hek, hek, hek." His laugh had dried up with the rest of his person. "My good fellow, what would rich clients find here? I have nothing to sell them." He walked unsteadily to one shelved wall. "You think these are books; rare books, worth their weight in gold." Evan's knuckles resounded on the hollow, false backs which concealed the vacancy of the shelves. "There aren't ten books in the store. All these are false—camouflage. That box I just put in the safe contains my last autograph, an Abraham Lincoln nobody believes in but me. Rich clients! I have plenty of names on my books but I never see them any more."

The artist watched his senior and heard the old man's voice break. It certainly looked like no supper for Tucker but he felt more active sorrow for Evan's plight than for his own. "Why don't you close the store?" the ex-doctor asked. That seemed the most sensible course to him. "I would," he added.

"Others have suggested that too," Evan admitted. "But I couldn't do that. What would I do all day? No, I've got to have a place of business. I can't be idle."

The tools of his trade started once more for the artist's pocket. "I wouldn't have asked if I'd known," he said, starting away. "I used to be rich—once."

"Oh," said Evan, "I have plenty of money. Here—" He counted out real silver pieces, several dollars' worth. "Get yourself something to eat."

Gratitude shone in Tucker's black eyes. He grasped Evan's hand and suddenly kissed it.

"Here!" said Evan.

"Isn't there someone in *your* family, sir? Haven't you a daughter or your wife who would like to sit for me?"

The bookman frowned in perplexity. Myrtle! Of course! It would please her a great deal. "There is! now that you mention it. Certainly there is!" He telephoned the Swan. His aged Eminence held the ivory-colored French hand-set to her ear. "Are you busy, my dear? I have a surprise for you."

"But, Evan, you've surprised me already."

"Oh, you mean your birthday. No. This is something different. There's an artist here."

"An artist *there!*"

Cardinal Ridell preened.

"A portrait person. Would you like to sit for him?"

The Swan raised her chin automatically. "What portrait person, Evan? Someone of consequence?"

The bookman looked at the shabby Tucker. His character would have to be synthetic. There was certainly little that was consequential in his appearance. "A genius," said Evan. "A temperamental genius."

Tucker started in mild alarm and raised one hand a little way in modest deprecation.

"Just a moment, Evan," Mrs. Fitzhugh turned to Cardinal John. "Someone wants to paint me," she said. "Do you mind?"

"I think it would be delightful," said John.

"When will he start?" she asked her husband.

"When will you start?"

"At once."

"Oh—but, very well. I'll be expecting him. I wonder why we haven't thought of it before."

"I've thought of it many times," Evan lied, "but I've never found the right man."

While the temperamental genius was on his way to the Fitzhugh home, the cardinal and Fritz tried out postures. They had settled on one they liked very well long before Tucker got there. He had to stop at a store for canvas, colors and more brushes. Then he disliked the pose they had invented very much. "It doesn't do you justice, madame." In reality it was a very good pose, becoming and appropriate, half reclining on a chaise longue, her ankles crossed, one arm bent back of her beautiful head.

Tucker objected only to avoid giving the lie to Evan. Objections displayed temperament. After arguing for an hour and very nearly coming to blows with His fussy Eminence, Allardice—as if inspired—placed the lady exactly as she had wished to be, with her feet reversed. "Now!" he exulted—but the light was gone.

Mr. Fitzhugh got home early. He was anxious to see how far the work had progressed. It was disappointing to find nothing done, but it was also understandable. He invited Tucker to remain for dinner. John was staying. In the course of the evening it was suggested that the artist "move" in until the picture was finished. He would thus grow to know the lady, witnessing her moods and transitions, her coloring and her weather. The painting, all agreed, the cardinal a bit skeptically, should thus become something more than a likeness. It should take on body and—with luck—a soul.

"No sooner said than done," Mr. Tucker said. "Here am I."

"But your things—"

"They too."

A liqueur was served in the music room where the Swan dwelt reminiscently over the keys, running almost without pause from Spanish serenades to lullabies and dances without fire. The cool shell lights of the room were not adjusted for reading, but His Eminence managed to make out a few headlines, standing near a wall bracket, chewing an unlighted cigar.

Tucker finished the story of his downfall, speaking only to Evan. "Now, everybody is painting—or dancing or writing—acting. Have you noticed? All the bourgeoisie have taken to the fine arts. Your plumber's son's a sculptor; your barber writes plays—it's almost too much to bear."

A plaintive love song, tender, lamentatious, came from the piano as if impelled by no human agency. John burst out suddenly, laughing. He came forward, removing his cigar from his mouth. "Listen to this! Listen, Fitz."

Myrtle stopped playing.

"Second Oldest Inhabitant Objects. Nantucket, June 20. Declaring that under existing conditions he had nothing to live for, Jerome Macy, 143 years of age, the second oldest inhabitant of this town, appeared before the Council and petitioned that body to order his execution. 'Ever since I was ninety,' said Mr. Macy, 'I have been looking forward to the time when I would be the oldest living resident of Nantucket. Not that I want my good friend Hobart

Starbuck to die. Not that I've ever been in a hurry. For ten years before that, I was the third oldest living inhabitant and before that, the fourth oldest. I have always been ready to wait my turn. Fact, that's the only reason I've hung on so long. But now it looks like I never was going to make it. Elias Coffin, who is just a boy compared to me, is in the same fix. He's the third oldest now, and it don't look like we was either of us going to move up, ever. I don't like this playing second fiddle and you can just do away with me unless you know more about it than I do and can say when if ever I'll be realizing my life's ambition.'

"The petition was tabled and no action taken."

"Isn't that amazing?"

"It just goes to show," said Evan. "We don't realize a tenth of the suffering this state of affairs has caused. Do we, Mr. Tucker?"

"They still have a Town Council there at least. That's something. I didn't know there were any such municipal bodies still active."

The three men fell to discussing the decay of politics. Mrs. Fitzhugh rose gracefully and left them.

Cook's radio was tuned in on the news broadcast. Wince gave his mistress his chair. "A human island is drifting ashore at Atlantic City, madame. We'll have more details in a moment."

As he spoke, the announcer came back:

"The *S.S. General William Booth* and a fleet of volunteer vessels are on their way to Atlantic City, New Jersey, where an exceptionally high tide is threatening to cover the beach with an enormous human island estimated to have an area of ten square miles! Think of it! Admiral Muftit of the Red Cross-Salvation Army and Navy believes this island is inhabited by a colony of Chinese lepers since its description tallies with that of one sighted by him after the battle of May twenty-fourth. When last seen this island was drifting toward our shores.

"The boardwalk is already jammed with spectators and the beach is aswarm with volunteer workers, intent upon pushing the awful object back to the open sea. This station is setting up an emergency observation post on the beach and a detailed description of the struggle will be broadcast within an hour by an eyewitness! Don't go 'way.

"Word comes from Oskaloosa, Iowa, that a party of Vigilantes today apprehended and lynched the ringleaders of a secret society advocating earth-burial of comatants. The Vigilantes of Oskaloosa are the city's best people and in a public manifesto they say: 'It is no false sympathy for these virtually-deceased which arouses this remonstration. It is, rather, our concern for ourselves and for posterity. Every inch of Iowa soil—the richest farming land on earth—is going to be needed either to grow food for the countless millions to come or to serve as foundations for their homes. There is no room in Oskaloosa for earth-burial. It may soon be necessary to reclaim the acreage hitherto used for that purpose. Several local cemeteries are now for sale as sites for apartment houses. We must all look to the future.'

"From the Grand Lodge of the Ancient Free and Accepted Masons today came the startling announcement that that order would immediately undertake to police the public highways. 'If the citizens of North America will undertake defense measures to preserve and to protect each his own home, we will endeavor to restore a measure of safety to city streets,' the announcement said in part. 'Swift justice will be administered by the local lodges which will meet every evening until further notice.'

"This decision was reached by the Grand Lodge after an analysis of a detailed report from every corner of the continent, showing that lawlessness had reached the proportions of a reign of terror in many communities.

"Not to be outdone by the Masons, the Benevolent and Protective Order of Elks announced an hour later that they would undertake to keep clean and in good repair the streets and roads of the entire continent. This has been a much-needed service since the abandonment of office by almost every municipal authority and the failure of county treasuries everywhere. Abandoned and wrecked automobiles have clogged hundreds of our roads and in many cities the streets have become general dumping grounds for broken furniture, glass, garbage, mattresses and tin cans by the ton. If the Elks can clean up the accumulated mess, they will deserve the heartfelt thanks of every right-thinking American.

"Just a minute folks.

"What's that?

"Oh, ho. My partner, here, wants to know what the Lambs are going to do for their country."

Mrs. Fitzhugh smiled wanly at her servants and returned to the music room.

He who was to paint her was just finishing a surgical anecdote. " 'Don't look now,' the nurse said, 'but your appendix is out!' "

Twenty years after the miracle.

That same evening Happy took Myra and his mother to the theater to see the sixteenth, seventeenth and eighteenth acts of a deadly epic by O'Neill. Although the author had not written the final scene, the producers had enough material in rehearsal to last another month, three acts the night. The title of the piece was *Mourning Becomes the Audience* and a television broadcast was used as an entr'acte instead of an orchestral din.

The wisecracking radio-news man had seen no part of this drama or he could not have asked what the Lambs were doing for their country.

The television was a newsreel and the assemblage was treated to a bird's-eye view of the Salvation Navy tugging a noissome, leprous island off the beach at Atlantic City.

"Look at all that business going to waste," said Happy. "Tch-tch-tch—tch-tch-tch. Just look."

"Always the merchant," said Mrs. Suderman.

A tipsy Irishman next to Happy nudged him. "Atlantic City's always looked like that to me, only *these* corpses' noses is better lookin'."

At the last sad curtain—for that evening—Happy led his

ladies to the elevator and the roof where a gyro-taxi lifted them through the Manhattan night and set them down in their own penthouse dooryard atop the Heaven on Earth Building, eighty staggered stories in the air.

"Well, I'm old-fashioned, I guess," said Happy's mother, "but I liked the old plays better than these talk-marathons we have today. I'm probably wrong."

"Of course you're wrong," said her son. "You don't appreciate art. Go to bed now, mother."

The old lady grumbled off toward her own room, pausing at a door halfway along the hall and looking furtively behind to see if she were watched. It was expressly forbidden. It was one of the first rules Happy had made when she was brought to live with them, but her curiosity was too strong to brook restraint if her son did not watch her. She opened the door to Willard's room and stepped inside.

The neon-lighted case revealed the same creature she always saw there and in precisely the same position. Mother Suderman watched his breathing closely. She was sure he was very tired of lying flat on his back for twenty years. He couldn't make it known, but horse-sense could tell a person that. They'd probably make a big to-do if she turned him over on his side. Didn't he look a little *green* tonight? Around the mouth. Maybe it was just the light.

Myra and Happy had forgotten her. They had forgotten Willard several years before. Gracie took care of him and Mrs. Suderman worried about him. There was nothing they could do.

Despite the multifarious hazards of life in the new jungle, a ton and a half of boredom had descended upon the home life of Heaven's president and his spouse. They were desperately tired of one another, yet life apart, life in any other perpetual company was unthinkable. Happy gave her everything. Six cars were available to her, jewels by the peck, she was gowned like a princess and servants were so numerous they got underfoot. There was a Suderman mansion at Bar Harbor, another at Palm Beach, a ranch in Wyoming and a lodge at Carmel. There were yachts and planes and a tallyho.

A stable, a kennel, an aviary. Everything money could buy had been provided her, yet with Happy Myra was bored. And he with her.

To ply their luxuries, they moved like an invading army, caparisoned, armored, equipped for flight or siege. By rail, road or air, it was thus all men of means went a journey, with scouts before and a guard behind, with portable kitchen and food supplies, for Robin Hood had been multiplied by a thousand and Jesse James was everywhere.

Still were they bored, for proximity to these necessities reduced their glamour and the step by backward step which brought each dark-age institution again into common use made them all to seem more natural than romantic. Expedients of imperative utility need the enchantment of distance or the transmutation of poetry to tint them. All are drab, some are a nuisance, when the Joneses and the Smythes live this way too.

Sick of the sight of each other and vexed by the cumbersome pediculae of pleasure, still there was a deep-seated, inner clinging, an attachment separation could not have severed, binding these two immortals indissolubly. They wrangled and growled unprettily, they bickered and snapped like a janitor's family, but you couldn't have torn them apart.

The motives of Mr. Henry Thorndike in his attentions to Myra never became clean-cut nor clear. As time went on and they persisted, their innocence was deduced if not proved, for Henry was some thirty-two or three years the lady's senior and Myra must soon confess fifty.

Ada Werfel's unremitting assaults upon Happy were less obscure as to intent. That banshee desired only the one thing and the office-supplies stock room was big enough.

Ada and Henry were foils for many a Suderman fence, but as they spoke, both, either and each realized that these recriminations were baseless.

Happy's money, which he showered over Myra with so coarse a sieve, came from the profits of Heaven. Lamson had never had any particular feeling for the business, so Happy had bought his share. Dan Sweeney remained a third owner, but Dan had no part in the development and growth of the institution. All that was Happy's doing. In addition to the income from the housing of comatants in Heaven itself, there was a still larger revenue from the designing, construction and servicing of outhouses. Architecture had been ransacked for classic designs and the moderne was popular and limitless. "Let the punishment fit the crime," was Happy's slogan, and by this he meant that the "tombs" or vaults should be appropriate to the nature of their occupants. Besides Taj Mahals in miniature of marble, bamboo pergolas, log cabins, igloos and tepees, there were also baby Parthenons, Viking ships, urns of intricate mechanism, stone wells, bowers, pueblos, turreted castles, cribs, shanties and box stalls. In the better neighborhoods, the residents vied with one another in the display of individuality and novelty. Heaven on Earth had branches in all principal cities and thousands of men and women were employed on regular routes to minister to the needs of the not-quite-deceased. Children playing in their dooryards would sing out to their mothers: "The angel is here to read grandpa!"

25

ALTHOUGH HE HAD FORGOTTEN the date of his birth, it was on Dr. Arnoldi's one hundred second anniversary that Happy and his bodyguard of four bravos arrived at 408 Canal with determination in every lineament. Happy expected resistance, but he meant to transplant the old man by force. If the four stalwarts couldn't carry him down the steps, he would summon four more. Dr. Arnoldi was moving to a more comfortable home where he would be cared for as he should be.

He had not dressed that day, but sat in his once-white pajamas with vodka and his unwashed breakfast dishes before him.

"*You,* my friend," he greeted Happy. "And your handsome retainers. Strapping fellows, aren't they?"

"How do you like the new uniforms?" Happy asked, trying to disarm the doctor.

"Very becoming. Wilhelm of Germany should see them.

He had a fine eye for a uniform—and a soldier's figure too."

"Do you think we can carry you downstairs, doctor? The five of us?"

"Carry me? I imagine so."

"We'll try, anyway. You are moving."

"Oh."

"I have a house on the river for you. Five rooms, plainly furnished. A man and a woman with more than ordinary sense to look after you."

"Thank you very much," said the doctor.

Happy waited for him to go on, waited for the rejection. The old man pushed the vodka a few inches toward Happy.

"If you'll get your own glass we can drink to your kindness."

"You mean you'll go?"

Dr. Arnoldi looked from broad chest to broad chest of the four huskies standing near the door. "Do you think I am mad enough to wrestle with your bodyguard at my age?"

Suderman laughed joyously and took a glass from the shelf. "I certainly didn't expect you to give in so easily. I've been planning this for a month but I was afraid to tell you about it."

"This neighborhood isn't what it used to be," said the doctor drily.

"Not since Chinatown was moved back to China, eh?"

"They came here, you know, for me."

"I know."

"A captain has been exacting twenty dollars a week ever since to permit me to stay."

"We'll settle his hash!" said Happy. "To your new home!" They drank.

"I think I could walk downstairs if I wished," the old man said a little loftily. "I pamper myself because I am lazy."

"Of course you do."

"But don't *you* pamper me. I refuse to develop crotchets."

"You drink too much, too," said Happy with a change of tone.

"Too much? Too much for what? For whom?"

"Too much for your own good."

"For my ultimate good or my present good?"

"Both."

"I could easily contradict you. I drink only as much as I want."

Happy sent one of his bravos to call moving people. The others carried books and bottles to the waiting cars.

The doctor's ancient and immemorial hat slipped over his hair, once white, faded now as yellow as his pajamas. A voluminous, tentlike, Inverness cape covered him. At the door Happy paused. "You've lived here a long time, doctor."

"My fancy has never been lively enough to animate walls, my romantic friend. I leave them without regret."

The doctor's half billiard cue and Happy's arm aided the ponderous descent. "How long has it been since you were out, doctor? You'll find things greatly changed."

"Oh."

"Everything is very different."

"All but one thing, perhaps."

"What's that?"

"Have men's eyes changed?"

"How?"

"Have men ceased to be fools?"

"Of course not."

"No."

"You didn't expect anything as radical as that in only twenty years!"

"I expect nothing," said Dr. Arnoldi.

As they sped uptown, passing plumed traffic cops, some with their swords drawn to enforce a restriction on left turns, the old man smiled at Happy.

"It reminds me of Spain in the old days. Every third man in uniform."

"The Knights of Columbus have taken over the traffic department. They make no arrests but they're very helpful at corners."

"There is a difference, isn't there? Autos move faster, the pedestrians more slowly. Am I right?"

Happy assented, "But I can't explain it. Why should the difference be so marked?"

They gathered further evidence as the car went through Times Square. "See how deliberately, lackadaisically, they step over those bodies in the gutter," said Harry. "I can understand that. The general listlessness is the reaction of a people which doesn't know where it's going."

"Chickens *dart* in bewilderment."

"This isn't bewilderment. It's fatalism. 'Take your time,' they seem to say, 'we've got plenty of that. There's no hurry. Nobody's going anywhere.' "

"Then the speed of cars?"

"Oh, that's a savage instinct. Have you ever driven an automobile? Know how?"

"No."

"Well, when you're driving a car, you are the sole master of a tremendous power, a force. Merely by pressing with your foot or moving your fingers, you cause a mass of steel to hurtle through the air faster and faster—faster than you have ever moved before. You are steering. Right, left, around corners; they can't stand it. With the steering wheel in their hands most men become savages, especially men who know little about motors. They have no clear picture of what intervenes between pressure on the accelerator and the additional speed. Their subconscious associates the leap of the car with the physical act of the foot or the hand. The car becomes a juggernaut! The driver a god! It's amazing to me that there aren't more so-called accidents than there are.

"Now that speed limits are unenforceable and street lights are on only half the time at night—well, *we* just stay home."

"The theory seems sound—" Dr. Arnoldi began.

"That's no theory," said Happy. "It's been proved again and again. And that reaction is not confined to the lower orders of intelligence either."

"Do you drive?"

"Yes!" Happy answered, "and I have a tough time maintaining a reasonable speed. You would too!"

"Yes, sir. If you learned to drive, I'll bet you'd be one of the fiercest demons on the road. It releases something."

"Oh, I hardly think so," the doctor remonstrated mildly. "I have nothing to release."

"You'd find something," said Happy. "Everybody does."

A street fight in which perhaps two hundred men and a score of women were involved caused Happy's cars to make a wide detour. Shots were fired and glass crashed. "A lot of that goes on now," Happy told his companion.

"What became of your roommate, Happy? The boy who almost insisted that I address his Comrades?"

"He was deported several years ago, I heard. He'll be back. Hmm. There's another thing. No matter how hard we try we can't lose anybody, certainly, any more. There's always a chance of meeting—anyone—everyone we have ever known."

"Yes," sighed Dr. Arnoldi. "There is that chance."

Their detour took them through a little-frequented street near the Washington-Memorial Bridge. Happy's chauffeur avoided several bodies in his path, but the next block was impassable, clogged with rusty bed springs, dozens of bottles, wash boilers and packing cases. The three automobiles stopped and when Happy saw the obstruction, he drew a revolver from a car pocket and handed it to the doctor. "This may be an ambush. It's being done. If anybody comes near the car, be ready."

The old Russian smiled. "What do they want, money?"

"Money. Sometimes the cars. My men will clear the street quickly." Happy himself held an automatic in his lap. "I told you things had changed."

"I've never shot a gun in my life. Do you think I shall know how?"

"You'll find out in a minute; here they come!"

From a passage between two tenement buildings, seven or eight men burst suddenly. At least two brandished revolvers, the rest were armed with clubs. Happy shot first, at the head of the leader. He faltered, staggered and fell. The bravos dropped their work in the street and closed with the highwaymen, using their blunt, ugly pistols with good effect. After the first fusillade, the three fellows who remained standing took to their heels. Dr. Arnoldi shot wildly once.

A uniformed member of Happy Suderman's party was stretched on the ground, blood soaking his new uniform.

"That was a mild skirmish, doctor," Happy said as they hurried the wounded man to a drug store on the New Jersey shore. "Out in the country is where they get you. I lost four men one time on the way to Maine."

"Yes. You told me."

They reached Dr. Arnoldi's new home without further mishap. He walked from room to room, obligingly, on Myra's arm. She had been there to welcome him. "And you came without a fuss! Isn't that fine?"

"I'm not stubborn," he scowled at her. "Why should I fuss to stay there?"

"We were afraid you would."

"That's stupid," said Dr. Arnoldi impatiently. "It would have cost me a great deal of effort to remain. It was much simpler to say 'yes'—and I got to shoot a gun."

The couple hired to care for him was introduced. "Can you make borsht?" he asked the woman with a touch of weariness. It was the necessity of being thus circumlocuitously polite and indirectly grateful that bored him most.

The answer was a Russian affirmative including many other dishes peculiar to his native land, dishes he had himself forgotten. "How have *you* escaped deportation? Please speak English."

Happy laughed. "They are part of a Soviet retaliation. Mr. Diernev was accused of being an English spy."

"So they sent him here?"

"To Canada, doctor. We were deported from Russia four years ago."

"Were the charges true?"

"Yes, doctor."

Arnoldi smiled. "We shall get along," he said, and turned to Myra. "You were ashamed of leaving me there. You wouldn't come back so you moved me."

"That's right," she confessed cheerfully, taking his hat

from his head. "Will you have some beer?"

He acknowledged the sally with a heavy wink and sat in a comfortable chair which afforded a view of the Hudson. From that prospect he turned his clever eyes again on Myra, then to Suderman. "Now I shall probably change my mind about being dead—and lose my self-respect entirely. It is very pleasant here."

"I'll leave directions for reaching this place on your door, down there, and if there is anyone you want notified, I'll have it done," Happy offered.

"The Salvation Army captain—?"

"I'm going to take care of him."

"I have had many callers, there, but, my friends, they have all demanded so much. They came expecting wisdom and left disappointed, I feel sure. One of them told me frankly that I was much overrated."

"No!"

"Indeed! And I had done nothing to deserve her scorn."

"A woman?"

"A young lady. She had a sheaf of papers. I thought she was taking the census.

" 'Do you believe red-headed people are quick-tempered?' she asked.

"I assured her I had no such belief—nor that they were slow to anger. I can't remember that I know a red-headed person.

" 'Do you know the meaning of these words: sagittary, bullpont, kakapo, commensal, spinge?'

"I did not. Not one of them.

" 'Do you jump when there is a sudden, unexpected noise near you?'

" 'Not much,' I said. 'Sometimes, perhaps.'

" 'If you saw a person standing in front of a fast train and there was a chance that you might save him by very seriously endangering your own life, would you be likely to do so?'

" 'I hope I should stand perfectly still.'

" 'If it were possible for you to commit suicide, would you like to have certain people come to watch you?'

" 'Dear lady,' I said, 'I have no desire to commit suicide, but, if I ever try, I shall be glad to have *you* come to watch me,' I said.

"She rose with a sniff. 'Well,' she said. 'If you are the *celebrated* Dr. Arnoldi, I'm sure you're greatly overrated'—and she left.

"I shouldn't care to have her call again, Happy. Not here."

Myra and Happy were weeping from laughter. "She was giving you an intelligence test!" Myra said between spasms—"and you failed!"

"I could have saved her the trouble," sighed the doctor. "I have never claimed to be intelligent."

The male half of the serving couple entered the room and unobtrusively signaled to Happy. Myra—and then the doctor—noticed, and followed the gaze of the two men to the middle of the river. Three bodies, grouped, floated there, moving toward the sea. The company watched them in silence for a moment, then each member turned away.

"That's not going to be a very pleasant sight," Myra apologized.

"I shan't mind it," Dr. Arnoldi assured her. "My eyes are so bad now that they were only whitish blurs on the water."

Happy shook himself. "I'll be damned if I can get used to it!" he ejaculated. "Call it atavism if you like, tell me it's only habit, *I* can't get used to it."

At Arnoldi's request, the Sudermans told Mr. Henry Thorndike where the doctor could be found. They could not reach Evan Fitzhugh although he had been included in the old man's invitation. "He's out with his autograph," said Marceline. "I'll tell him you called." But Henry told him first, making a special trip for the purpose. Mr. Thorndike refused to use the latest model automatic telephone. Its perfection never failed to startle him and he hated to be startled. It was so much like magic, punching the buttons, picking up the receiver and finding your party there. He'd walk a mile to avoid using the machine if he could.

"Evan! Dr. Arnoldi has *moved.*"

"Impossible!"

"No, sir. The chap who runs that Heaven place has moved him."

"Not comatant!"

"No, to a place in Jersey. I have the address. I've known the fellow's wife some time. She called me up. They've got him a cottage and some servants. She says he looks happy. Isn't that amazing?"

"I shan't believe it until I've seen it."

"Let's go look him up."

"Now? I was going home to watch Mr. Tucker work on my wife's portrait. He paints every day from about two-thirty until three or a little after, on sunny days."

"Half an hour a day?"

"The light—he says."

"Oh—"

"It doesn't come on very fast."

"I should think not, only half an hour a day! But, let it go. Watch him to-morrow. I want to see Arnoldi."

"I'll call my house."

"There's a good boy, Wince, run in and ask Mrs. Fitzhugh if she minds me not coming home for the painting. I'm going to see Dr. Arnoldi, tell her; if she doesn't mind."

"Yes, sir."

"And—Wince."

"Yes, sir."

"While you're in there—see if you can steal a peep at the Johnny's canvas. See what he's making of her. Don't let His Eminence notice your curiosity. He might not like it."

"Yes, sir."

Wince did his best. On entering the room where the Swan reclined in a beam of early afternoon sun, he walked around behind the crouching Tucker and emptied Cardinal Ridell's ash tray. Three times, he pussyfooted between Tucker and the wall, without seeming to look at the alleged portrait.

The Swan adjusted her neck for speech. "What is it, Wince?"

He stood close beside her before answering. "It's Mr.

Fitzhugh, madame. If you do not object, he will call on Dr. Arnoldi—and watch the painting tomorrow. He's holding on."

"If the light is right tomorrow," Tucker interposed.

"If the light is right," Wince bowed.

"Who is Dr. Arnoldi?" asked His Eminence. "Whom has Evan taken up with now?"

"I've heard the name before," said the sitter.

"Dr. Arnoldi—" Allardice Tucker murmured. "I seem to recall it too."

"I think he might have put it off," Ridell puffed. "Here *we* sit!"

"Yes," said the Swan. "Tell Evan that."

"Yes, madame."

"Mr. Fitzhugh? His Eminence thinks you might have put it off. Here *they* sit."

"Said that, did he?"

"Yes, sir."

"Did you get a look at the Johnny's daubing? What's it like?"

"Well, sir, if you ask *me,* he has an eyebrow there, just an eyebrow."

"Nothing else? Just an eyebrow?"

"It looked like an eyebrow to me, sir, a rather large one."

"But Myrtle—Mrs. Fitzhugh has no eyebrows worth mentioning! Are you sure, Wince?"

"It's either an eyebrow or a mustache, sir, and he seemed about to put a face around it."

"*Most* extraordinary," said Evan. "Most extraordinary."

"And Mr. Tucker was impatient with the light, sir. He remarked that it might not be all that he wished tomorrow."

Evan cleared his throat.

"Shall I say you'll be home, sir?"

"No!" the old bookman shouted suddenly. "Nothing of the kind. Tell His Eminence to go to the devil. I may not be home for days!"

"Very forceful. Very forceful indeed," Mr. Thorndike applauded, drawing on his gloves. "Your wife's confessor?"

"And old enough to know better!" said Evan. "Come."

A band of Elks stopped the Thorndike-Fitzhugh retinue at the toll house on the Washington Bridge. Their leader was directed to the car in which Evan and Henry sat. "We'll have to charge you gentlemen fifty cents a car to cross over here," the beadle said. "Sorry. That'll be three dollars."

"What's that for?" Thorndike demanded.

"Who are you?" asked Evan.

"I'm the toll man."

"How long has this been going on?"

"We just started today."

"Who gets this money? You don't intend to finish paying the contractors, do you?"

The Elk laughed. "I should say not. It's for a repair. There was a crack-up that took out a piece of rail down the line."

"Make *them* pay for it," Evan suggested. "We're not responsible."

Some of the secondary Elks looked threatening. A line of cars was forming behind the train of the two old men.

"Oh, come on," the leader cajoled. "Be good sports. You're using the bridge. What's three dollars?"

"It isn't the three dollars," said Mr. Thorndike. "It's the principle of the thing."

"Well, somebody has to pay for it," the beadle pouted. "If they don't, the bridge will fall down in time."

Eventually the old fellows coughed up. "It's a damned outrage," said Evan, "and I'm going to look you chaps up."

That racket became known and possession of every bridge to Brooklyn was contested by cliques of the criminal element who fought pitched battles with the Elks who were honestly working for the public good. Sometimes as many as three tolls were exacted on one bridge, entering, middling and leaving. *Pont* Williamsburg developed a population of its own. Men too stubborn or too poor to buy all these tickets, camped by the side of the road—high over the East River— and sent for their families. Periodically, these squatters were driven off one end or the other, gratis, or were thrown over the rail with all their paraphernalia. At the end of five years this built a dam of Fords and other debris, making navigation impossible. The evil spread. Transportation everywhere was impeded by "tollers", as they came to be called. It was impossible for railway engineers to ignore their demands to halt at an approach to a trestle, for—as many learned—a length or two of rail had often been removed about a mile farther on. The rails on the bridges were never tampered with for the same reason that gold-laying geese were nevermore killed after that one sad affair. If engineers pulled up and everyone paid according to his ability, the sections of rail were tacked back in place and the tollers wished their customers Godspeed.

Dr. Arnoldi had been raised on the vodka bottle and he had never let himself get out of practice. His age gave him from eighteen to twenty-three or -four years' more experience than the other two old coots, who were pretty well potted when they left. "The dinner," they assured him, "was delishush."

One of the bravos paid the Elk the three dollars for recrossing the bridge, paid it without waking his master, and they reached Evan's warren without mishap. The sleep and the swift breeze had sobered them somewhat. Henry consented to meet Evan's family.

"Where is everyone, Wince? I don't hear the piano."

"His Eminence has taken Madame and Mr. Tucker to the cock fights, sir. His Eminence was in something of a pet."

"In a pet, was he? I don't doubt it. Never been told to go to the devil before, *I'll* bet."

"It struck me that way, sir, as I delivered your message. It struck me as quite new to him."

"Tell me, Wince."

"He colored, sir."

"Colored, did he?"

"Yes, sir."

"What color?"

"We-ell—"

"Choleric—sort of? Pinkish? Jaundiced?"

"A shade on the purple side, *I* should say, sir."

"Hear that, Henry? He turned purple! Cock fights, eh?"

"Yes, sir, at the Y.M.C.A."

"Well, Wince, before they get back, I want to look at that eyebrow. You bring Scotch and soda in there, will you?"

"Yes, sir; but Mr. Tucker's going to be put out, sir, for you uncovering his canvas. He could scarcely bring himself to attend the cock fights for fear something would happen to it in his absence."

"He may be put out, Wince, after I've seen it. I am a new man tonight. Scotch and soda in the sun-room."

"Yes, sir," said the almost perfect butler.

The Swan and Mr. Tucker found the two old men tailor-fashion on the floor, studying the eyebrow and finishing the last swallow of that bottle of Scotch.

"Evan," said his wife reprovingly.

"Good evening, my dear. Where's John?"

"He has gone home. You must have hurt him."

"No!"

"He wasn't himself all evening."

Tucker fluttered and clucked like a hen with chicks over the exposed painting. "Mr. Fitzhugh," he repeated several times. "Mr. Fitzhugh!"

"Just a minute, son, before you cover that up. I'd like to know what it is."

"It's a start," said Tucker, dropping the sheet, "only a start."

"What'd I tell you?" asked Henry. "Didn't I say it was a start?"

Henry was presented to Allardice and Mrs. Fitzhugh.

"Who is this Dr. Arnoldi you are running around with, Evan? Have I met him?"

"No, my dear. You have not. He is a very old man, a Russian."

"Unique," said Thorndike. "Beyond good and evil. Only man I ever met who never has a desire."

"That sounds dreadful to me. Will you help them up, Mr. Tucker?"

"Dr. Arnoldi," said Evan, weaving to his feet, "has forgotten more about medicine than all the doctors in town will ever find out. He can kill a man."

The erstwhile portrait painter bridled, almost spilling Mr. Thorndike. "No, he can't," said Tucker. "I know he can't."

"When did he say that?" asked Henry. "That's the first I've heard about it."

"He told me he'd been thinking. You know what *that* means."

"About killing people?"

" 'I think I have a plan,' he said, while you were talking to that Heaven Johnny on the telephone. He said it to me."

"His plan won't work," Tucker asserted. "I know."

"What 'Heaven Johnny' does he mean, Mr. Thorndike? Are you acquainted with the Sudermans?" asked Mrs. Fitzhugh.

"Very well, indeed," said Henry, struggling for at least one sober breath. "Mrs. Suderman's first husband worked for me."

"One reads so much about him, *Happy* Suderman, in the papers. His advertisements are so clever. 'Happy wants to see you!' he had for one headline. 'Happy's Heaven on Earth means eternal happiness.' I'd so like to meet him. He must have a beautiful soul—and Mrs. Suderman too."

"If you will set a date, I am sure I can arrange it. Ha! That is clever, isn't it? 'Happy wants to see you!' Ho." When he did not hear Evan's laugh, Henry looked around for him. The bookman was dozing in a chair.

26

THE NEXT MORNING was Children's Welfare Morning for Fitz. The hope of the world assembled in the house and on the grounds and were there subjected to a discourse designed to arouse their collective sense of responsibility. Sometimes Cardinal Ridell talked, sometimes a passé celebrity, sometimes Fitz herself. The keynote of late, the keynote of all the talking had been Vision! They must look ahead, these young eyes, look into the future and take steps to prevent it. The month before, all the speakers had dwelt upon Virtue!—until the hope of the world threatened to strike and not attend any more lectures regardless of the swell feed they got after. The spokesman had stood right up on his hind legs—his father had been a lawyer while the law lasted—and spoke his mind and the mind of his group. "Mrs. Fitzhugh, this has gone far enough." He was ten. "At the Culbertsons' Welfare Morning the children are fed *before* the speaking. At the Allburgs' the lectures are about contraception and murder. We don't mind waiting until noon to eat, if you want us to, but we had a meeting and voted that we won't come here any more unless you quit talking always about right living. Father says there's no use sending me if *that's* all you're going to talk about." The elders convened and after deliberation called at Horace's home. His father was out, but his mother was glad to answer questions. "Like as not his father did tell him that," she admitted. "He was just a young attorney when this thing broke out. He's been a sneak-thief ever since and he's done right well."

Taken slightly aback, the cardinal hemmed. "Does—does he intend to—to make a—a sneak-thief of his son?"

"Well, I guess so. He's too slight for highway work. Did you ever see anything like the size of these bravos? They're big as a house!"

So the faculty of the Children's Welfare Mornings adjusted its views. The lecture program was changed, Vision being substituted for Virtue, and Back to the Farm for Back to Church. The strike was thus averted and attendance even increased.

"Look! Mrs. Fitzburgh," said Horace proudly, the morning after the cock fights, "I've brought the whole Packing House Gang."

The Swan looked them over in alarm. Thirty-five of the toughest devil-spawned brats and bastards ever spewed from Hell's Kitchen. Their average age was fourteen and they had wrested sustenance from the city of their birth by begging, stealing and ragpicking for half that number of years. There was not an open eye nor a clean mouth among them. They were not little wolves, but young jackals, hyenas, shifty and mean and foul. They formed a filthy spot in the garden around which eddied the neat and clean children whose faces were more familiar to Fitz. She looked them over once and adjusted her neck; then she looked them over again. She tried it once more, and still a third time, lifting her chin and her brows, wiggling her head—still the word refused to be born.

It was John's turn to speak. Where was John? Fitz flew to a telephone. "John! Where are you?"

"I'm here."

"I know. But it's Welfare Morning!"

"I'm not coming."

"Riddy!"

"No. Evan has abused me. I shan't come there again until he has apologized."

"John—you must! There—there is a swarm of—of children here—the—the Packing House Gang! They need you, John."

"The Packing House Gang! They don't need *me*. You better go away for a few days—until they leave. Try to get out of the house without them seeing you."

"That isn't Christian, John Ridell!"

"Christian! Christian! If they see you leaving they'll take the paint off your car! They're worse than locusts in Africa. They *swarm*."

"And you'd leave me among them—exposed to this danger? Oh! How I have misjudged you!"

"Oh, *damn!*" said the cardinal. "I'm coming."

The garden billowed restlessly. Mrs. Fitzhugh did not show herself. Behind a portiere, she watched the pranks of the children, the breaking down of shrubs, the trampling of flowers, the crashing of fences. Wince came to ask for instructions. "Just let them alone, Wince," she whispered. "Perhaps they'll get tired and go away." But her hopes on that score were obliterated when a voice rose from the midst of the rowdy element: "Hey! Hey you! When do we eat?"

Ten voices took it up. "When do we eat? When do we

Tiffany Thayer

eat?"

"Ragamuffin ingrates!" said the Swan, to herself, "you *don't* eat—now!"

The gardener, discovering the vandalism at about that moment, sallied among the children with a spade waving over his head. "Ye spalpeens!" he screamed, "ye witherin', blitherin' stomp and scatters! Stay to the walks! Keep to the grass! Off o' them flowers, y' dromendaries!" His horticultural zeal deprived him of discretion and judgment. The tom-tom rhythm of the chant: *When do we eat? When do we eat?* had entered the blood of the hitherto well-behaved Welfaristas. The clean little boys and the neat little girls began to hum the tune and finally to join in the shouting. The Packing House Gang looked at the spade brandisher in mild astonishment at his temerity, but without awe.

The gardener's transitions were extremely comic. When no child ran from him and his bellowing was ignored, he bore down on the nearest three, speaking with reasoning authority. Their hard little squint eyes were agates set in the marble of their heads. "*Do* you hear, now!" They heard! They started grimly toward him. "To the walks. I'll bash you!" He raised the spade.

Five or six Packing Housers drew a close circle closer around him. The spade bounced off a head—and that was the signal.

They took his spade; they took his clothes, his hair, his ears, his nails. They left him stripped and bleeding mid the ruin of his flower beds and, with blood on their palates and the fumes of a kill in their nostrils, they started for the kitchen. The well-behaved were swept along on surges of impunity. The months of virtue preaching, the years of parental restraint were obliterated by sight of this one concrete demonstration of untrammeled freedom.

Cook had locked herself and two maids in her room when she heard them coming. They ate everything in sight. Truffles and various canapés in glass, they smashed on the floor and gobbled. A fight over a squab precipitated a dish and butter fight which terminated at the music room door because by the time they had penetrated the house so far, every dish and glass was broken and all the butter had been flung too high on the walls and ceilings to be easily available.

Fitz in noble naïveté had refused to quit the house. Trembling Tucker had fled, but the Swan put Wince on the telephone calling for help, and she sat at the piano. As the thunder and crash of the dish and butter fight grew louder and louder, the Swan began to play. The dulcet simpering of a French lullaby, one of her favorites, issued with sweet calm from the grand box and she adjusted her neck for song. She thought she identified, by a more than ordinarily patrician tinkle of its parts, the destruction of her Haviland game set, then a Dresden bowl. She sang.

To charm the savage breast. To still the roaring beast. To quiet the tumult and to impress these primitive throwbacks, Myrtle Fitzhugh sang.

They filled the room. They mounted the furniture. They packed tight around the piano and the bench and the Swan. She looked slightly up from force of habit, and sang over their heads—in French.

Victory seemed in her grasp. They jostled. They kicked. Their harsh shoes played havoc with satin upholstery and polished floors, but they listened. Playing for her life, for her health—at least, Fitz would not let the song end or pause. From one ditty into another she ran, racing with time, to hold this pigmy mob until succor came.

"Say," one Packing Houser said, "can you play *Yes, We Have no Cadavers?*"

She pretended not to hear.

"Play *We Ain't Gonna Die No More, No More,* lady."

The Swan sang louder, switching to a Lutheran hymn.

"Don't you know *any* hot stuff?" they demanded.

The hymn—

"Aw, t'hell with it!"

Their grimy, greasy fingers profaned her, and, still singing, they stuffed her in the top of the piano and tried to shut the lid.

With rare attention to detail, the gang proceeded to finish

the wreck of the house. It was remarkable, or, perhaps it was not, that Tucker's start on Mrs. Fitzhugh's portrait was not harmed. His paints were gone, however, having been squirted from the tubes in brilliant streaks all over the place and down the drive. The trail of the departing children could even be followed for several miles, by the long worms of pigment with which they traced the sidewalk.

Some results of this untoward incident were still easily discernible when the Sudermans were brought by Mr. Henry Thorndike to dine. The Swan was still ruffled. She blamed it all on Cardinal Ridell and treated him distantly as punishment. Any grievance he may have tried to nurture against Evan was drowned in this greater enormity of his own. He was permitted to watch the sitting in the afternoon, but his comments and suggestions were greeted coolly.

Tucker was quite set up by the awe his eyebrow had inspired in the little savages. "No other work of art was sufficiently powerful in appeal to stay their hands. Not even a beautiful woman, singing with her soul, could stop them. But," he twiddled a brush at his canvas, "they couldn't destroy this. Something they did not understand, made them turn away."

His Eminence turned away, allowing the expression of his face to tell the artist why. Riddy had no more to say after that.

It was singular, but not unnatural withal, that even Evan had not encountered Happy Suderman at any time between their first meeting and this dinner party. Evan did not know that the young man of the strange behavior at 408 Canal, the chap who had locked them in to get rid of Ada Werfel, was the owner of Heaven on Earth. In more than twenty years that coincidence had not become apparent to the custodian of that last dubious Lincoln autograph.

On greeting his guests, at Myrtle's elbow, Evan started in recognition. "Tell me, tell me," he said, turning to Thorndike. "It's the mad Johnny!"

"Mad Johnny, mad Johnny? *What* mad Johnny?"

"He locked me in!"

"What? Where?"

"Locked us up!"

"Oh," said Happy, extending his hand, "hullo."

"Ho!" Evan said to his wife. "Fancy that. Mr. Suderman is the chap who locked the girl in—in—"

Too late Evan remembered some circumspection, looked sheepishly at Myra and flushed brilliantly.

"Never mind," Myra consoled the old man. "I understand."

Mr. Fitzhugh continued to be astonished at this turn of chance all through the cocktails. What astounded Myra, however, was finding Dr. Tucker at this board. There seemed to be no intimation of incognito. The name was Tucker, but without degrees, and his work was portrait painting. Always dapper, Evan's funds had dressed the little fellow well again and he was barbered daily.

"Weren't you a doctor once?" Myra asked mercilessly at table. "I think I remember you—many years ago."

Tucker looked around—and especially at Wince—with frightened eyes. "Yes," he acknowledged. "I was. I remember you too. You were Mrs. Kent." He lowered his voice. "I left the profession."

"Yes, for painting."

"I live in constant dread of being found out by some society, found out and forced to return to it."

"They need doctors badly," said Mr. Thorndike. "I see where some ex-senator, quite an organizer, forgotten his name, fell ill on the eve of a *coup.*"

"A *coup?*"

"He had a considerable armed force, was about to take over New England and the North Atlantic States. Thought he could bring about some kind of order. Took sick, and now his army is breaking up because he is in bed."

Tucker snorted. "That's the sort of thing I am afraid of. There will be lots of that in the next ten years; petty generals, small kings, principalities everywhere. They'll want to attach good surgeons to every Tom, Dick and Harry who can assemble a mob. I'm through with it—and I'd be greatly obliged to you—to all of you—if you'd forget who I am. I am an artist, not a surgeon, and I do not wish to change."

"You left your profession very abruptly; didn't you, doctor? Mr. Kent never regained consciousness after your last operation."

Happy looked quizzically at his "wife".

"Didn't he?" Tucker asked, truly puzzled. "I've forgotten exactly what was done—but he should have come out of that. Where is he?"

"At home."

"Comatant?"

"Yes."

"I'll have to take another look at him. No reason he shouldn't have come out of that all right."

The talk drifted to the Swan's bruises, to "Heaven on Earth", through the habits of comatants to the predicament of mankind in general. Happy tried to avoid the more gruesome details of his business, but the Swan was morbidly insistent.

"Some swell," he shrugged, "others shrink. We have a statistical department which records everything minutely. If anything approaching normal mortality ever returns to earth, our data will be valuable as a record. The big medical centers all have men on our staff, experimenting. They are no nearer an explanation today than they were twenty years ago."

"Which are the very worst cases to handle, Mr. Suderman?" Mrs. Fitzhugh was seeking something.

"Brain concussion is pretty bad. They have violent reflexes at the most unexpected times. Several have I broken the glass out of their cases."

"It's funny to see some of them recover. Lots of them do. Heart failure and pneumonia cases often get over it in a few weeks or a month. We don't do anything to keep them from getting well."

"How about the aged?" the Swan asked softly. "Do you have any people who have—merely worn out?"

"Dozens. They just sleep. Some snore, some groan, I some wake up, but most of them just sleep."

"And grow older—in their sleep? Whiter hair? More

wrinkles?"

"Oh, yes. We have a complete beauty salon for those. We can dye the hair, and cut it, of course; manicure the nails. Massage and facial treatments are available. There's really nothing wanting."

"Smallpox—and other contagious diseases?"

"Well, we have a special wing for them, but the Red Cross-Salvation Army keeps it pretty well cleaned out. They ship them to foreign countries, to poison water supplies and contaminate cities."

The cardinal had been silent a good while. "Would you believe Man could fall so low? Really, we are returning to barbarism."

"Worse than that, Your Eminence. We are returning to the jellyfish. It is only a matter of time."

"The jellyfish! Impossible. How?"

"I am wary of detailed predictions, Your Eminence, but if we don't get off this planet, that's where we are headed, mark my words."

"Off this planet?" said Evan. "Now, really—"

"Why not?" asked Happy. "All the land we know about on earth was discovered by men forced out of their crowded homes by something or other. It wasn't overpopulation in every case, but that would have followed if the new lands had not been found.

"This isn't hearsay or guesswork. I haven't invented the theory. Russia and Japan are colonizing the Arctic. They aren't dumping any surplus men in the ocean any more and they aren't sending their expectant mothers here. They are sending them, well equipped, to the Arctic Circle.

"England and Belgium have settled the Amazon—thickly, with convicts of about the same caliber as the Pilgrim Fathers. Many recover from the jungle fevers in short order and adapt themselves to their environment. I've seen reports which attest that the babies born in these colonies never have fever. And the Soviet is bragging—Norway too—that the infants born near the North Pole have more hairy bodies than any Siberia has ever produced."

"Granted, granted," said Evan. "We know the human race is adapting itself to the new system, but how are we going to get off the planet? Who is going first? Would *you* get in one of these rocket ships I read about?"

"There are Christopher Columbuses and Leif Ericsons born in every age, Mrs. Fitzhugh. It won't be hard to man a rocket for the moon or Mars. In theory, such a sky-ship, propelled by explosives, has been perfected many years. It has been only the danger to life on this planet which has delayed the first takeoff. It will take a discharge of tremendous force to lift the rocket. A series of explosions must follow—in the air. It will tear a gigantic hole in the earth as it leaves, and, if it is shot from the Sahara, the succeeding explosions will fill our atmosphere with fumes and ash, perhaps debris. Even then, the greatest danger is in re-alighting. Suppose the moon or Mars is reached. The scientists who don't know why we have stopped dying say that the rocket will land with scarcely a bump—there—due to the difference in gravity. It will take but a slight explosion to start the rocket back. *But!* Ah, there's the rub. That is why it hasn't been attempted.

"Every second after the rocket starts the *return* trip, its speed will increase. Old Earth will be pulling it for all she's worth. Who can say where the ship will land? Suppose it hit here on Manhattan! It would crush thousands—and surely kill the occupants.

To overcome the pull of Earth, the rocket can discharge more explosives—directly at the earth—to break the fall, but how about the poor people underneath? One blast from one cylinder—on our heads! Can you imagine the result? It could blow a county right off the map."

The company stared in collective and mutual cogitation. No one spoke.

"My God, I talk a lot, don't I? Myra! Why don't you stop me when I start raving?"

"It doesn't matter, now," said Myra vacantly. "No matter where it landed, so long as it didn't hit us—we wouldn't care."

"We'll be driven to it," said Cardinal Ridell. "It may take

another century, but if the old order does not return, Mr. Suderman is right, we shall have to colonize the planets."

It was five years—or six—after this conversation when the first rocket ship was built. The *Back to the Farm* movement and its cousin *Reclaim Waste Land,* had not yet populated all the American desert. One hundred miles from nowhere, in Arizona, the preparations took three years more. The enormous steel cigar was as delicate in mechanism as a fine watch, as precisely put together as a submarine. An arrangement of springs and shock absorbers surrounded the ship at all possible points of contact with the ground. Steel parts, electrical appliances, explosives, oxygen and respiratory devices, were hauled away from the railroad far into the sandy waste. Its construction and outfitting had cost eight million dollars—8,000,000 *good* dollars—and countless pounds of scrip, paid in bales.

There were three big meteorologists interested passionately in the enterprise. They would captain the crew. Four of the employees who had worked on the construction and fitting of the unique air vessel were anxious to go along to see their handiwork in actual operation. To complete the quota of twelve persons, volunteers were called for, through radio and newspapers—and for the five berths there were half a million applicants.

At the last moment it was decided that three of the five should be healthy, strong, young women, for—if they should be unable to return—it was Professor Damien's sudden inspiration that they should wish to breed on the planet Mars, to people their colony with human beings, to leave as dark a blot as possible on any stellar land they found. The professor did not put it so frankly—not even to himself—but that was the idea.

The selection of the three women from among the multitude willing to take a sky ride and to become brood mares aloft delayed the rocket's red glare another month. From a chance thought, this idea grew in significance when it was discovered that some really high-class material offered. It was finally necessary to forget eugenics, mental powers and

breadth of pelvis and to take along the three winners of a na-
tion-wide beauty contest. As Professor Damien said, "We
better take the cuties, otherwise we'll never take off."

Miss San Antonio, Miss Bronx and Miss Hollywood were
the dubious winners. No one on Earth ever learned whether
they were happy about their success or not for the expedition
was never heard from again after it kicked a gigantic crater
in the desert and shot into space. It may have been this ship
which became the Flying Dutchman of the air, no one could
say surely, for after the first aerial torpedo was launched,
Others followed rapidly. It was an expensive way to get rid
of people, but it was effectual for several hundred years.
Then some of them began coming back.

27

THE SUDERMANS and the Fitzhughs saw a good deal of each
other after their first meeting, and Allardice Tucker never
failed to ask after Willard Kent's health. Loss of that case
was a cankerous memory to the vain little man and he tried
to fret out a way to continue his treatment of that particular
case without jeopardizing his freedom from the medical profession. Myra ignored hints. She even resented the fellow's
constant reminders of her first husband. He had been so well
forgotten so long.

Events conspired, however, in this wise:

The portrait of the Swan, ten years after it had been
started with a classic eyebrow, mid-canvas, was as nearly
finished as it would ever be. It resembled Fitz very little. A
solemn unveiling ceremony was held and the house was full
of people.

Evan pursed his lips and half closed his eyes as one
should in the presence of oil paintings. The only improve-
ment on that practice suggested by Tucker's work was to
close the eyes entirely. "Finished, is it?" said Evan.

Tucker rocked back and forth, heel and toe, heel and toe.
"Rather apparent, I should say."

"I never should have guessed it," said Evan. "You've

made her wopper-jawed."

"For the sake of composition," Tucker explained. "I needed an oval movement there."

"Do her eyes track, Evan?" asked Mr. Henry Thorndike. "I have a feeling that her eyes don't just exactly track."

"Track!" said the alleged artist. "They almost speak."

"Where's her mouth?" some curious individual inquired at large.

His Eminence, Cardinal John Ridell glowered. "Too young," he said cattily. "You've tried to keep her too young." In disfavor since the Packing House Gang invasion, John never missed an opportunity to be nasty. "No character. Face of a virgin."

The Swan turned slowly away and glided sadly from the room.

"You don't understand," said unabashed Tucker. "You people are not artists. It is the necessity for painting for patrons like you which keeps a genius like me starving. This painting is a soul-struggle."

"Oh," said Evan.

Happy disengaged himself from a group and followed Mrs. Fitzhugh. Myra was absorbed in Tucker's dissertation and did not miss him for some time.

"It's not a portrait, then?" asked Henry.

"Only in a sense. Naturally, I can't come to a man like Mr. Fitzhugh and say, 'I want to paint a soul-struggle of your wife.' It wouldn't make sense."

"No," they agreed, "it wouldn't."

"Who's soul is struggling?" asked the cardinal, "and what with?"

"It is *my* soul, struggling with itself."

The room was hushed.

"My eyes tell me to make a likeness. I know my patron and my sitter desire a likeness, something almost photographic. My artistic sense, my love for beauty and harmony, my devotion to the tenets of art demand something entirely different. A mouth in the lower half of that oval movement would disturb my idea. It would be harsh and glaring, indelicate, inharmonious. Within myself I battle. The mouth must be there! The mouth must not be there! This ear is straight in life—in my composition it must—incline. I incline it.

"Oh, you don't know how I suffer, painting this way, mixing my blood with the color on the palate. Striving, ever striving to satisfy both sides of me. That is why I say this work is a soul-struggle. It is the record of my travail."

About half the guests were impressed.

"You can see it was painful," said Evan.

"Think of suffering like that for ten years!" said a woman standing next to Myra.

"Only half an hour a day," said His Eminence.

Myra looked around for Happy.

Thus events conspired. Boredom in the Suderman home. The tiff between Evan and John. The house-wrecking. The failure of the portrait. "When are you leaving?" Evan asked the soul-struggler.

Myra wandered off in search of her husband. She came upon them unexpectedly in the conservatory. Happy, even at seventy-four, was still considerable consolation, and under the hot glass, shielded by tropical vegetation, he had been telling the Swan in his own way that Cardinal Ridell was a liar; that she had not aged a day and that Tucker's portrait of her was a daub not worth a glance from one of her eyes as fair as the dawn.

"Well!" said Myra, which is as good a thing to say at a time like that as anything *you* can think of. "Well!" And she was gone.

"Who was that?" asked the Swan dreamily.

"An old lady," said Happy. "Never mind."

"Did she see us?"

"Perhaps," he admitted. "It doesn't matter."

"No-o," sighed the Swan. "It doesn't matter, does it?"

Myra made it seem to matter on their way home. She maintained a stony silence, answering Happy's remarks on the subject with twists of her mouth and vicious cuts and jabs with her eyes.

"Come on, cheer up," said Happy. "You don't really care

about that and you know it. Be honest. Admit that you have to make a perceptible effort to resent what you saw— because it's 'the thing to do'. Admit it."

Myra stared straight forward and said nothing. As soon as she was in their penthouse, she went to Willard's room. She could not remember when she had been there last. With a wry mouth, she watched his even breathing, pulling off her tight gloves with little jerks of her head in time with her fingers.

Gracie had just left the room, after ministering to the comatant and smoothing his bed for the night. Myra looked for a long time on the unconscious man who had grown old flat on his back, and withdrew.

Events *must* have conspired, because, later that evening, Mrs. Suderman, that is, Happy's mother, when she sneaked her wonted glance at Willard before retiring, yielded to the desire she had so often felt and *turned the poor cuss on his side*.

Happy had flown across the river to Dr. Arnoldi's. There he was sure of a calm evening of conversation, free from passion or hypocrisy.

Myra flounced from room to room of her home, throwing magazines from her in disgust, and finally settling herself with tweezers and mirror for a good old-fashioned evening with her eyebrows. Someone at the Fitzhughs had said hers were like that woman's. The old fascination for tweezing was gone. She considered waking the mother of that goat of a Happy. There would be some satisfaction in telling a member of the Suderman family exactly what she thought of the scion.

Poor Willard! she thought in the hall. She had neglected him. There was no way to make up for it She opened his door only a crack and looked in.

To that climax events had tended. Myra ran screaming to the telephone. Dr. Tucker was about to retire, but he would gladly serve her. She must be calm and not touch the body. He would hurry.

As the disappointing artist hurried acrosstown to see a patient he had left more than thirty years before, Dr. Arnoldi was making a confession to Happy. "It must be my age," he said, dripping absinthe into his vodka through a tablet of sugar. "I'm curious—for probably the first time since I left Grenoble. I'm curious."

"About what?"

"Two things; the flavor of human flesh—and the effect of digestion upon this unquenchable life spark. I want to eat a man to see if it will kill him."

Happy rubbed his eyes and yawned. "Pardon me. Well, why don't you try it?"

"I've hesitated."

"So should I, I think."

"Yes, I've hesitated. I'm afraid the good cook you got me would not relish the work. She's narrow, a little, you know."

"Cannibalism! *Back* we go. Would you ever, ever have thought it, doctor? As you and I discussed the possible consequences of this—did you imagine that it would carry us straight back over the road men trod to get where he was thirty-four years ago?

"We are scarcely out of the shock days yet. Still the course we must inevitably take is indicated. Our institutions fail, learning is a mockery. Law goes to hell and our public utilities stagger.

"Nations close their doors to commerce. Provincialism, more absolute than at any time since Bell and Morse, spreads its walls and cuts its cables. It's a jerky backward progression, but do you see its sweep?"

"I see it," said Arnoldi.

"We're back of the Boer War already. And I learned only the other day that it is now the fashion to make eunuchs of young bravos. What are the Chinese but slaves to Japan? What are our own large cities but tiny kingdoms, waiting for strong men to rise and rule them? Hordes of savages roam at will. Robber barons infest the countryside. Mexico, Louisiana and Georgia have quit building houses. The women—"

"Quit building houses?"

"Yes. The dwellings are all mausoleums. The healthy

people are living entirely in the open."

"Tribes," Dr. Arnoldi smiled at his glass.

"And feudalism. Now you suggest cannibalism as a way out."

"It may be," the doctor nodded ponderously. "Don't you think it may be? Living is but a slow dying, we once said, a metamorphosis, a burning. Digestion is a burning. Rot is a burning.

"Since all other elements have quit their natural functions and reject us as unburnable, perhaps we can burn each other. Perhaps we can *blend* life, thus, instead of terminating it.

"If I ate you—and somehow got your life in my stomach, isn't it possible that it would be incorporated into my system by the same metabolic process that extracts the strength from meat juices and the energy from vegetables?"

"Not—if you eat me—ahem—let's talk about eating somebody *else*."

"You're facetious. I'm not. I've been thinking."

"I can see you have."

"Fecal matter is nothing but ash. I doubt that life, taken in by mouth, would pass through the fire of the human stomach and be carried out by the stool. I doubt it—and I should like to test it."

"Why not?" said Happy. "They've tried everything else."

"Lives could thus be blended, if I am right. Your heavy eater, myself, for instance, could be made the repository of—well—a small village."

"Wow!" Happy ejaculated. "And how does *he* feel?"

"By experiment, perhaps, we could determine at last if there is a seat of life, a truly vital part, which may be eaten. At first, I think it will be necessary to consume every vestige of the body to be sure the life itself is taken in."

"Well, it's a funny way to become pregnant. Just suppose—now—a baby develops in your stomach. Think of becoming a father—and a mother too—at your age!"

"*You* think of it," said Dr. Arnoldi, "while I find a body for my experiment."

"Bodies! My God, I've got thousands."

Both men were silent a moment, thinking. "We could ask Myra," said Happy. "All he does is lie there. I think that would be very appropriate. He was one of the very first. Maybe he will be the means of leading us out of the jam he led us into."

"It's a delicate question."

"It's more delicate just now. You'd have to ask her because she's sore at me . . . Ho! Lordy! I beg your pardon, lady, but could you spare me your husband for dinner?!"

"Even if she's willing, there's still the problem of the cook. Mrs. Diernev would be horror-stricken, I feel sure."

"Tell her it's antelope! You'll dissect it yourself?"

"Yes. I might have to have some help. I'm not strong any more."

"I'll bet that a meal or two of strong men will bring back your schoolgirl complexion! Think, doctor, this diet may be rejuvenating! Why didn't I think of this before?"

"I don't know," said Dr. Arnoldi. "Why didn't you?"

"I'm going to join you, you know. There's a girl who works for me that I've had my eye on—"

"Antelopes don't have fingers," said Dr. Arnoldi.

"Oh, doctor, you aren't going to let a little thing like a stubborn cook impede the wheels of Science! When are they off?"

"Thursday."

"On Thursday, then!" They drained their glasses, "If Myra won't give in—say! There's no need of asking her! She never goes near him! I'll bet she hasn't gone in that room for two or three years, maybe more. I'll just have him moved."

"You are a zealot," said Arnoldi, measuring vodka, "When we get back to the Inquisition in our return through history, you will make an admirable Chief Inquisitor."

"Zealot yourself! If I deliver Willard Kent here, you'll do your share!"

"One lump or two?" asked the doctor with his sugar tongs poised.

"Thursday," said Happy, "but have a room ready at once. I don't know exactly when I shall make the delivery."

"Butcher!" The Russian was sardonic.

They talked until nearly dawn, and drank, and parted in more mutual admiration than had been theirs before.

The penthouse was very quiet. Happy wrote a memo ordering Willard's removal to a room in Heaven—and went to sleep.

When Allardice Tucker arrived with his baggage that morning, his patient was not to be found. The alarums and furor in the hall brought Happy out in a dressing-gown. Myra was still in negligee. "Willard's gone," she said frantically. "Happy, Willard's *gone!*"

"Well, he can't have gone far. Have you looked everywhere?"

"He moved last night! He rolled over. Now he's gone."

"He rolled over!" Happy was incredulous.

"I saw him," Myra insisted. "I saw him."

"Saw him *move?*"

"Yes!"

"Jesus." Happy dressed and scooted to his office. He summoned the internes who had moved Willard and learned his whereabouts. "Was he quiet?"

"Sure."

"You didn't detect any movement?"

"Naw."

"Deliver him to this address at once."

So that Myra's husband was shanghaied on the eve of another operation. Old lady Suderman had nothing to say. She was scared stiff. It was her doings and she was beside herself. If they found out she had been messing around in that room after Happy had told her not to—it would just be too bad. Search parties were formed under Happy's guidance and the story made page one in the evening papers.

In the midst of her troubles, Myra called on her old friend, Dr. Arnoldi. She found him in a white apron, a white cap and rubber gloves, looking like a snow-covered hill. "*You,* my dear."

"Doctor! Why that get-up? Are you operating? Think of that! It did you good to move."

"Yes," said the doctor. "I'm beginning to think it did."

"Did I interrupt?"

"There's no hurry. I was just about to start."

"I can come back. I just wanted to tell you about Willard."

"Willard?"

"You remember—Willard?"

"Oh, yes. Yes, I remember."

"He's disappeared!"

Arnoldi turned his rubber gloves wrong-side-out taking them off. "Is that so?"

"He came to life—and walked away."

"No."

"Yes! Isn't it amazing?"

"Amazing if true," the old man murmured. "Will you have beer, my dear?"

"I'm keeping you from your operation."

"Perhaps it's just as well. Since you have come, I wonder if I'm the man for this particular operation. Perhaps I shan't perform it."

"Oh, you *must*. I'm sorry I came and I'm leaving this instant. You go right ahead."

"I've changed my mind," said Dr. Arnoldi. "You might as well stay."

His manner made Myra curious. "What have you got up your sleeve? Are you trying to kill a man too?"

"Silly, isn't it?" the old man asked. "Ambition at my age."

"How were you going to do it?"

"I'd rather not talk about it, Myra. I've changed my mind."

"You certainly act strangely. I think I'll come back some other time when you are less professional. Anyway, I've got to go look for Willard."

"Willard's here," said the doctor. "I was going to operate—on Willard."

"Oh—! Now! Isn't that just like you and Happy? Planning a surprise for me! You never did like Dr. Tucker, did you?"

"I don't remember."

"How is Willard. Is he conscious?"

Dr. Arnoldi shook his head. "He wasn't a moment ago."

"Let me see him. Oh, you two!"

The doctor opened the door for her. Willard on a table, covered with a sheet.

"He hasn't changed a bit, but he *did* roll over. What has changed your mind? If you think Dr. Tucker doesn't know his business, why don't you go ahead?"

"I'm not strong enough to go ahead, Myra, if you love this man. When I agreed—to—operate—I didn't know he—mattered to you."

Myra studied the upturned face on the table. "Oh, well, I don't know what it is. It would be a shame to revive him now. He's slept the best part of his life away. There's nothing much ahead for any of us to look forward to. If he hadn't rolled over I never would have thought of it."

"Ask Happy to send for him, please. Tell him I lost my courage."

"No, I won't say that. I'll tell him I wouldn't let you do it, that I decided not to have it done."

"That's an excellent way to put it," Dr. Arnoldi agreed hopelessly. "That you decided not to have it done."

The woman looked at her friend intently. "I can't get over how changed you are." They moved into another room.

"Emotion has never been becoming to me. I am all right as long as I don't feel."

"No one can help feeling. Even you."

"That is a discovery I have made—again—just now." He dropped his enormous white bulk into a chair.

It took Myra thirty or more embarrassed minutes to get out of the cottage and away. Never before had she been ill at ease in the Russian's presence. She worried about that all the way home.

28

SHOOTING TRAINLOADS of human beings at the moon, serving them for veal in all the restaurants, dumping thousands and thousands of them into the sea, availed man nothing.

Colonies in Arctic and Antarctic regions produced a hairy brood in two hundred years, hardy and hairy and so bearlike that, sometimes, in rut, the real bears forgot themselves.

In two hundred years, tropical colonists could scarcely be distinguished from monkeys, and the monkeys didn't mind. Even the temperate zones reared children with more than ordinarily bestial natures and as the comatant population of the world approached, equaled and passed the total wholly alive, the cities were given over entirely to the living dead. Great nomad hordes moved from place to place, feeding upon each other, cropping the remains of vegetation close to the ground, eating roots and grubs and ants yet growing ever weaker and weaker.

"Heaven on Earth" was but a sluggish anthill and its founders were long since departed, gone with a tribe called Long Teeth, for the fangs they had developed, although the Sudermans and the Fitzhughs had lost theirs along the years. Old lady Suderman pulsed in the penthouse, deserted there at the exodus.

While gold could still buy labor and materials, rockets had left Earth regularly, carrying broods of "rich" men and breeding females into the sky. Some of these rockets returned, but they made haste to depart as quickly as possible when the unchanged predicament of humankind was seen.

The Long Teeth were a giant species, all young and strong. They carried Dr. Arnoldi with them as a deity because a folk tale identified him as the inventor of cannibalism and to cannibalism they owed their strength and stature. His retinue of oldlings they resented. Three puny, toothless, doddering hags—Myra, the Swan and Ada Werfel; six stumbling, incompetent males—Happy, His Eminence, Mr. Henry Thorndike, Tucker, Evan and Dan Sweeney. They ate Dan first, as a sort of experiment. When no godly wrath was displayed by the heavy Arnoldi, they ate the cardinal. The Swan watched the last morsel disappear with very old tears in her eyes. "Good-bye, Riddy," she whispered as one of the braves swallowed.

A short time later, Myra received undue notice from the

culinary department and Happy urged his old friends to desert the tribe. They conspired to steal Dr. Arnoldi from his litter and to hide in a grotto when the horde moved on.

They wandered alone after that, subsisting on stubble and flies for a number of years, roasting Tucker one dawn when they found the first unextinguished camp fire they had seen in many months. Shortly thereafter they came upon a tribe of man-apes, squatting around a great steel cigar. These creatures had no words, but through a window of the rocket, Happy saw a full-human face. By signs he sought a parley.

"Take us with you," Happy croaked, "take us away."

The man was joined at the porthole by others of his crew. "What for? What can you do?"

"We are human. We still live. Is age a crime? Be merciful!"

"Merciful! Ha! We'd get fat being merciful. It's no cinch living on Mars. You have to be cunning."

"It's better than *this,* isn't it?"

"Oh, yes, but not so easy that we can carry useless carcasses back there to feed."

"Is there no death there? Take us back that we may die."

"The natives die, but not us. Earthlings don't die."

"Oh, hell," said Evan.

"What's in that box?" asked the man.

Evan held up the flat steel case. "In this? An autograph of Abraham Lincoln, but I've lost the key to it."

The men from Mars laughed cruelly.

"When are you going back?" asked Happy.

"As soon as our party returns with power. Where are we, anyway?"

"About the middle of Tennessee. We came through Nashville about a week ago."

"Do you suppose there's any nitroglycerin in Nashville?"

"I don't know," said Happy.

"Any transportation?"

"None."

"No railroads running?"

"No coal. All the engines are rusted apart."

"Autos?"

"No gasoline."

"Horses!"

"Eaten."

"We may be here a long time."

"Haven't you any power at all?"

"Not enough. We'd drop back."

As they talked, the plain surrounding the rocket had become ever more populous. From every quarter, groups arrived, until hundreds of thousands of half-animal creatures
milled around the machine and struggled for a closer view.
Wrangling and snapping marked the arrival of each new
group and when feeding time came blood flew in every direction.

"You see what we're up against," said Happy. "If we
weren't so old and tough they'd wipe us out. You wouldn't
like to shelter us in there overnight, would you?" Then, as if
offering credentials, "This is Dr. Arnoldi."

"Comatant?"

"No, not quite. He's conscious about half the time."

The men in the rocket considered together. "We're afraid
these beasts will storm the hatch if we open it. If it weren't
for that we'd be glad to have you."

Some vicious, smear-nosed beasts came smelling around
the Swan.

"Have you guns?" Happy called. "They're going I to get
some of us if you don't help."

Ada Werfel clung to Mrs. Fitzhugh. Evan stood guard
with a threatening look which was practically lost through
the thick mat of his brows. He held his little steel case like a
club.

The resolution of the Martians weakened, and charity, the
most stupid of all human blunders, entered their hearts. Despite elaborate precautions to prevent any of the strong,
young, hairy folk from entering the rocket with the decrepit
group, four or five squeezed through the hatch as Arnoldi's
bulky form was hoisted in.

So few were not dangerous, but their inquisitive snouts

and fingers worked over switches and valves which controlled the car.

"You better shoot those boys," said Ada with an inscrutable gleam in her eye. "They'll break something."

Happy nodded, "You better."

Mr. Henry Thorndike smiled at a young officer. "I don't suppose you have any food to spare." He spoke as one certain of refusal.

Charity, mercy, pity—opened the rocket's larder, but a rattle of gunfire drew everyone's attention as the young savages were shot away from the controls. Henry left the provender with what—in a younger man—would have been a bound. Ada was ahead of him. They sucked and lapped the fresh blood of the wounded men, chomping the flesh with their hardened gums.

"Throw 'em all out," the ship's commander ordered. "I was a fool to let them in."

"I beg your pardon, sir," said his first mate. "If we open the hatch again, we are liable to be overpowered. Hear them?"

The multitude was roaring.

"You're right, but drag those beasts away. I can't stand it."

Whereon a battle ensued within the torpedo, the old carnivora clinging desperately to their fallen victims.

"We'll hop," said the commander, "only a few miles, and drop them while we're up. To your posts!" The crew faltered, but it obeyed. With such a burst of flame as all the cannons of history could not have equaled, with a head-splitting roar, the car took flight, burying hundreds of charred savages in the crater it left behind.

Trouble developed immediately. High over the Atlantic Ocean a sorry puff indicated the end of ascent. There was no way to go but down. The heavy rocket paused for but a wink at the end of its impetus, then nosed straight down. Even equipped with dirigibility, it would have been difficult to avoid hitting a human island in that day. An almost unbroken crust of bodies covered all the seven seas. The great cigar crushed through the surface of the mulling, intertwined mass, but it did not sink. The mile-deep pile of buoyant men and women received the shock of its visitor and returned to its wonted pastimes of dallying with sharks and seals, catching tender sardines for the little scaly boys and girls who clung to their mothers' fins.

The bruised occupants of the rocket made their way out of the car and stood on the slimy, living pavement of the strangest municipality any eye had ever seen.

"It beats Mars," said one wide-eyed youth, born on that planet, "Look!"

Through crevices, mucid and rank with seaweed, the seal-men and seal-women flopped out to inspect their guests. A flock of half-feathered, penguin-like critters stalked down from a mound of bodies and stood as solemn as aldermen, waiting for the mayor to open the town meeting.

Dr. Arnoldi opened his eyes slowly and looked around. He took in all the hybrids in sight, then closed his eyes with a weary sigh. Happy watched him. "Is there anything I can do for you, doctor?"

It took a long time for a whispered "No" to reach the light of day. "No." A very long pause. "Unless these silly creatures have reinvented brewing. Do they speak?"

Attempts at communication were met with caws and barks.

"Apparently not," said Happy, "but Ada seems to understand them." Two males with webbed feet and dorsal fins had singled Miss Werfel out for their attentions.

Myra sniffed and took the Swan's hand in hers. "Let us form a pact, darling, no matter what that woman does, that you and I will lay no fish eggs, nor great auk either!"

Fitz looked at the rocket's first mate who had not yet found his tongue. "I promise, my dear. I promise."

The circle of penguin-men opened to permit an ancient without feathers, scales or hair to slither between them and up to the commander of the Martians.

In a high-pitched, whining voice, this patriarch spoke. "You'll have to throw those shoes away, first. That's the law.

No shoes. They cause unrest among the downtrodden."

Ada Werfel turned away from her finned swains. "Happy! It's *That* Sonofabitch!"

Dr. Arnoldi groaned.

29

IN THE YEAR 3000 A.D., there was not a stem nor a stalk nor a leaf of grass on God's entire footstool. There was no longer room to walk between the milling feet of the voracious giants who covered all the solid portions of the globe—and burrowed under it. There was not an inch of uninhabited soil and no room to swim in the sea.

Whales were extinct, as were all mammals and the structure of the larger fishes had become at least half human.

Higher and higher the slimy piles grew, croaking, squealing, crawling—all over the globe, like a solid sphere of maggots. It is hopeless to try to find a familiar face there, hopeless and unpleasant. Rest content that, however, deep he is buried, whoever his immediate companions may be, the sage old Dr. Arnoldi is answering their questions: "I don't know. Perhaps. It may be. There is nothing impossible about it. It doesn't matter much, either way."

EPILOGUE

Almighty God, Our Heavenly Father, Maker of Heaven and Earth, Jupiter, Zeus, Chronos, Hera, Allah, Dis, Aidoneus, Jarvos, Moceos, Epona, Nuello, Huitzilopochtli, Tezacatlipoca, QuetzalcoatI, Tlaloc, Chalchihuitlicue, Xiehtecutli, Centeotl, Tlazolteotl, Mictlan, Ixtilton, Omacatl, Yacatecutli, Mixcoatl, Xipe, Tzitzimitles, Damona, Esus, Priapus, Drune-meton, Silvana, Dervones, Adsalluta, Deva, Belisama, Axona, Vintios, Taranucus, Sulis, Cocidius, Adsmerius, Dumiatis, Caletos, Moccus, Ollovidius, Albiorix, Lencitius, Vitucadrus, Ogmios, Uxellimus, Borvo, Grannos, Mogons, Bubastes, Ops, Poseidon, Hades, Mephisto, Hephsestos, Dionysus, Ares, Phoebus, Apollo, Aphrodite, Eros, Pallas Athena, Hermes, Demeter, Persephone, Artemis, Diana, Ceres, Mercury, Minerva, Cupid, Venus, Mars, Bacchus, Vulcan, Pluto, Beelzebub, Satan, Neptune, Juno, Javeh, Rhea, Saturn, Hymen, Rumilia, Ishtar, Orpheus, Osiris, Attis, Adonis, Zagreus, Zabazius, Mithra, Mary, Jesus, Ahura-Mazda, Sutekh, Resheph, Anath, Ashtoreth, El, Nergal, Nebo, Ninib, Melek, Ahijab, Ptah, Anubis, Baal, Lucifer, Astarte, Hadad, Addu, Shalem, Dagon, Sharrab, Yau, Amon-Re, Sebech, Molech, Bile, Ler, Arianrod, Nimrod, Morrigu, Govannon, Gundfled, Sokk-mimi, Memetona, Dagda, Kerridwen, Pwyll, Ogyrvan, Dia, Vaticanus, Edulia, Adeona, Lucina, Gwydion, Manawydan, Nuada Argetlam, Tadg, Goibniu, Odin, Thor, Wotan, Llaw Gyffes, Lleu, Ogma, Mider, Rigautona, Marzia, Cunina, Potina, Statilmus, Robigus, Furrina, Vediovis, Consus, Enki, Engurra, Belus, Dimmer, Ahriman, Mu-ul-lil, Ubargisi, Ubilulu, Gasan-lil, U-dimmer-an-kia, Enurestu, Usabsib, U-Mersi, Tammuz, Ban, Mulu-hursang, Anu, Beltis, Nusku, Nizu, Sahi, Aa, Allatu, Sin, Abil-Addu, Apsu, Dagan, Elali, Isura, Mami, Nin-mah, Zaraqu, Suquamunu, Zagaga, Meditriña, Tilmun,

Zerpanitu, Merodach, Uki, Daukc, Gasanabzu, Elum, Elohim, U-Tin-dirki, Marduk, Nin-lilla, Nin, Istar, Lagas, U-urugal, Sirtumu, Ea, Nirig, Samas, Ma-banba-anna, Eu-Mersi, Amurru, Assur, Aku, Beltu, Dumuzi-abzu, Kuski-banda, Kaawanu, Ninazu, Lugal-Amarada, Quarrada, Uragala, Ueras, Vesta, Isis or Pan (which are all the names by which I have learned that men address You); oh Thou Giver and Takeraway of ideas; hear me!

For years I have taken no thought of myself, but have sat patient as Job and set words end to end through long days and longer nights, revealing the wonders You have put in my head. I have never complained and never faltered, even when I thought some of Thy notions were pretty sick. But, Almighty Ruler, All-Merciful and All-Knowing, there is a limit even to my endurance. On my knees, prostrate, I beseech Thee, Old Grandpa, the next time You have an idea like *this* to give away, You send it to H.G. Wells, because I won't bother with it.

Amen.

RAMBLE HOUSE's

Harry Stephen Keeler Webwork Mysteries

(RH) indicates the title is available ONLY in the RAMBLE HOUSE edition

The Ace of Spades Murder
The Affair of the Bottled Deuce (RH)
The Amazing Web
The Barking Clock
Behind That Mask
The Book with the Orange Leaves
The Bottle with the Green Wax Seal
The Box from Japan
The Case of the Canny Killer
The Case of the Crazy Corpse (RH)
The Case of the Flying Hands (RH)
The Case of the Ivory Arrow
The Case of the Jeweled Ragpicker
The Case of the Lavender Gripsack
The Case of the Mysterious Moll
The Case of the 16 Beans
The Case of the Transparent Nude (RH)
The Case of the Transposed Legs
The Case of the Two-Headed Idiot (RH)
The Case of the Two Strange Ladies
The Circus Stealers (RH)
Cleopatra's Tears
A Copy of Beowulf (RH)
The Crimson Cube (RH)
The Face of the Man From Saturn
Find the Clock
The Five Silver Buddhas
The 4th King
The Gallows Waits, My Lord! (RH)
The Green Jade Hand
Finger! Finger!
Hangman's Nights (RH)
I, Chameleon (RH)
I Killed Lincoln at 10:13! (RH)
The Iron Ring
The Man Who Changed His Skin (RH)
The Man with the Crimson Box
The Man with the Magic Eardrums
The Man with the Wooden Spectacles
The Marceau Case
The Matilda Hunter Murder

The Monocled Monster
The Murder of London Lew
The Murdered Mathematician
The Mysterious Card (RH)
The Mysterious Ivory Ball of Wong Shing Li (RH)
The Mystery of the Fiddling Cracksman
The Peacock Fan
The Photo of Lady X (RH)
The Portrait of Jirjohn Cobb
Report on Vanessa Hewstone (RH)
Riddle of the Travelling Skull
Riddle of the Wooden Parrakeet (RH)
The Scarlet Mummy (RH)
The Search for X-Y-Z
The Sharkskin Book
Sing Sing Nights
The Six From Nowhere (RH)
The Skull of the Waltzing Clown
The Spectacles of Mr. Cagliostro
Stand By—London Calling!
The Steeltown Strangler
The Stolen Gravestone (RH)
Strange Journey (RH)
The Strange Will
The Straw Hat Murders (RH)
The Street of 1000 Eyes (RH)
Thieves' Nights
Three Novellos (RH)
The Tiger Snake
The Trap (RH)
Vagabond Nights (Defrauded Yeggman)
Vagabond Nights 2 (10 Hours)
The Vanishing Gold Truck
The Voice of the Seven Sparrows
The Washington Square Enigma
When Thief Meets Thief
The White Circle (RH)
The Wonderful Scheme of Mr. Christopher Thorne
X. Jones—of Scotland Yard
Y. Cheung, Business Detective

Keeler Related Works

A To Izzard: A Harry Stephen Keeler Companion by Fender Tucker — Articles and stories about Harry, by Harry, and in his style. Included is a compleat bibliography.

Wild About Harry: Reviews of Keeler Novels — Edited by Richard Polt & Fender Tucker — 22 reviews of works by Harry Stephen Keeler from *Keeler News*. A perfect introduction to the author.

The Keeler Keyhole Collection: Annotated newsletter rants from Harry Stephen Keeler, edited by Francis M. Nevins. Over 400 pages of incredibly personal Keeleriana.

Fakealoo — Pastiches of the style of Harry Stephen Keeler by selected demented members of the HSK Society. Updated every year with the new winner.

Strands of the Web: Short Stories of Harry Stephen Keeler — 29 stories, just about all that Keeler wrote, are edited and introduced by Fred Cleaver.

RAMBLE HOUSE's Loon Sanctuary

A Clear Path to Cross — Sharon Knowles short mystery stories by Ed Lynskey.

A Jimmy Starr Omnibus — Three 40s novels by Jimmy Starr.

A Niche in Time and Other Stories — Classic SF by William F. Temple

A Roland Daniel Double: The Signal and The Return of Wu Fang — Classic thrillers from the 30s.

A Shot Rang Out — Three decades of reviews and articles by today's Anthony Boucher, Jon Breen. An essential book for any mystery lover's library.

A Smell of Smoke — A 1951 English countryside thriller by Miles Burton.

A Snark Selection — Lewis Carroll's *The Hunting of the Snark* with two Snarkian chapters by Harry Stephen Keeler — Illustrated by Gavin L. O'Keefe.

A Young Man's Heart — A forgotten early classic by Cornell Woolrich.

Alexander Laing Novels — *The Motives of Nicholas Holtz* and *Dr. Scarlett*, stories of medical mayhem and intrigue from the 30s.

An Angel in the Street — Modern hardboiled noir by Peter Genovese.

Automaton — Brilliant treatise on robotics: 1928-style! By H. Stafford Hatfield.

Away From the Here and Now — Clare Winger Harris stories, collected by Richard A. Lupoff

Beast or Man? — A 1930 novel of racism and horror by Sean M'Guire. Introduced by John Pelan.

Black Hogan Strikes Again — Australia's Peter Renwick pens a tale of the 30s outback.

Black River Falls — Suspense from the master, Ed Gorman.

Blondy's Boy Friend — A snappy 1930 story by Philip Wylie, writing as Leatrice Homesley.

Blood in a Snap — The *Finnegan's Wake* of the 21st century, by Jim Weiler.

Blood Moon — The first of the Robert Payne series by Ed Gorman.

Bogart '48 — Hollywood action with Bogie by John Stanley and Kenn Davis

Calling Lou Largo! — Two Lou Largo novels by William Ard.

Cornucopia of Crime — Francis M. Nevins assembled this huge collection of his writings about crime literature and the people who write it. Essential for any serious mystery library.

Corpse Without Flesh — Strange novel of forensics by George Bruce

Crimson Clown Novels — By Johnston McCulley, author of the Zorro novels, *The Crimson Clown* and *The Crimson Clown Again*.

Dago Red — 22 tales of dark suspense by Bill Pronzini.

Dark Sanctuary — Weird Menace story by H. B. Gregory

David Hume Novels — *Corpses Never Argue, Cemetery First Stop, Make Way for the Mourners, Eternity Here I Come*. 1930s British hardboiled fiction with an attitude.

Dead Man Talks Too Much — Hollywood boozer by Weed Dickenson.

Death Leaves No Card — One of the most unusual murdered-in-the-tub mysteries you'll ever read. By Miles Burton.

Death March of the Dancing Dolls and Other Stories — Volume Three in the Day Keene in the Detective Pulps series. Introduced by Bill Crider.

Deep Space and other Stories — A collection of SF gems by Richard A. Lupoff.

Detective Duff Unravels It — Episodic mysteries by Harvey O'Higgins.

Diabolic Candelabra — Classic 30s mystery by E.R. Punshon

Dime Novels: Ramble House's 10-Cent Books — *Knife in the Dark* by Robert Leslie Bellem, *Hot Lead* and *Song of Death* by Ed Earl Repp, *A Hashish House in New York* by H.H. Kane, and five more.

Don Diablo: Book of a Lost Film — Two-volume treatment of a western by Paul Landres, with diagrams. Intro by Francis M. Nevins.

Dope and Swastikas — Two strange novels from 1922 by Edmund Snell

Dope Tales #1 — Two dope-riddled classics; *Dope Runners* by Gerald Grantham and *Death Takes the Joystick* by Phillip Condé.

Dope Tales #2 — Two more narco-classics; *The Invisible Hand* by Rex Dark and *The Smokers of Hashish* by Norman Berrow.

Dope Tales #3 — Two enchanting novels of opium by the master, Sax Rohmer. *Dope* and *The Yellow Claw*.

Double Hot — Two 60s softcore sex novels by Morris Hershman.

Dr. Odin — Douglas Newton's 1933 racial potboiler comes back to life.

Evangelical Cockroach — Jack Woodford writes about writing.

Evidence in Blue — 1938 mystery by E. Charles Vivian.

Fatal Accident — Murder by automobile, a 1936 mystery by Cecil M. Wills.

Fighting Mad — Todd Robbins' 1922 novel about boxing and life

Finger-prints Never Lie — A 1939 classic detective novel by John G. Brandon.

Freaks and Fantasies — Eerie tales by Tod Robbins, collaborator of Tod Browning on the film FREAKS.

Gadsby — A lipogram (a novel without the letter E). Ernest Vincent Wright's last work, published in 1939 right before his death.

Gelett Burgess Novels — *The Master of Mysteries, The White Cat, Two O'Clock Courage, Ladies in Boxes, Find the Woman, The Heart Line, The Picaroons* and *Lady Mechante*. Recently added is A Gelett Burgess Sampler, edited by Alfred Jan. All are introduced by Richard A. Lupoff.

Geronimo — S. M. Barrett's 1905 autobiography of a noble American.

Hake Talbot Novels — *Rim of the Pit, The Hangman's Handyman*. Classic locked room mysteries, with mapback covers by Gavin O'Keefe.

Hands Out of Hell and Other Stories — John H. Knox's eerie hallucinations

Hell is a City — William Ard's masterpiece.

Hollywood Dreams — A novel of Tinsel Town and the Depression by Richard O'Brien.

Hostesses in Hell and Other Stories — Russell Gray's most graphic stories

House of the Restless Dead — Strange and ominous tales by Hugh B. Cave

I Stole $16,000,000 — A true story by cracksman Herbert E. Wilson.

Inclination to Murder — 1966 thriller by New Zealand's Harriet Hunter.

Invaders from the Dark — Classic werewolf tale from Greye La Spina.

J. Poindexter, Colored — Classic satirical black novel by Irvin S. Cobb.

Jack Mann Novels — Strange murder in the English countryside. *Gees' First Case, Nightmare Farm, Grey Shapes, The Ninth Life, The Glass Too Many, Her Ways Are Death, The Kleinert Case* and *Maker of Shadows*.

Jake Hardy — A lusty western tale from Wesley Tallant.

Jim Harmon Double Novels — *Vixen Hollow/Celluloid Scandal, The Man Who Made Maniacs/Silent Siren, Ape Rape/Wanton Witch, Sex Burns Like Fire/Twist Session, Sudden Lust/Passion Strip, Sin Unlimited/Harlot Master, Twilight Girls/Sex Institution*. Written in the early 60s and never reprinted until now.

Joel Townsley Rogers Novels and Short Stories — By the author of *The Red Right Hand: Once In a Red Moon, Lady With the Dice, The Stopped Clock, Never Leave My Bed*. Also two short story collections: *Night of Horror* and *Killing Time*.

John Carstairs, Space Detective — Arboreal Sci-fi by Frank Belknap Long

Joseph Shallit Novels — *The Case of the Billion Dollar Body, Lady Don't Die on My Doorstep, Kiss the Killer, Yell Bloody Murder, Take Your Last Look*. One of America's best 50's authors and a favorite of author Bill Pronzini.

Keller Memento — 45 short stories of the amazing and weird by Dr. David Keller.

Killer's Caress — Cary Moran's 1936 hardboiled thriller.

Lady of the Yellow Death and Other Stories — More stories by Wyatt Blassingame.

League of the Grateful Dead and Other Stories — Volume One in the Day Keene in the Detective Pulps series.

Library of Death — Ghastly tale by Ronald S. L. Harding, introduced by John Pelan

Malcolm Jameson Novels and Short Stories — *Astonishing! Astounding!, Tarnished Bomb, The Alien Envoy and Other Stories* and *The Chariots of San Fernando and Other Stories*. All introduced and edited by John Pelan or Richard A. Lupoff.

Man Out of Hell and Other Stories — Volume II of the John H. Knox weird pulps collection.

Marblehead: A Novel of H.P. Lovecraft — A long-lost masterpiece from Richard A. Lupoff. This is the "director's cut", the long version that has never been published before.

Master of Souls — Mark Hansom's 1937 shocker is introduced by weirdologist John Pelan.

Max Afford Novels — *Owl of Darkness, Death's Mannikins, Blood on His Hands, The Dead Are Blind, The Sheep and the Wolves, Sinners in Paradise* and *Two Locked Room Mysteries and a Ripping Yarn* by one of Australia's finest mystery novelists.

Money Brawl — Two books about the writing business by Jack Woodford and H. Bedford-Jones. Introduced by Richard A. Lupoff.

More Secret Adventures of Sherlock Holmes — Gary Lovisi's second collection of tales about the unknown sides of the great detective.

Muddled Mind: Complete Works of Ed Wood, Jr. — David Hayes and Hayden Davis deconstruct the life and works of the mad, but canny, genius.

Murder among the Nudists — A mystery from 1934 by Peter Hunt, featuring a naked Detective-Inspector going undercover in a nudist colony.

Murder in Black and White — 1931 classic tennis whodunit by Evelyn Elder.

Murder in Shawnee — Two novels of the Alleghenies by John Douglas: *Shawnee Alley Fire* and *Haunts*.

Murder in Silk — A 1937 Yellow Peril novel of the silk trade by Ralph Trevor.

My Deadly Angel — 1955 Cold War drama by John Chelton.

My First Time: The One Experience You Never Forget — Michael Birchwood — 64 true first-person narratives of how they lost it.

Mysterious Martin, the Master of Murder — Two versions of a strange 1912 novel by Tod Robbins about a man who writes books that can kill.

Norman Berrow Novels — *The Bishop's Sword, Ghost House, Don't Go Out After Dark, Claws of the Cougar, The Smokers of Hashish, The Secret Dancer, Don't Jump Mr. Boland!, The Footprints of Satan, Fingers for Ransom, The Three Tiers of Fantasy, The Spaniard's Thumb, The Eleventh Plague, Words Have Wings, One Thrilling Night, The Lady's in Danger, It Howls at Night, The Terror in the Fog, Oil Under the Window, Murder in the Melody, The Singing Room.* This is the complete Norman Berrow library of locked-room mysteries, several of which are masterpieces.

Old Faithful and Other Stories — SF classic tales by Raymond Z. Gallun

Old Times' Sake — Short stories by James Reasoner from Mike Shayne Magazine.

One Dreadful Night — A classic mystery by Ronald S. L. Harding

Pair O' Jacks — A mystery novel and a diatribe about publishing by Jack Woodford

Perfect .38 — Two early Timothy Dane novels by William Ard. More to come.

Prince Pax — Devilish intrigue by George Sylvester Viereck and Philip Eldridge

Prose Bowl — Futuristic satire of a world where hack writing has replaced football as our national obsession, by Bill Pronzini and Barry N. Malzberg.

Red Light — The history of legal prostitution in Shreveport Louisiana by Eric Brock. Includes wonderful photos of the houses and the ladies.

Researching American-Made Toy Soldiers — A 276-page collection of a lifetime of articles by toy soldier expert Richard O'Brien.

Reunion in Hell — Volume One of the John H. Knox series of weird stories from the pulps. Introduced by horror expert John Pelan.

Ripped from the Headlines! — The Jack the Ripper story as told in the newspaper articles in the *New York* and *London Times*.

Robert Randisi Novels — *No Exit to Brooklyn* and *The Dead of Brooklyn.* The first two Nick Delvecchio novels.

Rough Cut & New, Improved Murder — Ed Gorman's first two novels.

R.R. Ryan Novels — Freak Museum and The Subjugated Beast, two horror classics.

Ruled By Radio — 1925 futuristic novel by Robert L. Hadfield & Frank E. Farncombe.

Rupert Penny Novels — *Policeman's Holiday, Policeman's Evidence, Lucky Policeman, Policeman in Armour, Sealed Room Murder, Sweet Poison, The Talkative Policeman, She had to Have Gas* and *Cut and Run* (by Martin Tanner.) Rupert Penny is the pseudonym of Australian Charles Thornett, a master of the locked room, impossible crime plot.

Sacred Locomotive Flies — Richard A. Lupoff's psychedelic SF story.

Sam — Early gay novel by Lonnie Coleman.

Sand's Game — Spectacular hard-boiled noir from Ennis Willie, edited by Lynn Myers and Stephen Mertz, with contributions from Max Allan Collins, Bill Crider, Wayne Dundee, Bill Pronzini, Gary Lovisi and James Reasoner.

Sand's War — More violent fiction from the typewriter of Ennis Willie

Satan's Den Exposed — True crime in Truth or Consequences New Mexico — Award-winning journalism by the *Desert Journal.*

Satans of Saturn — Novellas from the pulps by Otis Adelbert Kline and E. H. Price

Satan's Sin House and Other Stories — Horrific gore by Wayne Rogers

Secrets of a Teenage Superhero — Graphic lit by Jonathan Sweet

Sex Slave — Potboiler of lust in the days of Cleopatra by Dion Leclerq, 1966.

Shadows' Edge — Two early novels by Wade Wright: *Shadows Don't Bleed* and *The Sharp Edge.*

Sideslip — 1968 SF masterpiece by Ted White and Dave Van Arnam.

Slammer Days — Two full-length prison memoirs: *Men into Beasts* (1952) by George Sylvester Viereck and *Home Away From Home* (1962) by Jack Woodford.

Slippery Staircase — 1930s whodunit from E.C.R. Lorac.

Sorcerer's Chessmen — John Pelan introduces this 1939 classic by Mark Hansom.

Star Griffin — Michael Kurland's 1987 masterpiece of SF drollery is back.

Stakeout on Millennium Drive — Award-winning Indianapolis Noir by Ian Woollen.

The House of the Vampire — 1907 poetic thriller by George S. Viereck.

The Illustrious Corpse — Murder hijinx from Tiffany Thayer

The Incredible Adventures of Rowland Hern — Intriguing 1928 impossible crimes by Nicholas Olde.

The Julius Caesar Murder Case — A classic 1935 re-telling of the assassination by Wallace Irwin that's much more fun than the Shakespeare version.

The Koky Comics — A collection of all of the 1978-1981 Sunday and daily comic strips by Richard O'Brien and Mort Gerberg, in two volumes.

The Lady of the Terraces — 1925 missing race adventure by E. Charles Vivian.

The Lord of Terror — 1925 mystery with master-criminal, Fantômas.

The Melamare Mystery — A classic 1929 Arsene Lupin mystery by Maurice Leblanc

The Man Who Was Secrett — Epic SF stories from John Brunner

The Man Without a Planet — Science fiction tales by Richard Wilson

The N. R. De Mexico Novels — Robert Bragg, the real N.R. de Mexico, presents *Marijuana Girl, Madman on a Drum, Private Chauffeur* in one volume.

The Night Remembers — A 1991 Jack Walsh mystery from Ed Gorman.

The One After Snelling — Kickass modern noir from Richard O'Brien.

The Organ Reader — A huge compilation of just about everything published in the 1971-1972 radical bay-area newspaper, *THE ORGAN*. A coffee table book that points out the shallowness of the coffee table mindset.

The Poker Club — Three in one! Ed Gorman's ground-breaking novel, the short story it was based upon, and the screenplay of the film made from it.

The Private Journal & Diary of John H. Surratt — The memoirs of the man who conspired to assassinate President Lincoln.

The Secret Adventures of Sherlock Holmes — Three Sherlockian pastiches by the Brooklyn author/publisher, Gary Lovisi.

The Shadow on the House — Mark Hansom's 1934 masterpiece of horror is introduced by John Pelan.

The Sign of the Scorpion — A 1935 Edmund Snell tale of oriental evil.

The Singular Problem of the Stygian House-Boat — Two classic tales by John Kendrick Bangs about the denizens of Hades.

The Smiling Corpse — Philip Wylie and Bernard Bergman's odd 1935 novel.

The Spider: Satan's Murder Machines — A thesis about Iron Man

The Stench of Death: An Odoriferous Omnibus by Jack Moskovitz — Two complete novels and two novellas from 60's sleaze author, Jack Moskovitz.

The Story Writer and Other Stories — Classic SF from Richard Wilson

The Strange Case of the Antlered Man — 1935 dementia from Edwy Searles Brooks

The Strange Thirteen — Richard B. Gamon's odd stories about Raj India.

The Technique of the Mystery Story — Carolyn Wells' tips about writing.

The Threat of Nostalgia — A collection of his most obscure stories by Jon Breen

The Time Armada — Fox B. Holden's 1953 SF gem.

The Tongueless Horror and Other Stories — Volume One of the series of short stories from the weird pulps by Wyatt Blassingame.

The Tracer of Lost Persons — From 1906, an episodic novel that became a hit radio series in the 30s. Introduced by Richard A. Lupoff.

The Trail of the Cloven Hoof — Diabolical horror from 1935 by Arlton Eadie. Introduced by John Pelan.

The Triune Man — Mindscrambling science fiction from Richard A. Lupoff.

The Unholy Goddess and Other Stories — Wyatt Blassingame's first DTP compilation

The Universal Holmes — Richard A. Lupoff's 2007 collection of five Holmesian pastiches and a recipe for giant rat stew.

The Werewolf vs the Vampire Woman — Hard to believe ultraviolence by either Arthur M. Scarm or Arthur M. Scram.

The Whistling Ancestors — A 1936 classic of weirdness by Richard E. Goddard and introduced by John Pelan.

The White Owl — A vintage thriller from Edmund Snell

The White Peril in the Far East — Sidney Lewis Gulick's 1905 indictment of the West and assurance that Japan would never attack the U.S.

The Wizard of Berner's Abbey — A 1935 horror gem written by Mark Hansom and introduced by John Pelan.

The Wonderful Wizard of Oz — by L. Frank Baum and illustrated by Gavin L. O'Keefe

Through the Looking Glass — Lewis Carroll wrote it; Gavin L. O'Keefe illustrated it.

Time Line — Ramble House artist Gavin O'Keefe selects his most evocative art inspired by the twisted literature he reads and designs.

Tiresias — Psychotic modern horror novel by Jonathan M. Sweet.

Totah Six-Pack — Fender Tucker's six tales about Farmington in one sleek volume.

Trail of the Spirit Warrior — Roger Haley's historical saga of life in the Indian Territories.

Two Kinds of Bad — Two 50s novels by William Ard about Danny Fontaine

Two Suns of Morcali and Other Stories — Evelyn E. Smith's SF tour-de-force

Ultra-Boiled — 23 gut-wrenching tales by our Man in Brooklyn, Gary Lovisi.

Up Front From Behind — A 2011 satire of Wall Street by James B. Kobak.

Victims & Villains — Intriguing Sherlockiana from Derham Groves.

Wade Wright Novels — *Echo of Fear*, *Death At Nostalgia Street*, *It Leads to Murder* and *Shadows' Edge*, a double book featuring *Shadows Don't Bleed* and *The Sharp Edge*.

Walter S. Masterman Novels — *The Green Toad*, *The Flying Beast*, *The Yellow Mistletoe*, *The Wrong Verdict*, *The Perjured Alibi*, *The Border Line*, *The Bloodhounds Bay* and *The Curse of Cantire*. Masterman wrote horror and mystery, some introduced by John Pelan.

We Are the Dead and Other Stories — Volume Two in the Day Keene in the Detective Pulps series, introduced by Ed Gorman. When done, there may be as many as 11 in the series.

Welsh Rarebit Tales — Charming stories from 1902 by Harle Oren Cummins

West Texas War and Other Western Stories — by Gary Lovisi.

Whip Dodge: Man Hunter — Wesley Tallant's saga of a bounty hunter of the old West.

Win, Place and Die! — The first new mystery by Milt Ozaki in decades. The ultimate novel of 70s Reno.

You'll Die Laughing — Bruce Elliott's 1945 novel of murder at a practical joker's English countryside manor.

RAMBLE HOUSE

Fender Tucker, Prop.   Gavin L. O'Keefe, Graphics
www.ramblehouse.com   fender@ramblehouse.com
228-826-1783   10329 Sheephead Drive, Vancleave MS 39565

www.ingramcontent.com/pod-product-compliance
Lightning Source LLC
Chambersburg PA
CBHW031218020726
47499CB00002B/628